# THE
# ORANGE-YELLOW
# DIAMOND

## CHAPTER ONE
## THE PRETTY PAWNBROKER

On the southern edge of the populous parish of Paddington, in a parallelogram bounded by Oxford and Cambridge Terrace on the south, Praed Street on the north, and by Edgware Road on the east and Spring Street on the west, lies an assemblage of mean streets, the drab dulness of which forms a remarkable contrast to the pretentious architectural grandeurs of Sussex Square and Lancaster Gate, close by. In these streets the observant will always find all those evidences of depressing semi-poverty which are more evident in London than in any other English city. The houses look as if laughter was never heard within them. Where the window blinds are not torn, they are dirty; the folk who come out of the doors wear anxious and depressed faces. Such shops as are there are mainly kept for the sale of food of poor quality: the taverns at the corners are destitute of attraction or pretension. Whoever wanders into these streets finds their sordid shabbiness communicating itself: he escapes, cast down, wondering who the folk are who live in those grey, lifeless cages; what they do, what they think; how life strikes them. Even the very sparrows which fight in the gutters for garbage are less lively than London sparrows usually are; as for the children who sit about the doorsteps, they look as if the grass, the trees, the flowers, and the sunlight of the adjacent Kensington Gardens were as far away as the Desert of Gobi. Within this slice of the town, indeed, life is lived, as it were, in a stagnant backwash, which nothing and nobody can stir.

In an upper room of one of the more respectable houses in one of the somewhat superior streets of this neighbourhood, a young man stood looking out of the window one November afternoon. It was then five o'clock, and the darkness was coming: all day a gentle, never-ceasing rain had been bringing the soot down from the dark skies upon the already dingy roofs. It was a dismal and miserable prospect upon which the watcher looked out, but not so miserable nor so dismal as the situation in which he just then found himself. The mean street beneath him was not more empty of cheerfulness than his pockets were empty of money and his stomach of food. He had spent his last penny on the previous day: it, and two other coppers, had gone on a mere mouthful of food and drink: since their disappearance he had eaten nothing. And he was now growing faint with hunger—and to add to his pains, some one, downstairs, was cooking herrings. The smell of the frying-pan nearly drove him ravenous.

He turned from the window presently and looked round at the small room behind him. It was a poor, ill-furnished place—cleanliness, though of a dingy sort, its only recommendation. There was a bed, and a washstand, and a chest of drawers, and a couple of chairs—a few shillings would have purchased the lot at any second-hand dealer's. In a corner stood the occupant's trunk—all the property he had in the world was in it, save a few books which were carefully ranged on the chimney-piece, and certain writing materials that lay on a small table. A sharp eye, glancing at the books and the writing materials, and at a few sheets of manuscript scattered on the blotting-pad, would have been quick to see that here was the old tale, once more being lived out, of the literary aspirant who, at the very beginning of his career, was finding, by bitter experience, that, of all callings, that of literature is the most precarious.

A half-hesitating tap at the door prefaced the entrance of a woman—the sort of woman who is seen in those streets by the score—a tallish, thinnish woman, old before her time, perpetually harassed, always anxious, always looking as if she expected misfortune. Her face was full of anxiety now as she glanced at her lodger—who, on his part, flushed all over his handsome young face with conscious embarrassment. He knew very well what the woman wanted—and he was powerless to respond to her appeal.

"Mr. Lauriston," she said in a half whisper, "when do you think you'll be able to let me have a bit of money? It's going on for six weeks now, you know, and I'm that put to it, what with the rent, and the rates—"

Andrew Lauriston shook his head—not in denial, but in sheer perplexity.

"Mrs. Flitwick," he answered, "I'll give you your money the very minute I get hold of it! I told you the other day I'd sold two stories—well, I've asked to be paid for them at once, and the cheque might be here by any post. And I'm expecting another cheque, too—I'm surprised they aren't both here by this time. The minute they arrive, I'll settle with you. I'm wanting money myself—as badly as you are!"

"I know that, Mr. Lauriston," assented Mrs. Flitwick, "and I wouldn't bother you if I wasn't right pressed, myself. But there's the landlord at me—he wants money tonight. And—you'll excuse me for mentioning it—but, till you get your cheques, Mr. Lauriston, why don't you raise a bit of ready money?"

Lauriston looked round at his landlady with an air of surprised enquiry.

"And how would I do that?" he asked.

"You've a right good gold watch, Mr. Lauriston," she answered. "Any pawnbroker—and there's plenty of 'em, I'm sure!—'ud lend you a few pounds on that. Perhaps you've never had occasion to go to a pawnbroker before? No?—well, and I hadn't once upon a time, but I've had to, whether or no, since I came to letting lodgings, and if I'd as good a watch as yours is, I wouldn't go without money in my pocket! If you've money coming in, you can always get your goods back—and I should be thankful for something, Mr. Lauriston, if it was but a couple o' pounds. My landlord's that hard—"

Lauriston turned and picked up his hat.

"All right, Mrs. Flitwick," he said quietly. "I'll see what I can do. I—I'd never even thought of it."

When the woman had gone away, closing the door behind her, he pulled the watch out of his pocket and looked at it—an old-fashioned, good, gold watch, which had been his father's. No doubt a pawnbroker would lend money on it. But until then he had never had occasion to think of pawnbrokers. He had come to London nearly two years before, intending to make name, fame, and fortune by his pen. He had a little money to be going on with—when he came. It had dwindled steadily, and it had been harder to replace it than he had calculated for. And at last there he was, in that cheap lodging, and at the end of his resources, and the cheque for his first two accepted stories had not arrived. Neither had a loan which, sorely against his will, he had been driven to request from the only man he could think of—an old schoolmate, far away in Scotland. He had listened for the postman's knock, hoping it would bring relief, for four long days—and not one letter had come, and he was despairing and heartsick. But—there was the watch!

He went out presently, and on the stair, feebly lighted by a jet of gas, he ran up against a fellow-lodger—a young Jew, whom he knew by the name of Mr. Melchior Rubinstein, who occupied the rooms immediately beneath his own. He was a quiet, affable little person, with whom Lauriston sometimes exchanged a word or two—and the fact that he sported rings on his fingers, a large pin in his tie, and a heavy watch-chain, which was either real gold or a very good imitation, made Lauriston think that he would give him some advice. He stopped him—with a shy look, and an awkward blush.

"I say!" he said. "I—the fact is, I'm a bit hard up—temporarily, you know—and I want to borrow some money on my watch. Could you tell me where there's a respectable pawnbroker's?"

Melky—known to every one in the house by that familiar substitute for his more pretentious name—turned up the gas-jet and then held out a slender, long-fingered hand. "Let's look at the watch," he said curtly, in a soft, lisping voice. "I know more than a bit about watches, mister."

Lauriston handed the watch over and watched Melky inquisitively as he looked at it, inside and out, in a very knowing and professional way.

Melky suddenly glanced at him. "Now, you wouldn't like to sell this here bit of property, would you, Mr. Lauriston?" he enquired, almost wheedlingly. "I'll give you three quid for it—cash down."

"Thank you—but I wouldn't sell it for worlds," replied Lauriston.

"Say four quid, then," urged Melky. "Here!—between friends, I'll give you four-ten! Spot cash, mind you!"

"No!" said Lauriston. "It belonged to my father. I don't want to sell—I want to borrow."

Melky pushed the watch back into its owner's hand.

"You go round into Praed Street, mister," he said, in business-like fashion. "You'll see a shop there with Daniel Multenius over it. He's a relation o' mine—he'll do what you want. Mention my name, if you like. He'll deal fair with you. And if you ever want to sell, don't forget me."

Lauriston laughed, and went down the stairs, and out into the dismal evening. It was only a step round to Praed Street, and within five minutes of leaving Melky he was looking into Daniel Multenius's window. He remembered now that he had often looked into it, without noticing the odd name above it. It was a window in which there were all sorts of curious things, behind a grille of iron bars, from diamonds and pearls to old ivory and odds and ends of bric-à-brac. A collector of curiosities would have found material in that window to delay him for half-an-hour—but Lauriston only gave one glance at it before hastening down a dark side-passage to a door, over which was a faintly-illuminated sign, showing the words: PLEDGE OFFICE.

He pushed open that door and found himself before several small, boxed-off compartments, each just big enough to contain one person. They were all empty at that moment; he entered one, and seeing nobody about, tapped gently on the counter. He expected to see some ancient and Hebraic figure present itself—instead, light steps came from some recess of the shop, and Lauriston found himself gazing in surprise at a young and eminently pretty girl, who carried some fancy needle-work in her hand, and looked over it at him out of a pair of large, black eyes. For a moment the two gazed at each other, in silence.

"Yes?" said the girl at last. "What can I do for you?"

Lauriston found his tongue.

"Er—is Mr. Multenius in?" he asked. "I—the fact is, I want to see him."

"Mr. Multenius is out," answered the girl. "But I'm in charge—if it's business."

She was quietly eyeing Lauriston over, and she saw his fresh-complexioned face colour vividly.

"I do my grandfather's business when he's out," she continued. "Do you

want to borrow some money?"
Lauriston pulled out the watch, with more blushes, and pushed it towards her.
"That's just it," he answered. "I want to borrow money on that. A friend of mine—fellow-lodger—Mr. Melky Rubinstein—said I could borrow something here. That's a real good watch, you know."
The girl glanced at her customer with a swift and almost whimsical recognition of his innocence, and almost carelessly picked up the watch.
"Oh, Melky sent you here, did he?" she said, with a smile. "I see!" She looked the watch over, and snapped open the case. Then she glanced at Lauriston. "How much do you want on this?" she asked.

## CHAPTER TWO
### MRS. GOLDMARK'S EATING-HOUSE

Lauriston thrust his hands in his pockets and looked at the girl in sheer perplexity. She was a very pretty, dark girl, nearly as tall as himself, slender and lissom of figure, and decidedly attractive. There was evident sense of fun and humour in her eyes, and about the corners of her lips: he suddenly got an idea that she was amused at his embarrassment.
"How much can you lend me?" he asked. "What—what's it worth?"
"No, that's not it!" she answered. "It's—what do you want to borrow?
You're not used to pledging things, are you?"
"No," replied Lauriston. "This is the first time. Can—can you lend me a few pounds?"
The girl picked up the watch again, and again, examined it.
"I'll lend you three pounds fifteen on it," she said suddenly, in business-like tones. "That do?"
"Thank you," replied Lauriston. "That'll do very well—I'm much obliged. I suppose I can have it back any time."
"Any time you bring the money, and pay the interest," replied the girl. "Within twelve calendar months and seven days." She picked up a pen and began to fill out a ticket. "Got any copper?" she asked presently.
"Copper?" exclaimed Lauriston. "What for?"
"The ticket," she answered. Then she gave him a quick glance and just as quickly looked down again. "Never mind!" she said. "I'll take it out of the loan. Your name and address, please."
Lauriston presently took the ticket and the little pile of gold, silver, and copper which she handed him. And he lingered.
"You'll take care of that watch," he said, suddenly. "It was my father's, you see."
The girl smiled, reassuringly, and pointed to a heavily-built safe in the rear.
"We've all sorts of family heirlooms in there," she observed. "Make

yourself easy."

Lauriston thanked her, raised his hat, and turned away—unwillingly. He would have liked an excuse to stop longer—and he did not quite know why. But he could think of none, so he went—with a backward look when he got to the door. The pretty pawnbroker smiled and nodded. And the next moment he was out in the street, with money in his pocket, and a strange sense of relief, which was mingled with one of surprise. For he had lived for the previous four days on a two-shilling piece—and there, all the time, close by him, had been a place where you could borrow money, easily and very pleasantly.

His first thought was to hurry to his lodgings and pay his landlady. He owed her six weeks' rent, at ten shillings a week—that would take three pounds out of the money he had just received. But he would still have over fourteen shillings to be going on with—and surely those expected letters would come within the next few postal deliveries. He had asked the editor who had taken two short stories from him to let him have a cheque for them, and in his inexperience had expected to see it arrive by return of post. Also he had put his pride in his pocket, and had written a long letter to his old schoolmate, John Purdie, in far-away Scotland, explaining his present circumstances, and asking him, for old times' sake, to lend him some money until he had finished and sold a novel, which, he was sure, would turn out to be a small gold-mine. John Purdie, he knew, was now a wealthy young man—successor to his father in a fine business; Lauriston felt no doubt that he would respond. And meantime, till the expected letters came, he had money—and when you have lived for four days on two shillings, fourteen shillings seems a small fortune. Certainly, within the last half-hour, life had taken on a roseate tinge—all due to a visit to the pawnshop.

Hurrying back along Praed Street, Lauriston's steps were suddenly arrested. He found himself unconsciously hurrying by an old-fashioned eating-house, from whence came an appetizing odour of cooking food. He remembered then that he had eaten nothing for four-and-twenty hours. His landlady supplied him with nothing: ever since he had gone to her he had done his own catering, going out for his meals. The last meal, on the previous evening, had been a glass of milk and a stale, though sizable bun, and now he felt literally ravenous. It was only by an effort that he could force himself to pass the eating-house; once beyond its door, he ran, ran until he reached his lodgings and slipped three sovereigns into Mrs. Flitwick's hands.

"That'll make us right to this week end, Mrs. Flitwick," he said. "Put the receipt in my room."

"And greatly obliged I am to you, Mr. Lauriston," answered the landlady. "And sorry, indeed, you should have had to put yourself to the trouble, but—"

"All right, all right—no trouble—no trouble at all," exclaimed Lauriston. "Quite easy, I assure you!"

He ran out of the house again and back to where he knew there was food. He was only one-and-twenty, a well-built lad, with a healthy appetite, which, until very recently, had always been satisfied, and just then he was feeling that unless he ate and drank, something—he knew not what—would happen. He was even conscious that his voice was weakening, when, having entered the eating-house and dropped into a seat in one of the little boxes into which the place was divided, he asked the waitress for the food and drink which he was now positively aching for. And he had eaten a plateful of fish and two boiled eggs and several thick slices of bread and butter, and drunk the entire contents of a pot of tea before he even lifted his eyes to look round him. But by that time he was conscious of satisfaction, and he sat up and inspected the place to which he had hurried so eagerly. And in the same moment he once more saw Melky.

Melky had evidently just entered the little eating-house. Evidently, too, he was in no hurry for food or drink. He had paused, just within the entrance, at a desk which stood there, whereat sat Mrs. Goldmark, the proprietress, a plump, pretty young woman, whose dark, flashing eyes turned alternately from watching her waitresses to smiling on her customers as they came to the desk to pay their bills. Melky, his smart billy-cock hat cocked to one side, his sporting-looking overcoat adorned with a flower, was evidently paying compliments to Mrs. Goldmark as he leaned over her desk: she gave him a playful push and called to a waitress to order Mr. Rubinstein a nice steak. And Melky, turning from her with a well satisfied smile, caught sight of Lauriston, and sauntered down to the table at which he sat.

"Get your bit of business done all right?" he asked, confidentially, as he took a seat opposite his fellow-lodger and bent towards him. "Find the old gent accommodating?"

"I didn't see him," answered Lauriston. "I saw a young lady."

"My cousin Zillah," said Melky. "Smart girl, that, mister—worth a pile o' money to the old man—she knows as much about the business as what he does! You wouldn't think, mister," he went on in his soft, lisping tones, "but that girl's had a college education—fact! Old Daniel, he took her to live with him when her father and mother died, she being a little 'un then, and he give her—ah, such an education as I wish I'd had—see?

She's quite the lady—is Zillah—but sticks to the old shop—not half, neither!"

"She seems very business-like," remarked Lauriston, secretly pleased that he had now learned the pretty pawnbroker's name. "She soon did what I wanted."

"In the blood," said Melky, laconically. "We're all of us in that sort o' business, one way or another. Now, between you and me, mister, what did she lend you on that bit o' stuff?"

"Three pounds fifteen," replied Lauriston.

"That's about it," assented Melky, with a nod. He leaned a little nearer. "You don't want to sell the ticket?" he suggested. "Give you a couple o' quid for it, if you do."

"You seem very anxious to buy that watch," said Lauriston, laughing. "No—I don't want to sell the ticket—not I! I wouldn't part with that watch for worlds."

"Well, if you don't, you don't," remarked Melky. "And as to wanting to buy—that's my trade. I ain't no reg'lar business—I buy and sell, anything that comes handy, in the gold and silver line. And as you ain't going to part with that ticker on no consideration, I'll tell you what it's worth, old as it is. Fifteen quid!"

"That's worth knowing, any way," said Lauriston. "I shall always have something by me then, while I have that. You'd have made a profit of a nice bit, then, if I'd sold it to you?"

"It 'ud be a poor world, mister, if you didn't get no profit, wouldn't it?" assented Melky calmly. "We're all of us out to make profit. Look here!—between you and me—you're a lit'ry gent, ain't you? Write a bit, what? Do you want to earn a fiver—comfortable?"

"I should be very glad," replied Lauriston.

"There's a friend o' mine," continued Melky, "wholesale jeweller, down Shoreditch way, wants to get out a catalogue. He ain't no lit'ry powers, d'you see? Now, he'd run to a fiver—cash down—if some writing feller 'ud touch things up a bit for him, like. Lor' bless you!—it wouldn't take you more'n a day's work! What d'ye say to it?"

"I wouldn't mind earning five pounds at that," answered Lauriston.

"Right-oh!" said Melky. "Then some day next week, I'll take you down to see him—he's away till then. And—you'll pay me ten per cent. on the bit o' business, won't you, mister? Business is business, ain't it?"

"All right!" agreed Lauriston. "That's a bargain, of course."

Melky nodded and turned to his steak, and Lauriston presently left him and went away. The plump lady at the desk gave him a smile as she handed him his change.

"Hope to see you again, sir," she said.

Lauriston went back to his room, feeling that the world had changed. He had paid his landlady, he had silver and copper in his pocket, he had the chance of earning five pounds during the coming week—and he expected a cheque for his two stories by every post. And if John Purdie made him the loan he had asked for, he would be able to devote a whole month to finishing his novel—and then, perhaps, there would be fame and riches. The dismal November evening disappeared in a dream of hope.

But by the end of the week hope was dropping to zero again with Lauriston. No letters had arrived—either from John Purdie or the editor. On the Sunday morning he was again face to face with the last half-crown. He laid out his money very cautiously that day, but when he had paid for a frugal dinner at a cheap coffee-shop, he had only a shilling left. He wandered into Kensington Gardens that Sunday afternoon, wondering what he had best do next. And as he stood by the railings of the ornamental water, watching the water-fowls' doings, somebody bade him good-day, and he turned to find the pretty girl of the pawnshop standing at his side and smiling shyly at him.

## CHAPTER THREE
### THE DEAD MAN

Lauriston was thinking about Zillah at the very moment in which she spoke to him: the memory of her dark eyes and the friendly smile that she had given him as he left the pawnshop had come as a relief in the midst of his speculations as to his immediate future. And now, as he saw her real self, close to him, evidently disposed to be friendly, he blushed like any girl, being yet at that age when shyness was still a part of his character. Zillah blushed too—but she was more self-possessed than Lauriston.

"I've been talking to my Cousin Melky about you," she said quickly.
"Or, rather, he's been talking to me. He says he's going to introduce
you to a man who wants his catalogue put in shape—for five pounds.
Don't you do it for five pounds! I know that man—charge him ten!"
Lauriston moved away with her down the walk.
"Oh, but I couldn't do that, now!" he said eagerly. "You see I promised
I'd do it for five."
Zillah gave him a quick glance.
"Don't you be silly!" she said. "When anybody like Melky offers you five pounds for anything, ask them double. They'll give it. You don't know much about money matters, do you?"
Lauriston laughed, and gaining confidence, gave the girl a knowing look.
"Not much," he admitted, "else I wouldn't have had to do that bit of

business with you the other day."

"Oh—that!" she said indifferently. "That's nothing. You'd be astonished if you knew what sort of people just have to run round to us, now and then—I could tell you some secrets! But—I guessed you weren't very well up in money matters, all the same. Writing people seldom are."

"I suppose you are?" suggested Lauriston.

"I've been mixed up in them all my life, more or less," she answered. "Couldn't help being, with my surroundings. You won't think me inquisitive if I ask you something? Were you—hard up—when you came round the other night?"

"Hard up's a mild term," replied Lauriston, frankly. "I hadn't a penny!"

"Excepting a gold watch worth twelve or fifteen pounds," remarked Zillah, drily. "And how long had you been like that?"

"Two or three days—more or less," answered Lauriston. "You see, I've been expecting money for more than a week—that was it."

"Has it come?" she asked.

"No—it hasn't," he replied, with a candid blush. "That's a fact!"

"Will it come—soon?" she demanded.

"By George!—I hope so!" he exclaimed. "I'll be hard up again, if it doesn't."

"And then you offer to do for five what you might easily get ten for!" she said, almost reproachfully. "Let me give you a bit of advice—never accept a first offer. Stand out for a bit more—especially from anybody like my cousin Melky."

"Is Melky a keen one, then?" enquired Lauriston.

"Melky's a young Jew," said Zillah, calmly. "I'm not—I'm half-and-half—a mixture. My mother was Jew—my father wasn't. Well—if you want money to be going on with, and you've got any more gold watches, you know where to come. Don't you ever go with empty pockets in London while you've got a bit of property to pledge! You're not a Londoner, of course?"

"I'm a Scotsman!" said Lauriston.

"To be sure—I knew it by your tongue," asserted Zillah. "And trying to make a living by writing! Well, you'll want courage—and money. Have you had any luck?"

"I've sold two stories," answered Lauriston, who by that time was feeling as if the girl was an old friend. "They come to twenty pounds for the two, at the rate that magazine pays, and I've asked for a cheque—it's that I'm waiting for. It ought to come—any time."

"Oh, but I know that game!" said Zillah. "I've two friends—girls—who write. I know how they have to wait—till publication, or till next pay-day. What a pity that some of you writers don't follow some other profession that would bring in a good income—then you could do your writing to please yourselves, and not be dependent on it. Haven't you thought of that?"

"Often!" answered Lauriston. "And it wouldn't do—for me, anyway. I've made my choice. I'll stick to my pen—and swim or sink with it. And I'm not going to sink!"

"That's the way to talk—to be sure!" said the girl. "But—keep yourself in money, if you can. Don't go without money for three days when you've anything you can raise money on. You see how practical I am! But you've got to be in this world. Will you tell me something?"

"It strikes me," answered Lauriston, looking at her narrowly and bringing the colour to her cheeks, "that I'm just about getting to this—that I'd tell you anything! And so—what is it?"

"How much money have you left?" she asked softly.

"Precisely a shilling—and a copper or two," he answered.

"And—if that cheque doesn't arrive?" she suggested.

"Maybe I'll be walking round to Praed Street again," he said, laughing. "I've a bit of what you call property, yet."

The girl nodded, and turned towards a side-walk that led across the Gardens.

"All right," she said. "Don't think me inquisitive—I don't like to think of—of people like you being hard up: I'm not wrapped up in business as much as all that. Let's talk of something else—tell me what you write about."

Lauriston spent the rest of that afternoon with Zillah, strolling about Kensington Gardens. He had lived a very lonely life since coming to London, and it was a new and pleasant experience to him to have an intelligent companion to talk to. There was a decided sense of exhilaration within him when he finally left her; as for Zillah, she went homewards in a very thoughtful mood, already conscious that she was more than half in love with this good-looking lad who had come so strangely into her life. And at the corner of Praed Street she ran up against Mr. Melky Rubinstein, and button-holed him, and for ten minutes talked seriously to him. Melky, who had good reasons of his own for keeping in his cousin's favour, listened like a lamb to all she had to say, and went off promising implicit obedience to her commandments.

"Zillah ain't half gone on that chap!" mused Melky, as he pursued his way. "Now, ain't it extraordinary that a girl who'll come into a perfect fortune should go and fall head over ears in love with a red-headed young feller what ain't got a penny to bless hisself with! Not but what he ain't got good looks—and brains. And brains is brains, when all's said!"

That night, as Lauriston sat writing in his shabby little room, a knock came at his door—the door opened, and Melky slid in, laying his finger to the side of his large nose in token of confidence.

"Hope I ain't interrupting," said Melky. "I say, mister, I been thinking about that catalogue business. Now I come to sort of reflect on it, I think my friend'll go to ten pound. So we'll say ten pound—what? And I'll take you to see him next Friday. And I say, mister—if a pound or two on account 'ud be of any service—say the word, d'ye see?"

With this friendly assurance, Melky plunged his hand into a hip-pocket, and drew out some gold, which he held towards Lauriston on his open palm.

"Two or three pound on account, now, mister?" he said, ingratiatingly. "You're welcome as the flowers in May!"

But Lauriston shook his head; he had already decided on a plan of his own, if the expected remittance did not arrive next morning.

"No, thank you," he answered. "It's uncommonly good of you—but I can manage very well indeed—I can, really! Next Friday, then—I'll go with you. I'm very much obliged to you."

Melky slipped his money into his pocket—conscious of having done his part. "Just as you like, mister," he said. "But you was welcome, you know. Next Friday, then—and you can reckon on cash down for this job."

The Monday morning brought neither of the expected letters to Lauriston. But he had not spoken without reason when he said to Zillah that he had a bit of property to fall back upon—now that he knew how ready money could easily be raised. He had some pledgeable property in his trunk—and when the remittances failed to arrive, he determined to avail himself of it. Deep down in a corner of the trunk he had two valuable rings—all that his mother had left him, with the exception of two hundred pounds, with which he had ventured to London, and on which he had lived up to then. He got the rings out towards the end of Monday afternoon, determining to take them round to Daniel Multenius and raise sufficient funds on them to last him for, at any rate, another month or two. He had little idea of the real value of such articles, and he had reasons of his own for not showing the rings to Melky Rubinstein; his notion was to wait until evening, when he would go to the pawnshop at about the same time as on his previous visit, in the hope of finding Zillah in charge again. After their meeting and talk of the afternoon before, he felt that she would do business with him in a sympathetic spirit—and if he could raise twenty pounds on the rings he would be free of all monetary anxiety for many a long week to come.

It was half-past five o'clock of that Monday evening when Lauriston, for the second time, turned into the narrow passage which led to the pawnshop door. He had already looked carefully through the street window, in the hope of seeing Zillah inside the front shop. But there was no Zillah to be seen; the front shop was empty. Nor did Zillah confront him when he stepped into the little boxed-in compartment in the pawnshop. There was a curious silence in the place—broken only by the quiet, regular ticking of a clock. That ticking grew oppressive during the minute or two that he waited expecting somebody to step forward. He rapped on the counter at last—gently at first, then more insistently. But nobody came. The clock—hidden from his sight—went on ticking.

Lauriston bent over the counter at last and craned his neck to look into the open door of a little parlour which lay behind the shop. The next instant, with no thought but of the exigencies of the moment, he had leapt over the partition and darted into the room. There, stretched out across the floor, his head lying on the hearthrug, his hands lying inert and nerveless at his sides, lay an old man, grey-bearded, venerable—Daniel Multenius, no doubt. He lay very still, very statuesque—and Lauriston, bending over and placing a trembling hand on the high, white forehead, knew that he was dead.

He started up—his only idea that of seeking help. The whole place was so still that he knew he was alone with the dead in it. Instinctively, he ran through the front shop to the street door—and into the arms of a man who was just entering.

## CHAPTER FOUR
## THE PLATINUM SOLITAIRE

The newcomer, an elderly, thick-set man, who, in spite of his plain clothes, looked as if he were an official of some sort and carried some documents in his hand, at which he was glancing as he entered, started and exclaimed as Lauriston, in his haste, ran up against him. "Hullo!" he said. "What's the matter? You seem in a hurry, young fellow!"

Lauriston, almost out of breath with excitement, turned and pointed to the open door of the little parlour.

"There's an old man—lying in there—dead!" he whispered. "A grey-bearded old man—is it the pawn-broker—Mr. Multenius?"

The man stared, craned his neck to glance in the direction which Lauriston's shaking finger indicated, and then started forward. But he suddenly paused, and motioned Lauriston to go first—and before following him he closed the street door.

"Now then, where?" he said. "Dead, do you say?" He followed Lauriston into the parlour, uttered a sharp exclamation as he caught sight of the recumbent figure, and, bending down, laid a hand on the forehead. "Dead, right enough, my lad!" he muttered. "Been dead some minutes, too. But—where's the girl—the grand-daughter? Have you seen anybody?"

"Not a soul!" answered Lauriston. "Since I came in, the whole place has been as still as—as it is now!"

The man stared at him for a second or two, silently; then, as if he knew the ins and outs of the establishment, he strode to an inner door, threw it open and revealed a staircase.

"Hullo there!" he called loudly. "Hullo! Miss Wildrose! Are you there?"

This was the first time Lauriston had heard Zillah's surname: even in the midst of that startling discovery, it struck him as a very poetical one. But he had no time to reflect on it—the man turned back into the parlour.

"She must be out," he said. "Do you say you found him?"

"Yes—I found him," answered Lauriston. "Just now."

"And what were you doing here?" asked the man. "Who are you?"

Lauriston fancied he detected a faint note of suspicion in these questions, and he drew himself up, with a flush on his face.

"My name's Andrew Lauriston," he answered. "I live close by. I came in on—business. Who are you?"

"Well, if it comes to that, my lad," said the man, "I'm Detective-Sergeant Ayscough—known well enough around these parts! I came to see the old gentleman about these papers. Now—what was your business, then?"

He was watching Lauriston very keenly, and Lauriston, suddenly realizing that he was in an awkward position, determined on candour.

"Well, if you really want to know," he said, "I came to borrow some money—on these rings."

And he opened his left hand and showed the detective the two rings which he had taken from his trunk—not half-an-hour before.

"Your property?" asked Ayscough.

"Of course they're my property!" exclaimed Lauriston. "Whose else should they be?"

Ayscough's glance wandered from the rings to a table which stood, a little to one side, in the middle of the parlour. Lauriston turned in that direction, also. Two objects immediately met his eye. On the table stood a small tray, full of rings—not dissimilar in style and appearance to those which he held in his hand: old-fashioned rings. The light from the gas-brackets above the mantel-piece caught the facets of the diamonds in those rings and made little points of fire; here and there he saw the

15

shimmer of pearls. But there was another object. Close by the tray of old rings lay a book—a beautifully bound book, a small quarto in size, with much elaborate gold ornament on the back and side, and gilt clasps holding the heavy leather binding together. It looked as if some hand had recently thrown this book carelessly on the table.

But Ayscough gave little, if any, attention to the book: his eyes were fixed on the rings in the tray—and he glanced from them to Lauriston's rings.

"Um!" he said presently. "Odd that you have a couple of rings, young man, just like—those! Isn't it?"

"What do you mean?" demanded Lauriston, flushing scarlet. "You don't suggest—"

"Don't suggest anything—just now," answered the detective, quietly. "But you must stop here with me, until I find out more. Come to the door—we must have help here."

Lauriston saw there was nothing to do but to obey, and he followed Ayscough to the street door. The detective opened it, looked out, and waiting a few minutes, beckoned to a policeman who presently strolled along. After a whispered word or two, the policeman went away, and Ayscough beckoned Lauriston back into the shop.

"Now," he said, "there'll be some of our people and a surgeon along in a few minutes—before they come, just tell me your story. You're an honest-looking young chap—but you must admit that it looks a bit queer that I should find you running out of this shop, old Multenius dead inside his parlour, and you with a couple of rings in your possession which look uncommonly like his property! Just tell me how it came about."

Lauriston told him the plain truth—from the pawning of the watch to the present visit. Ayscough watched him narrowly—and at the end nodded his head.

"That sounds like a straight tale, Mr. Lauriston," he said. "I'm inclined to believe every word you say. But I shall have to report it, and all the circumstances, and you'll have to prove that these two rings were your mother's, and all that—and you must stay here till the doctor comes with our people. Queer that the old man should be alone! I wonder where his grand-daughter is?"

But just then the street door opened and Zillah came in, a big bunch of flowers under one arm, some small parcels in the other. At the sight of the two men she started; crimsoned as she saw Lauriston; paled again as she noticed that Ayscough was evidently keeping an eye on him.

"Mr. Ayscough!" she exclaimed. "What's this?—is something the matter? What are you doing here?" she went on hurriedly, turning to Lauriston.

"Inside the shop! What's happened?—tell me, one of you?"

The detective purposely kept himself and Lauriston between Zillah and the open door at the rear of the shop. He made a kindly motion of his head towards her.

"Now, my dear!" he said. "Don't get upset—your grandfather was getting a very old man, you know—and we can't expect old gentlemen to live for ever. Take it quietly, now!"

The girl turned and laid her flowers and parcels on the counter. Lauriston, watching her anxiously, saw that she was nerving herself to be brave.

"That means—he's dead?" she said. "I am quiet—you see I'm quiet. Tell me what's happened—you tell me," she added, glancing at Lauriston. "Tell me—now!"

"I came in and found no one here, and I looked round through the door into the parlour there," answered Lauriston, "and I saw your grandfather lying on the floor. So I jumped over the counter and went to him."

Zillah moved forward as if to go into the parlour. But the detective stopped her, glancing from her to Lauriston.

"You know this young man, Miss Wildrose?" he asked. "You've met him before?"

"Yes," replied Zillah, confidently. "He's Mr. Lauriston. Let me go in there, please. Can nothing be done?"

But Ayscough only shook his head. There was nothing to be done—but to await the arrival of the doctor. They followed the girl into the parlour and stood by while she bent over the dead man. She made no demonstration of grief, and when Ayscough presently suggested that she should go upstairs until the doctor had come, she went quietly away.

"Hadn't we better lift him on that sofa?" suggested Lauriston.

"Not till our people and the police-surgeon have seen him," answered Ayscough, shaking his head. "I want to know all about this—he may have died a natural death—a seizure of some sort—and again, he mayn't—They'll be here in a minute."

Lauriston presently found himself a passive spectator while a police-inspector, another man in plain clothes, and the doctor examined the body, after hearing Ayscough's account of what had just happened. He was aware that he was regarded with suspicion—the inspector somewhat brusquely bade him stay where he was: it would, indeed, have been impossible to leave, for there was a policeman at the door, in which, by his superior's orders, he had turned the key. And there was a general, uncomfortable sort of silence in the place while the doctor busied himself about the body.

"This man has been assaulted!" said the doctor, suddenly turning to the inspector. "Look here!—he's not only been violently gripped by the right arm—look at that bruise—but taken savagely by the throat. There's no doubt of that. Old and evidently feeble as he was, the shock would be quite enough to kill him. But—that's how it's been done, without a doubt."

The inspector turned, looking hard at Lauriston.

"Did you see anybody leaving the place when you entered?" he asked.

"There was no one about here when I came in—either at the street door or at the side door," replied Lauriston, readily. "The whole place was quiet—deserted—except for him. And—he was dead when I found him."

The inspector drew Ayscough aside and they talked in whispers for a few minutes, eyeing Lauriston now and then; eventually they approached him.

"I understand you're known here, and that you live in the neighbourhood," said the inspector. "You'll not object if the sergeant goes round with you to your lodgings—you'll no doubt be able to satisfy him about your respectability, and so on. I don't want to suggest anything—but—you understand?"

"I understand," replied Lauriston. "I'll show or tell him anything he likes. I've told you the plain truth."

"Go with him now," directed the inspector; "you know what to do, Ayscough!"

Half an hour later, when the dead man had been carried to his room, and the shop and house had been closed, Melky Rubinstein, who had come in while the police were still there, and had remained when they had gone, stood talking to Zillah in the upstairs sitting-room. Melky was unusually grave: Zillah had already gathered that the police had some suspicion about Lauriston.

"I'll go round there and see what the detective fellow's doing with him," said Melky. "I ain't got no suspicion about him—not me! But—it's an awkward position—and them rings, too! Now, if he'd only ha' shown 'em to me, first, Zillah—see?"

"Do go, Melky!" urged Zillah tearfully. "Of course, he'd nothing to do with it. Oh!—I wish I'd never gone out!"

Melky went downstairs. He paused for a moment in the little parlour, glancing meditatively at the place where the old man had been found dead. And suddenly his keen eyes saw an object which lay close to the fender, half hidden by a tassel of the hearthrug, and he stooped and picked it up—a solitaire stud, made of platinum, and ornamented with a curious device.

**CHAPTER FIVE**

**THE TWO LETTERS**
Once outside the shop, Lauriston turned sharply on the detective.
"Look here!" he said. "I wish you'd just tell me the truth. Am I suspected? Am I—in some way or other—in custody?"
Ayscough laughed quietly, wagging his head.
"Certainly not in custody," he answered. "And as to the other—well, you know, Mr. Lauriston, supposing we put it in this way?—suppose you'd been me, and I'd been you, half-an-hour ago? What would you have thought if you'd found me in the situation and under the circumstances in which I found you? Come, now!"
"Yes," replied Lauriston, after a moment's reflection. "I suppose it's natural that you should suspect me—finding me there, alone with the old man. But—"
"It's not so much suspicion in a case of this sort, as a wish to satisfy one's self," interrupted the detective. "You seem a gentleman-like young fellow, and you may be all right. I want to know that you are—I'd like to know that you are! It would be no satisfaction to me to fasten this business on you, I can assure you. And if you like to tell me about yourself, and how you came to go to Multenius's—why, it would be as well."
"There's not much to tell," answered Lauriston. "I came from Scotland to London, two years ago or thereabouts, to earn my living by writing. I'd a bit of money when I came—I've lived on it till now. I've just begun to earn something. I've been expecting a cheque for some work for these last ten or twelve days, but I was running short last week—so I went to that place to pawn my watch—I saw the young lady there. As my cheque hadn't arrived today, I went there again to pawn those rings I told you about and showed you. And—that's all. Except this—I was advised to go to Multenius's by a relation of theirs, Mr. Rubinstein, who lodges where I do. He knows me."
"Oh, Melky Rubinstein!" said Ayscough. "I know Melky—sharp chap he is. He sold me this pin I'm wearing. Well, that seems quite a straightforward tale, Mr. Lauriston. I've no doubt all will be satisfactory. You've friends in London, of course?"
"No—none," replied Lauriston. "And scarcely an acquaintance. I've kept to myself—working hard: I've had no time—nor inclination, either—to make friends. Here's the house where I lodge—it's not much of a place, but come in."
They had reached Mrs. Flitwick's house by that time, and Mrs. Flitwick herself was in the narrow, shabby passage as they entered. She

immediately produced two letters.

"Here's two letters for you, Mr. Lauriston," she said, with a sharp glance at Ayscough. "One of 'em's a registered—I did sign for it. So I kept 'em myself, instead of sending 'em up to your room."

"Thank you, Mrs. Flitwick," said Lauriston. He took the letters, saw that the writing on the registered envelope was his old friend John Purdie's, and that the other letter was from the magazine to which he had sold his stories, and turned to Ayscough. "Come up to my room," he continued. "We'll talk up there."

Ayscough followed him up to his room—once inside, and the door shut, Lauriston tore open the letter from the magazine, and extracted a printed form and a cheque for twenty guineas. He took one look at them and thrust them into the detective's hands.

"There!" he said, with a sigh of mingled relief and triumph. "There's a proof of the truth of one statement I made to you! That's the expected cheque I told you of. Excuse me while I look at the other letter."

Out of the registered letter came a bank-note—for twenty pounds—and a hastily scribbled note which Lauriston eagerly read. "Dear old Andie," it ran, "I've only just got your letter, for I've been from home for a fortnight, and had no letters sent on to me. Of course you'll make me your banker until your book's finished—and afterwards, too, if need be. Here's something to be going on with—but I'm coming to London in a day or two, as it happens, and will go into the matter—I'll call on you as soon as I arrive. Excuse this scrawl—post time. Always yours, John Purdie."

Lauriston thrust that letter, too, into Ayscough's hands.

"If I've no friends in London, there's proof of having one in my own country!" he exclaimed. "Ah!—if those letters had only come before I went off to Praed Street!"

"Just so!" agreed the detective, glancing the letters and their accompaniments over. "Well, I'm glad you're able to show me these, Mr. Lauriston, anyway. But now, about those rings—between you and me, I wish they hadn't been so much like those that were lying in that tray on the old man's table. It's an unfortunate coincidence!—because some folks might think, you know, that you'd just grabbed a couple of those as you left the place. Eh?"

"My rings have been in that trunk for two or three years," asserted Lauriston. "They were my mother's, and I believe she'd had them for many a year before she died. They may resemble those that we saw in that tray, but—"

"Well, I suppose you can bring somebody—if necessary, that is—to prove that they were your mother's, can't you?" asked Ayscough. "That'll make matters all right—on that point. And as for the rest—it's very lucky you know Melky Rubinstein, and that the girl knew you as a customer. But, my faith!—I wish you'd caught a glimpse of somebody leaving that shop! For there's no doubt the old man met his death by violence."

"I know nothing of it," said Lauriston, "I saw no one."

Just then Melky came in. He glanced at the cheque and the bank-notes lying on the table, and nodded to Lauriston as if he understood their presence. Then he turned to Ayscough, almost anxiously.

"I say, Mr. Ayscough!" he said, deprecatingly. "You ain't going to be so unkind as to mix up this here young fellow in what's happened. S'elp me, Mr. Ayscough, I couldn't believe anything o' that sort about him, nohow—nor would my cousin, Zillah, what you know well enough, neither; he's as quiet as a lamb, Mr. Ayscough, is Mr. Lauriston—ain't I known him, lodging here as he does, this many a month? I'll give my word for him, anyway, Mr. Ayscough! And you police gentlemen know me. Don't you now, Mr. Ayscough?"

"Very well indeed, my boy!" agreed the detective, heartily. "And I'll tell you what—I shall have to trouble Mr. Lauriston to go round with me to the station, just to give a formal account of what happened, and a bit of explanation, you know—I'm satisfied myself about him, and so, no doubt, will our people be, but you come with us, Melky, and say a word or two—say you've known him for some time, d'ye see—it'll help."

"Anything to oblige a friend, Mr. Ayscough," said Melky. He motioned to Lauriston to put his money in his pocket. "Glad to see your letters turned up," he whispered as they went downstairs. "I say!—a word in your ear—don't you tell these here police chaps any more than you need—I'll stand up for you."

The detective's report, a little questioning of Lauriston, and Melky's fervent protestations on Lauriston's behalf, served to satisfy the authorities at the police-station, and Lauriston was allowed to go— admonished by the inspector that he'd be wanted at the inquest, as the most important witness. He went out into the street with Melky.

"Come and have a bit o' supper at Mrs. Goldmark's," suggested Melky. "I shall have my hands full tonight at the poor old man's, but I ain't had nothing since dinner."

Lauriston, however, excused himself. He wanted to go home and write letters—at once. But he promised to look round at the pawnshop later in the evening, to see if he could be of any use, and to give Melky a full account of his finding of the old pawnbroker.

"Ah!" remarked Melky, as they pushed at the door of the eating-house. "And ain't it going to be a nice job to find the man that scragged him?—I don't think! But I'm going to take a hand at that game, mister!—let alone the police."

Mrs. Goldmark was out. She had heard the news, said the waitress who was left in charge, and had gone round to do what she could for Miss Zillah. So Melky, deprived of the immediate opportunity of talk with Mrs. Goldmark, ordered his supper, and while he ate and drank, cogitated and reflected. And his thoughts ran chiefly on the platinum solitaire stud which he had carefully bestowed in his vest pocket.

It was Melky's firm belief—already—that the stud had been dropped in Daniel Multenius's back parlour by some person who had no business there—in other words by the old man's assailant. And ever since he had found the stud, Melky had been wondering and speculating on his chances of finding its owner. Of one thing he was already certain: that the owner, whoever he was, was no ordinary person. Ordinary, everyday persons do not wear studs or tie-pins on chains made of platinum—the most valuable of all the metals. How came a solitaire stud, made of a metal far more valuable than gold, and designed and ornamented in a peculiar fashion, to be lying on the hearthrug of old Daniel Multenius's room? It was not to be believed that the old man had dropped it there—no, affirmed Melky to himself, with conviction, that bit of personal property had been dropped there, out of a loose shirt-cuff by some man who had called on Daniel not long before Andie Lauriston had gone in, and who for some mysterious reason had scragged the old fellow. And now the question was—who was that man?

"Got to find that out, somehow!" mused Melky. "Else that poor chap'll be in a nice fix—s'elp me, he will! And that 'ud never do!"

Melky, in spite of his keenness as a business man, and the fact that from boyhood he had had to fight the world by himself, had a peculiarly soft heart—he tended altogether to verge on the sentimental. He had watched Lauriston narrowly, and had developed a decided feeling for him—moreover, he now knew that his cousin Zillah, hitherto adamant to many admirers, had fallen in love with Lauriston: clearly, Lauriston must be saved. Melky knew police ways and methods, and he felt sure that whatever Ayscough, a good-natured man, might think, the superior authorities would view Lauriston's presence in the pawnshop with strong suspicion. Therefore—the real culprit must be found. And he, Melky Rubinstein—he must have a go at that game.

He finished his supper, thinking hard all the time he ate and drank; finally he approached the desk to pay his bill. The young woman whom Mrs. Goldmark had left in charge lifted the lid of the desk to get some change—and Melky's astonished eyes immediately fell on an object which lay on top of a little pile of papers. That object was the duplicate of the platinum solitaire which Melky had in his pocket. Without ceremony—being well known there—he at once picked it up.

"What's this bit of jewellery?" he demanded.

"That?" said the waitress, indifferently. "Oh, one of the girls picked it up the other day off a table where a stranger had been sitting—we think he'd dropped it. Mrs. Goldmark says it's valuable, so she put it away, in case he comes again. But we haven't seen him since."

Melky took a good look at the second stud. Then he put it back in the desk, picked up his change, and went away—in significant silence.

## CHAPTER SIX
## THE SPANISH MANUSCRIPT

Lauriston, walking back to his room after leaving Melky at the door of the eating-house, faced the situation in which an unfortunate combination of circumstances had placed him. Ayscough had been placable enough; the authorities at the police-station had heard his own version of things with attention—but he was still conscious that he was under a certain amount of suspicion. More than that, he felt convinced that the police would keep an eye on him that night. Ayscough, indeed, had more than hinted that that would probably be done. For anything he knew, some plain-clothes man might be shadowing him even then—anyway, there had been no mistaking the almost peremptory request of the inspector that he should report himself at the police station in the morning. It was no use denying the fact—he was suspected, in some degree.

He knew where the grounds of suspicion lay—in his possession of two rings, which were undoubtedly very similar to the rings which lay in the tray that he and the detective had found on the table in the back-parlour of the pawnshop. It needed no effort on the part of one who had already had considerable experience in the construction of plots for stories, to see how the police would build up a theory of their own. Here, they would say, is a young fellow, who on his own confession, is so hard up, so penniless, indeed, that he has had to pawn his watch. He has got to know something of this particular pawnshop, and of its keepers—he watches the girl leave; he ascertains that the old man is alone; he enters, probably he sees that tray of rings lying about; he grabs a couple of the rings; the old man interrupts him in the act; he seizes the old man, to silence his outcries; the old man, feeble enough at any time, dies under the shock. A clear, an unmistakable case!

What was he, Lauriston, to urge against the acceptance of such a theory? He thought over everything that could be said on his behalf. The friendliness of Zillah and her cousin Melky towards him could be dismissed—that, when it came to it, would weigh little against the cold marshalling of facts which a keen legal mind would put into the opposite scale. His own contention that it was scarcely probable that he should have gone to the pawnshop except to pledge something, and that that something was the rings, would also be swept aside, easily enough: his real object, the other side would say, had been robbery when the old man was alone: what evidence had he that the two rings which he had in his hand when Ayscough found him hurrying out of the shop were really his? Here, Lauriston knew he was in a difficulty. He had kept these two rings safely hidden in his old-fashioned trunk ever since coming to London, and had never shown them to a single person—he had, indeed, never seen them himself for a long time until he took them out that afternoon. But where was his proof of that! He had no relations to whom he could appeal. His mother had possessed an annuity; just sufficient to maintain her and her son, and to give Lauriston a good education: it had died with her, and all that she had left him, to start life on, was about two hundred pounds and some small personal belongings, of which the rings and his father's watch and chain were a part. And he remembered now that his mother had kept those rings as securely put away as he had kept them since her death—until they came into his hands at her death he had only once seen them; she had shown them to him when he was a boy and had said they were very valuable. Was it possible that there was any one, far away in Scotland, who had known his mother and who would come forward—if need arose—and prove that those rings had been her property? But when he had put this question to himself, he had to answer it with a direct negative—he knew of no one.

There was one gleam of hope in this critical situation. John Purdie was coming to London. Lauriston had always felt that he could rely on John Purdie, and he had just received proof of the value of his faith in his old schoolmate. John Purdie would tell him what to do: he might even suggest the names of some of Mrs. Lauriston's old friends. And perhaps the need might not arise—there must surely be some clue to the old pawnbroker's assailant; surely the police would go deeper into the matter. He cheered up at these thoughts, and having written replies to the two welcome letters and asked John Purdie to see him immediately on his arrival in town, he went out again to the post-office and to fulfil his promise to Melky to call at the pawnshop.

Lauriston was naturally of quick observation. He noticed now, as he stepped out into the ill-lighted, gloomy street that a man was pacing up and down in front of the house. This man took no notice of him as he passed, but before he had reached Praed Street, he glanced around, and saw that he was following him. He followed him to Spring Street post-office; he was in his rear when Lauriston reached the pawnshop. Idly and perfunctorily as the man seemed to be strolling about, Lauriston was sure that he was shadowing him—and he told Melky of the fact when Melky admitted him to the shop by the private door.

"Likely enough, mister," remarked Melky. "But I shouldn't bother myself about it if I were you. There'll be more known about this affair before long. Now, look here," he continued, leading the way into the little back-parlour where Lauriston had found Daniel Multenius lying dead, "here's you and me alone—Zillah, she's upstairs, and Mrs. Goldmark is with her. Just you tell me what you saw when you came in here, d'you see, Mr. Lauriston—never mind the police—just give me the facts. I ain't no fool, you know, and I'm going to work this thing out."

Lauriston gave Melky a complete account of his connection with the matter: Melky checked off all the points on his long fingers. At the end he turned to the table and indicated the finely-bound book which Lauriston had noticed when he and the detective had first looked round.

"The police," said Melky, "made Zillah lock up that tray o' rings that was there in a drawer what she had to clear out for 'em, and they've put a seal on it till tomorrow. They've got those rings of yours, too, mister, haven't they?"

"They said it would be best for me to leave them with them," answered Lauriston. "Ayscough advised it. They gave me a receipt for them, you know."

"All right," remarked Melky. "But there's something they ain't had the sense to see the importance of—that fine book there. Mister!—that there book wasn't in this parlour, nor in this shop, nor in this house, at a quarter to five o'clock this afternoon, when my cousin Zillah went out, leaving the poor old man alone. She'll swear to that. Now then, who brought it here—who left it here? Between the time Zillah went out, mister, and the time you come in, and found what you did find, somebody—somebody!—had been in here and left that book behind him! And—mark you!—it wasn't pawned, neither. That's a fact! And—it's no common book, that. Look at it, Mr. Lauriston—you'd ought to know something about books. Look at it!—s'elp me if I don't feel there's a clue in that there volume, whoever it belongs to!"

Lauriston took the book in his hands. He had only glanced at it casually before; now he examined it carefully, while Melky stood at his elbow, watching. The mysterious volume was certainly worthy of close inspection—a small quarto, wonderfully bound in old dark crimson morocco leather, and ornamented on sides and back with curious gold

25

arabesque work: a heavy clasp, also intricately wrought, held the boards together. Lauriston, something of a book lover, whose natural inclination was to spend his last shilling on a book rather than on beef and bread, looked admiringly at this fine specimen of the binder's art as he turned it over.

"That's solid gold, isn't it?" he asked as he unfastened the clasp.

"You know."

"Solid gold it is, mister—and no error," assented Melky. "Now, what's inside? It ain't no blooming account-book, I'll bet!"

Lauriston opened the volume, to reveal leaves of old vellum, covered with beautiful fine writing. He had sufficient knowledge of foreign languages to know what he was looking at.

"That's Spanish!" he said. "An old Spanish manuscript—and I should say it's worth a rare lot of money. How could it have come here?"

Melky took the old volume out of Lauriston's hands, and put it away in a corner cupboard.

"Ah, just so, mister!" he said. "But we'll keep that question to ourselves—for awhile. Don't you say nothing to the police about that there old book—I'll give Zillah the tip. More hangs round that than we know of yet. Now look here!—there'll be the opening of the inquest tomorrow. You be careful! Take my tip and don't let 'em get more out of you than's necessary. I'll go along with you. I'm going to stop here tonight—watch-dog, you know. Mrs. Goldmark and another friend's going to be here as well, so Zillah'll have company. And I say, Zillah wants a word with you—stop here, and I'll send her down."

Lauriston presently found himself alone with Zillah in the little parlour. She looked at him silently, with eyes full of anxiety: he suddenly realized that the anxiety was for himself.

"Don't!" he said, moving close to her and laying his hand on her arm.

"I'm not afraid!"

Zillah lifted her large dark eyes to his.

"Those rings?" she said. "You'll be able to account for them? The police, oh, I'm so anxious about you!"

"The rings are mine!" he exclaimed. "It doesn't matter what the police say or think, or do, either—at least, it shan't matter. And—you're not to be anxious I've got a good friend coming from Scotland—Melky told you I'd had two lots of good news tonight, didn't he?"

A moment later Lauriston was in the street—conscious that, without a word spoken between them, he and Zillah had kissed each other. He went away with a feeling of exaltation—and he only laughed when he saw a man detach himself from a group on the opposite side of the street

26

and saunter slowly after him. Let the police shadow him—watch his lodgings all night, if they pleased—he had something else to think of. And presently, not even troubling to look out of his window to see if there was a watcher there, he went to bed, to dream of Zillah's dark eyes.

But when morning came, and Lauriston realized that a fateful day was before him, his thoughts were not quite so rosy. He drew up his blind—there, certainly was a man pacing the opposite sidewalk. Evidently, he was not to escape surveillance; the official eye was on him! Supposing, before the day was out, the official hand was on him, too?

He turned from the window as he heard his newspaper thrust under his door. He had only one luxury—a copy of the *Times* every morning. It was a three-penny *Times* in those days, but he had always managed to find his weekly eighteen pence for it. He picked it up now, and carelessly glanced at its front page as he was about to lay it aside. The next moment he was eagerly reading a prominent advertisement:

"Lost in a Holborn to Chapel Street Omnibus, about 4 o'clock yesterday afternoon, a Spanish manuscript, bound in old crimson morocco. Whoever has found the same will be most handsomely rewarded on bringing it to Spencer Levendale, Esq., M.P., 591, Sussex Square, W."

Lauriston read this twice over—and putting the paper in his pocket, finished his dressing and went straight to the police-station.

**CHAPTER SEVEN**
**THE MEMBER OF PARLIAMENT**

Melky Rubinstein came out of the side-passage by Multenius's shop as Lauriston neared it; he, too, had a newspaper bulging from his coat pocket, and at sight of Lauriston he pulled it out and waved it excitedly.

"What'd I tell you, mister?" exclaimed Melky, as Lauriston joined him, the shadowing plain-clothes man in his rear. "D'ye see this?" He pointed to an advertisement in his own paper, which he had marked with blue pencil. "There y'are, Mr. Lauriston!—that identical old book what's inside the parlour—advertised for—handsome reward, too, in the *Daily Telegraph*! Didn't I say we'd hear more of it?"

Lauriston pulled out the *Times* and indicated the Personal Column.

"It's there, too," he said. "This man, Mr. Levendale, is evidently very anxious to recover his book. And he's lost no time in advertising for it, either! But—however did it get to Multenius's?"

"Mister!" said Melky, solemnly. "We'll have to speak to the police—now. There's going to be a fine clue in that there book. I didn't mean to say nothing to the police about it, just yet, but after this here advertisement, t'ain't no use keeping the thing to ourselves. Come on round to the police-station."

"That's just where I was going," replied Lauriston. "Let's get hold of Ayscough."

Ayscough was standing just inside the police-station when they went up the steps; he, too, had a newspaper in his hands, and at sight of them he beckoned them to follow him into an office in which two or three other police officials were talking. He led Lauriston and Melky aside.

"I say!" he said. "Here's a curious thing! That book we noticed on the table in Multenius's back room last night—that finely bound book—it's advertised for in the *Daily Mail*—handsome reward offered."

"Yes, and in the *Times*, too—and in the *Daily Telegraph*," said Lauriston. "Here you are—just the same advertisement. It's very evident the owner's pretty keen about getting it back."

Ayscough glanced at the two newspapers, and then beckoned to a constable who was standing near the door.

"Jim!" he said, as the man came up. "Just slip across to the newsagent's over there and get me the *News*, the *Chronicle*, the *Standard*, the *Morning Post*. If the owner's as keen as all that," he added, turning back to Lauriston, "he'll have put that advertisement in all the morning papers, and I'd like to make sure. What's known about that book at the shop?" he asked, glancing at Melky. "Does your cousin know anything?"

Melky's face assumed its most solemn expression.

"Mister!" he said earnestly. "There ain't nothing known at the shop about that there book, except this here. It wasn't there when my cousin Zillah left the old man alone at a quarter to five yesterday afternoon. It was there when this here gentleman found the old man. But it hadn't been pledged, nor yet sold, Mr. Ayscough—There'd ha' been an entry in the books if it had been taken in pawn, or bought across the counter—and there's no entry. Now then—who'd left it there?"

Another official had come up to the group—one of the men who questioned Lauriston the night before. He turned to Lauriston as Melky finished.

"You don't know anything about this book?" he asked.

"Nothing—except that Mr. Ayscough and I saw it lying on the table in the back room, close by that tray of rings," replied Lauriston. "I was attracted by the binding, of course."

"Where's the book, now?" asked the official.

"Put safe away, mister," replied Melky. "It's all right. But this here gentleman what's advertising for it—"

Just then the constable returned with several newspapers and handed them over to Ayscough, who immediately laid them on a desk and turned to the advertisements, while the others crowded round him.

"In every one of 'em," exclaimed Ayscough, a moment later. "Word for word, in every morning newspaper in London! He must have sent that advertisement round to all the offices last night. And you'll notice," he added, turning to the other official, "that this Mr. Levendale only lost this book about four o'clock yesterday afternoon: therefore, it must have been taken to Multenius's shop between then and when we saw it there."

"The old man may have found it in the 'bus," suggested a third police officer who had come up. "Looks as if he had."

"No, mister," said Melky firmly. "Mr. Multenius wasn't out of the shop at all yesterday afternoon—I've made sure o' that fact from my cousin. He didn't find no book, gentlemen. It was brought there."

Ayscough picked up one of the papers and turned to Melky and Lauriston.

"Here!" he said. "We'll soon get some light on this. You two come with me—we'll step round to Mr. Levendale."

Ten minutes later, the three found themselves at the door of one of the biggest houses in Sussex Square; a moment more and they were being ushered within by a footman who looked at them with stolid curiosity. Lauriston gained a general impression of great wealth and luxury, soft carpets, fine pictures, all the belongings of a very rich man's house—then he and his companions were ushered into a large room, half study, half library, wherein, at a massive, handsomely carved desk, littered with books and papers, sat a middle-aged, keen-eyed man, who looked quietly up from his writing-pad at his visitors.

"S'elp me!—one of ourselves!" whispered Melky Rubinstein at Lauriston's elbow. "Twig him!"

Lauriston was quick enough of comprehension and observation to know what Melky meant. Mr. Spencer Levendale was certainly a Jew. His dark hair and beard, his large dark eyes, the olive tint of his complexion, the lines of his nose and lips all betrayed his Semitic origin. He was evidently a man of position and of character; a quiet-mannered, self-possessed man of business, not given to wasting words. He glanced at the card which Ayscough had sent in, and turned to him with one word.

"Well?"

Ayscough went straight to the point.

"I called, Mr. Levendale, about that advertisement of yours which appears in all this morning's newspapers," he said. "I may as well tell you that that book of yours was found yesterday afternoon, under strange circumstances. Mr. Daniel Multenius, the jeweller and pawnbroker, of Praed Street—perhaps you know him, sir?"

"Not at all!" answered Levendale. "Never heard of him."

"He was well known in this part of the town," remarked Ayscough, quietly. "Well, sir—Mr. Multenius was found dead in his back-parlour yesterday afternoon, about five-thirty, by this young man, Mr. Lauriston, who happened to look in there, and I myself was on the spot a few minutes later. Your book—for it's certainly the same—was lying on the table in the parlour. Now, this other young man, Mr. Rubinstein, is a relation of Mr. Multenius's—from enquiries he's made, Mr. Levendale, it's a fact that the book was neither pawned nor sold at Multenius's, though it must certainly have been brought there between the time you lost it and the time we found the old gentleman lying dead. Now, we—the police—want to know how it came there. And so—I've come round to you. What can you tell me, sir?"

Levendale, who had listened to Ayscough with great—and, as it seemed to Lauriston, with very watchful—attention, pushed aside a letter he was writing, and looked from one to the other of his callers.

"Where is my book?" he asked.

"It's all right—all safe, mister," said Melky. "It's locked up in a cupboard, in the parlour where it was found, and the key's in my pocket."

Levendale turned to the detective, glancing again at Ayscough's card.

"All I can tell you, sergeant," he said, "is—practically—what I've told the public in my advertisement. Of course, I can supplement it a bit. The book is a very valuable one—you see," he went on, with a careless wave of his hand towards his book-shelves. "I'm something of a collector of rare books. I bought this particular book yesterday afternoon, at a well-known dealer's in High Holborn. Soon after buying it, I got into a Cricklewood omnibus, which I left at Chapel Street—at the corner of Praed Street, as a matter of fact: I wished to make a call at the Great Western Hotel. It was not till I made that call that I found I'd left the book in the 'bus—I was thinking hard about a business matter—I'd placed the book in a corner behind me—and, of course, I'd forgotten it, valuable though it is. And so, later on, after telephoning to the omnibus people, who'd heard nothing, I sent that advertisement round to all the morning papers. I'm very glad to hear of it—and I shall be pleased to reward you," he concluded, turning to Melky. "Handsomely!—as I promised."

But Melky made no sign of gratitude or pleasure. He was eyeing the rich man before him in inquisitive fashion.

"Mister!" he said suddenly. "I'd like to ask you a question."

Levendale frowned a little.

"Well?" he asked brusquely. "What is it?"

"This here," replied Melky. "Was that there book wrapped up? Was it brown-papered, now, when you left it?"

It seemed to Lauriston that Levendale was somewhat taken aback. But if he was, it was only for a second: his answer, then, came promptly enough.

"No, it was not," he said. "I carried it away from the shop where I bought it—just as it was. Why do you ask?"

"It's a very fine-bound book," remarked Melky. "I should ha' thought, now, that if it had been left in a 'bus, the conductor would ha' noticed it, quick."

"So should I," said Levendale. "Anything else?" he added, glancing at Ayscough.

"Well, no, Mr. Levendale, thank you," replied the detective. "At least not just now. But—the fact is, Mr. Multenius appears to have come to his death by violence—and I want to know if whoever took your book into his shop had anything to do with it."

"Ah!—however, I can't tell you any more," said Levendale. "Please see that my book's taken great care of and returned to me, sergeant. Good-morning."

Outside, Ayscough consulted his watch and looked at his companions.

"Time we were going on to the inquest," he remarked. "Come on—we'll step round there together. You're both wanted, you know."

"I'll join you at the Coroner's court, Mr. Ayscough," said Melky. "I've got a few minutes' business—shan't be long."

He hurried away by a short cut to Praed Street and turned into Mrs. Goldmark's establishment.

Mrs. Goldmark herself was still ministering to Zillah, but the young woman whom Melky had seen the night before was in charge. Melky drew her aside.

"I say!" he said, with an air of great mystery. "A word with you, miss!—private, between you and me. Can you tell me what like was that fellow what you believed to ha' lost that there cuff stud you showed me in Mrs. Goldmark's desk?—you know?"

"Yes!" answered the young woman promptly.

"Tall—dark—clean-shaved—very brown—looked like one of those Colonials that you see sometimes—wore a slouch hat."

"Not a word to nobody!" warned Melky, more mysteriously than ever. And nodding his head with great solemnity, he left the eating-house, and hurried away to the Coroner's Court.

## CHAPTER EIGHT
### THE INQUEST

Until he and Ayscough walked into this particular one, Lauriston had never been in a Coroner's Court in his life. He knew very little about what went on in such places. He was aware that the office of Coroner is of exceeding antiquity; that when any person meets his or her death under suspicious circumstances an enquiry into those circumstances is held by a Coroner, who has a jury of twelve men to assist him in his duties: but what Coroner and jury did, what the procedure of these courts was, he did not know. It surprised him, accordingly, to find himself in a hall which had all the outward appearance of a court of justice—a raised seat, on a sort of dais, for the Coroner; a box for the jury; a table for officials and legal gentlemen; a stand for witnesses, and accommodation for the general public. Clearly, it was evident that when any one died as poor old Daniel Multenius had died, the law took good care that everybody should know everything about it, and that whatever mystery there was should be thoroughly investigated.

The general public, however, had not as yet come to be greatly interested in the death of Daniel Multenius. Up to that moment the affair was known to few people beyond the police, the relations of the dead man, and his immediate neighbours in Praed Street. Consequently, beyond the interested few, there was no great assemblage in the court that morning. A reporter or two, each with his note-book, lounged at the end of the table on the chance of getting some good copy out of whatever might turn up; some of the police officials whom Lauriston had already seen stood chatting with the police surgeon and a sharp-eyed legal looking man, who was attended by a clerk; outside the open door, a group of men, evidently tradesmen and householders of the district, hung about, looking as if they would be glad to get back to their businesses and occupations. Melky, coming in a few minutes after Lauriston had arrived, and sitting down by him, nudged his elbow as he pointed to these individuals.

"There's the fellows what sits on the jury, mister!" whispered Melky. "Half-a-crown each they gets for the job—and a nice mess they makes of it, sometimes. They've the power to send a man for trial for his life, has them chaps—all depends on their verdict. But lor' bless yer!—they takes their tip from the Coroner—he's the fellow what you've got to watch."

Then Melky looked around more narrowly, and suddenly espied the legal-looking man who was talking to the police. He dug his elbow into Lauriston.

"Mister!" he whispered. "You be careful what you say when you get into that there witness-box. See that man there, a-talking to the detectives?—him with the gold nippers on his blooming sharp nose? That's Mr. Parminter!—I knows him, well enough. He's a lawyer chap, what the police gets when there's a case o' this sort, to ask questions of the witnesses, d'ye see? Watch him, Mr. Lauriston, if he starts a-questioning you!—he's the sort that can get a tale out of a dead cod-fish—s'elp me, he is! He's a terror, he is!—the Coroner ain't in it with him—he's a good sort, the Coroner, but Parminter—Lord love us! ain't I heard him turn witnesses inside out—not half! And here is the Coroner."

Lauriston almost forgot that he was an important witness, and was tempted to consider himself nothing but a spectator as he sat and witnessed the formal opening of the Court, the swearing-in of the twelve jurymen, all looking intensely bored, and the preliminaries which prefaced the actual setting-to-work of the morning's business. But at last, after some opening remarks from the Coroner, who said that the late Mr. Daniel Multenius was a well-known and much respected tradesman of the neighbourhood, that they were all sorry to hear of his sudden death, and that there were circumstances about it which necessitated a careful investigation, the business began—and Lauriston, who, for professional purposes, had heard a good many legal cases, saw, almost at once, that the police, through the redoubtable Mr. Parminter, now seated with his clerk at the table, had carefully arranged the presenting of evidence on a plan and system of their own, all of which, so it became apparent to him, was intended to either incriminate himself, or throw considerable suspicion upon him. His interest began to assume a personal complexion. The story of the circumstances of Daniel Multenius's death, as unfolded in the witness-box into which one person went after another, appeared to be the fairly plain one—looked at from one point of view: there was a certain fascination in its unfolding. It began with Melky, who was first called—to identify the deceased, to answer a few general questions about him, and to state that when he last saw him, a few hours before his death, he was in his usual good health: as good, at any rate, as a man of his years—seventy-five—who was certainly growing feeble, could expect to be in. Nothing much was asked of Melky, and nothing beyond bare facts volunteered by him: the astute Mr. Parminter left him alone. A more important witness was the police-surgeon, who testified that the deceased had been dead twenty minutes when he was called to him, that he had without doubt been violently assaulted, having been savagely seized by the throat and by the left arm, on both of which significant marks were plainly visible, and that the cause of death was shock following immediately on this undoubted violence. It was evident, said this witness, that the old man was feeble, and that he suffered from a weak heart: such an attack as that which he had described would be sufficient to cause death, almost instantly.

"So it is a case of murder!" muttered Melky, who had gone back to sit by

Lauriston. "That's what the police is leading up to. Be careful, mister!"
But there were three witnesses to call before Lauriston was called upon. It was becoming a mystery to him that his evidence was kept back so long—he had been the first person to find the old man's dead body, and it seemed, to his thinking, that he ought to have been called at a very early stage of the proceedings. He was about to whisper his convictions on this point to Melky, when a door was opened and Zillah was escorted in by Ayscough, and led to the witness-box.

Zillah had already assumed the garments of mourning for her grandfather. She was obviously distressed at being called to give evidence, and the Coroner made her task as brief as possible. It was—at that stage—little that he wanted to know. And Zillah told little. She had gone out to do some shopping, at half-past-four on the previous afternoon. She left her grandfather alone. He was then quite well. He was in the front shop, doing nothing in particular. She was away about an hour, when she returned to find Detective-Sergeant Ayscough, whom she knew, and Mr. Lauriston, whom she also knew, in the shop, and her grandfather dead in the parlour behind. At this stage of her evidence, the Coroner remarked that he did not wish to ask Zillah any further questions just then, but he asked her to remain in court. Mrs. Goldmark had followed her, and she and Zillah sat down near Melky and Lauriston—and Lauriston half believed that his own turn would now come.

But Ayscough was next called—to give a brief, bald, matter-of-fact statement of what he knew. He had gone to see Mr. Multenius on a business affair—he was making enquiries about a stolen article which was believed to have been pledged in the Edgware Road district. He told how Lauriston ran into him as he entered the shop; what Lauriston said to him; what he himself saw and observed; what happened afterwards. It was a plain and practical account, with no indication of surprise, bias, or theory—and nobody asked the detective any questions arising out of it.

"Ain't nobody but you to call, now, mister," whispered Melky. "Mind your p's and q's about them blooming rings—and watch that Parminter!"

But Melky was mistaken—the official eye did not turn upon Lauriston but, upon the public benches of the court, as if it were seeking some person there.

"There is a witness who has volunteered a statement to the police," said the Coroner. "I understand it is highly important. We had better hear him at this point. Benjamin Hollinshaw!"

Melky uttered a curious groan, and glanced at Lauriston.

"Fellow what has a shop right opposite!" he whispered. "S'elp me!—

34

what's he got to say about it?"

Benjamin Hollinshaw came forward. He was a rather young, rather self-confident, self-important sort of person, who strode up to the witness-box as if he had been doing things of importance and moment all his life, and was taking it quite as a matter of course that he should do another. He took the oath and faced the court with something of an air, as much as to imply that upon what he was about to say more depended than any one could conceive. Invited to tell what he knew, he told his story, obviously enjoying the telling of it. He was a tradesman in Praed Street: a dealer in second-hand clothing, to be exact; been there many years, in succession to his father. He remembered yesterday afternoon, of course. About half-past-five o'clock he was standing at the door of his shop. It was directly facing Daniel Multenius's shop door. The darkness had already come on, and there was also a bit of a fog in the street: not much, but hazy, as it were. Daniel Multenius's window was lighted, but the light was confined to a couple of gas-jets. There was a light in the projecting sign over the side entrance to the pawnshop, down the passage. For the first few minutes while he stood at his door, looking across to Multenius's, he did not see any one enter or leave that establishment. But he then saw a young man come along, from the Edgware Road direction, whose conduct rather struck him. The young man, after sauntering past Multenius's shop, paused, turned, and proceeded to peer in through the top panel of the front door. He looked in once or twice in that way. Then he went to the far end of the window and looked inside in the same prying fashion, as if he wanted to find out who was within. He went to various parts of the window, as if endeavouring to look inside. Finally, he stepped down the side-passage and entered the door which led to the compartments into which people turned who took things to pledge. He, Hollinshaw, remained at his shop door for some minutes after that—in fact, until the last witness came along. He saw Ayscough enter Multenius's front door and immediately pause—then the door was shut, and he himself went back into his own shop, his wife just then calling him to tea.

"You saw the young man you speak of quite clearly?" asked the Coroner.

"As clearly as I see you, sir," replied the witness.

"Do you see him here?"

Hollinshaw turned instantly and pointed to Lauriston.

"That's the young man, sir," he answered, with confidence.

Amidst a general craning of necks, Melky whispered to Lauriston.

"You'd ought to ha' had a lawyer, mister!" he said. "S'elp me, I'm a blooming fool for not thinking of it! Be careful—the Coroner's a-looking at you!"

As a matter of fact, every person in the court was staring at Lauriston, and presently the Coroner addressed him.

"Do you wish to ask this witness any questions?" he enquired.

Lauriston rose to his feet.

"No!" he replied. "What he says is quite correct. That is, as regards myself."

The Coroner hesitated a moment; then he motioned to Hollinshaw to leave the box, and once more turned to Lauriston.

"We will have your evidence now," he said. "And—let me warn you that there is no obligation on you to say anything which would seem to incriminate you."

## CHAPTER NINE
### WHOSE WERE THOSE RINGS?

Paying no attention to another attempted murmur of advice from Melky, who seemed to be on pins and needles, Lauriston at once jumped to his feet and strode to the witness-box. The women in the public seats glanced at him with admiring interest—such a fine-looking young fellow, whispered one sentimental lady to another, to have set about a poor old gentleman like Mr. Multenius! And everybody else, from the Coroner to the newspaper reporter—who was beginning to think he would get some good copy, after all, that morning—regarded him with attention. Here, at any rate, was the one witness who had actually found the pawnbroker's dead body.

Lauriston, his colour heightened a little under all this attention, answered the preliminary questions readily enough. His name was Andrew Carruthers Lauriston. His age—nearly twenty-two. He was a native of Peebles, in Scotland—the only son of the late Andrew Lauriston. His father was a minister of the Free Church. His mother was dead, too. He himself had come to London about two years ago—just after his mother's death. For the past few weeks he had lodged with Mrs. Flitwick, in Star Street—that was his present address. He was a writer of fiction—stories and novels. He had heard all the evidence already given, including that of the last witness, Hollinshaw. All that Hollinshaw had said was quite true. It was quite true that he had gone to Multenius's pawnshop about five-thirty of the previous afternoon, on his own business. He had looked in through both doors and window before entering the side-door: he wanted to know who was in the shop—whether it was Mr. Multenius, or his grand-daughter. He wanted to know that for a simple reason—he had never done business with Mr. Multenius, never even seen him that he remembered, but he had had one transaction with Miss Wildrose, and he wished, if possible, to do his business with her. As a matter of fact he saw nobody inside the shop when he looked in through the front door and the window—so he went round to the side-entrance.

All this had come in answer to questions put by the Coroner—who now paused and looked at Lauriston not unkindly.

"I daresay you are already aware that there is, or may be, some amount of suspicious circumstances attaching to your visit to this place yesterday afternoon," he said. "Do you care to tell the court—in your own way—precisely what took place, what you discovered, after you entered the pawnshop?"

"That's exactly what I wish to do," answered Lauriston, readily. "I've already told it, more than once, to the police and Mr. Multenius's relatives—I'll tell it again, as plainly and briefly as I can. I went into one of the compartments just within the side-door of the place. I saw no one, and heard no one. I rapped on the counter—nobody came. So I looked round the partition into the front shop. There was no one there. Then I looked round the other partition into the back parlour, the door of which was wide open. I at once saw an old man whom I took to be Mr. Multenius. He was lying on the floor—his feet were towards the open door, and his head on the hearth-rug, near the fender. I immediately jumped over the counter, and went into the parlour. I saw at once that he was dead—and almost immediately I hurried to the front door, to summon assistance. At the door I ran into Mr. Ayscough, who was entering as I opened the door. I at once told him of what I had found. That is the plain truth as to all I know of the matter."

"You heard nothing of any person in or about the shop when you entered?" asked the Coroner.

"Nothing!" replied Lauriston. "It was all perfectly quiet."

"What had you gone there to do?"

"To borrow some money—on two rings."

"Your own property?"

"My own property!"

"Had you been there before, on any errand of that sort?"

"Only once."

"When was that?"

"Last week," answered Lauriston. "I pawned my watch there."

"You have, in fact, been short of money?"

"Yes. But only temporarily—I was expecting money."

"I hope it has since arrived," said the Coroner.

"Mr. Ayscough was with me when it did arrive," replied Lauriston, glancing at the detective. "We found it—two letters—at my lodgings

37

when he walked round there with me after what I have just told you of."

"You had done your business on that previous occasion with the granddaughter?" asked the Coroner. "You had not seen the old man, then?"

"I never to my knowledge saw Mr. Multenius till I found him lying dead in his own parlour," answered Lauriston.

The Coroner turned from the witness, and glanced towards the table at which Mr. Parminter and the police officials sat. And Mr. Parminter slowly rose and looked at Lauriston, and put his first question—in a quiet, almost suave voice, as if he and the witness were going to have a pleasant and friendly little talk together.

"So your ambition is to be a writer of fiction?" he asked.

"I am a writer of fiction!" replied Lauriston.

Mr. Parminter pulled out a snuff-box and helped himself to a pinch.

"Have you published much?" he enquired, drily.

"Two or three stories—short stories."

"Did they bring in much money?"

"Five pounds each."

"Have you done anything else for a living but that since you came to London two years ago?"

"No, I haven't!"

"How much have you earned by your pen since you came, now?"

"About thirty pounds."

"Thirty pounds in two years. What have you lived on, then?"

"I had money of my own," replied Lauriston. "I had two hundred pounds when I left home."

"And that gave out—when?" demanded Mr. Parminter.

"Last week."

"And so—you took your watch to the pawnshop. And—yesterday—your expected money not having arrived, you were obliged to visit the pawnshop again? Taking with you, you said just now, two rings—your own property. Am I correct?"

"Quite correct—two rings—my own property."

Mr. Parminter turned and spoke to a police official, who, lifting aside a sheet of brown paper which lay before him, revealed the tray of rings which Lauriston and Ayscough had found on the table in Multenius's parlour. At the same time, Mr. Parminter, lifting his papers, revealed Lauriston's rings. He picked them up, laid them on the palm of his hand, and held them towards the witness.

"Are these the rings you took to the pawnshop?" he asked.

"Yes!" replied Lauriston. "They were my mother's."

Mr. Parminter indicated the tray.

"Did you see this tray lying in the parlour in which you found the dead man?" he enquired.

"I did."

"Did it strike you that your own rings were remarkably like the rings in this tray?"

"No, it did not," answered Lauriston. "I know nothing about rings."

Mr. Parminter quietly passed the tray of rings to the Coroner, with Lauriston's rings lying on a sheet of paper.

"Perhaps you will examine these things and direct the attention of the jurymen to them?" he said, and turned to the witness-box again. "I want to ask you a very particular question," he continued. "You had better consider it well before answering it—it is more important—to you—than may appear at first hearing. Can you bring any satisfactory proof that those two rings which you claim to be yours, really are yours?"

There followed on that a dead silence in court. People had been coming in since the proceedings had opened, and the place was now packed to the door. Every eye was turned on Lauriston as he stood in the witness-box, evidently thinking deeply. And in two pairs of eyes there was deep anxiety: Melky was nervous and fidgety; Zillah was palpably greatly concerned. But Lauriston looked at neither—and he finally turned to Mr. Parminter with a candid glance.

"The rings are mine," he answered. "But—I don't know how I can prove that they are!"

A suppressed murmur ran round the court—in the middle of it, the Coroner handed the rings to a police official and motioned him to show them to the jurymen. And Mr. Parminter's suave voice was heard again.

"You can't prove that they are yours."

"May I explain?" asked Lauriston. "Very well—there may be people, old friends, who have seen those two rings in my mother's possession. But I don't know where to find such people. If it's necessary, I can try."

"I should certainly try, if I were you," observed Mr. Parminter, drily.

"Now, when did those two rings come into your possession?"

"When my mother died," replied Lauriston.

"Where have you kept them?"

"Locked up in my trunk."

"Have you ever, at any time, or any occasion, shown them to any person? Think!"

"No," answered Lauriston. "I can't say that I ever have."

"Not even at the time of your mother's death?"

"No! I took possession, of course, of all her effects. I don't remember showing the rings to anybody."

"You kept them in your trunk until you took them out to raise money on them?"

"Yes—that's so," admitted Lauriston.

"How much money had you—in the world—when you went to the pawnshop yesterday afternoon?" demanded Mr. Parminter, with a sudden keen glance.

Lauriston flushed scarlet.

"If you insist on knowing," he said. "I'd just nothing."

There was another murmur in court—of pity from the sentimental ladies in the public seats, who, being well acquainted with the pawnshops themselves, and with the necessities which drove them there were experiencing much fellow-feeling for the poor young man in the witness-box. But Lauriston suddenly smiled—triumphantly.

"All the same," he added, glancing at Mr. Parminter. "I'd forty pounds, in my letters, less than an hour afterwards. Ayscough knows that!"

Mr. Parminter paid no attention to this remark. He had been whispering to the police inspector, and now he turned to the Coroner.

"I should like this witness to stand down for a few minutes, sir," he said. "I wish to have Miss Wildrose recalled."

The Coroner gently motioned Zillah to go back to the witness-box.

## CHAPTER TEN
## MELKY INTERVENES

Zillah had listened to Lauriston's answers to Mr. Parminter's searching questions with an anxiety which was obvious to those who sat near her. The signs of that anxiety were redoubled as she walked slowly to the box, and the glance she threw at the Coroner was almost appealing. But the Coroner was looking at his notes, and Zillah was obliged to turn to Mr. Parminter, whose accents became more mellifluous than ever as he addressed her; Mr. Parminter, indeed, confronting Zillah might have been taken for a kindly benevolent gentleman whose sole object was to administer condolence and comfort. Few people in court, however, failed to see the meaning of the questions which he began to put in the suavest and softest of tones.

"I believe you assisted your late grandfather in his business?" suggested Mr. Parminter.

"Just so! Now, how long had you assisted him in that way?"

"Ever since I left school—three years ago," replied Zillah.

"Three years—to be sure! And I believe you had resided with him for some years before that?"

"Ever since I was a little girl," admitted Zillah.

"In fact, the late Mr. Multenius brought you up? Just so!—therefore, of course, you would have some acquaintance with his business before you left school?"

"Yes—he taught me a good deal about it."

"You were always about the place, of course—yes? And I may take it that you gradually got a good deal of knowledge about the articles with which your grandfather had to deal? To be sure—thank you. In fact, you are entitled to regard yourself as something of an expert in precious stones and metals?"

"I know a good deal about them," replied Zillah.

"You could tell the value of a thing as accurately as your grandfather?"

"Ordinary things—yes."

"And you were very well acquainted with your grandfather's stock?"

"Yes."

Mr. Parminter motioned the official who had charge of it to place the tray of rings on the ledge of the witness-box.

"Oblige me by looking at that tray and the contents," he said. "You recognize it, of course? Just so. Now, do you know where that tray was when you went out, leaving your grandfather alone, yesterday afternoon?"

"Yes," replied Zillah, unhesitatingly. "On the table in the back-parlour—where I saw it when I came in. My grandfather had taken it out of the front window, so that he could polish the rings."

"Do you know how many rings it contained?"

"No. Perhaps twenty-five or thirty."

"They are, I see, laid loosely in the tray, which is velvet-lined. They were always left like that? Just so. And you don't know how many there were—nor how many there should be there, now? As a matter of fact, there are twenty-seven rings there—you can't say that is the right number?"

"No," answered Zillah, "and my grandfather couldn't have said, either. A ring might be dropped into that tray—or a ring taken out. They are all old rings."

"But—valuable?" suggested Mr. Parminter.

"Some—yes. Others are not very valuable."

"Now what do you mean by that word valuable? What, for instance, is the value of the least valuable ring there, and what is that of the most valuable?"

Zillah glanced almost indifferently at the tray before her.

"Some of these rings are worth no more than five pounds," she replied. "Some—a few—are worth twenty to thirty pounds; one or two are worth more."

"And—they are all old?"

"They are all of old-fashioned workmanship," said Zillah. "Made a good many years ago, all of them. The diamonds, or pearls, are all right, of course."

Mr. Parminter handed over the half-sheet of paper on which Lauriston's rings had been exhibited to the Coroner and the jurymen.

"Look at those rings, if you please," he said quietly. "Are they of the same sort, the same class, of rings as those in the tray?"

"Yes," admitted Zillah. "Something the same."

"What is the value of those rings—separately?" enquired Mr. Parminter. "Please give us your professional opinion."

Zillah bent over the two rings for a while, turning them about.

"This is worth about thirty, and that about fifty pounds," she replied at last.

"In other words, these two rings are similar in style and value to the best rings in that tray?"

"Yes."

"Do you recognize those two rings?"

"No—not at all."

Mr. Parminter paused a moment, and caught the jury's attention with a sharp glance of his eye before he turned again to the witness.

"Could you have recognized any of the rings in that tray?" he asked.

"No!" said Zillah. "I could not."

"Then you could not possibly say—one way or another, if those rings were taken out of that tray?"

"No!"

"The fact is that all those rings—the two on the half-sheet of notepaper, and twenty-seven on the tray—are all of the same class as regards age and style—all very much of a muchness?"

"Yes," admitted Zillah.

"And you can't—you are on your oath remember!—you can't definitely say that those two rings were not picked up from that tray, amongst the others?"

"No," replied Zillah. "But I can't say that they were! And—I don't believe they were. I don't believe they were our rings!"

Mr. Parminter smiled quietly and again swept the interested jurymen with his quick glance.

Then he turned to Zillah with another set of questions.

"How long have you known the last witness—Andrew Lauriston?" he enquired.

"Since one day last week," replied Zillah.

She had flushed at the mention of Lauriston's name, and Mr. Parminter was quick to see it.

"How did you get to know him?" he continued.
"By his coming to the shop—on business."
"To pawn his watch, I believe?"
"Yes."
"You attended to him?"
"Yes."
"You had never seen him before?"
"No."
"Ever seen him since?"
Zillah hesitated for a moment.
"I saw him—accidentally—in Kensington Gardens, on Sunday," she answered at last.
"Have any conversation with him?"
"Yes," admitted Zillah.
"About—pawnbroking?"
"No!" retorted Zillah. "About his work—writing."
"Did he tell you he was very hard up?"
"I knew that!" said Zillah. "Hadn't he pawned his watch?"
"Perhaps—you seem to be a very good business woman—perhaps you gave him some advice?"
"Yes, I did! I advised him, as long as he'd anything on which he could raise money, not to let himself go without money in his pocket."
"Excellent advice!" said Mr. Parminter, with a smile.
He leaned forward, looking at his witness more earnestly. "Now, did Lauriston, on Sunday, or when you saw him before, ever mention to you that he possessed two rings of some value?"
"No," replied Zillah.
Mr. Parminter paused, hesitated, suddenly bowed to the Coroner, and dropping back into his seat, pulled out his snuff-box. And the Coroner, motioning Zillah to leave the witness-box, interrupted Mr. Parminter in the midst of a pinch of snuff.
"I think it will be best to adjourn at this stage," he said. "It is obvious that we can't finish this today." He turned to the jurymen. "I propose to adjourn this enquiry for a week, gentlemen," he went on. "In the meantime—"
His attention was suddenly arrested by Melky Rubinstein, who, after much uneasiness and fidgeting, rose from his seat and made his way to the foot of the table, manifestly desiring to speak.
"What is it?" asked the Coroner. "Who are you? Oh!—the witness who identified the body. Yes?"
"Mr. Coroner!" said Melky, in his most solemn tones. "This here inquest

ain't being conducted right, sir! I don't mean by you—but these here gentlemen, the police, and Mr. Parminter there, is going off on a wrong scent. I know what they're after, and they're wrong! They're suppressing evidence, Mr. Coroner." Melky turned on Ayscough. "What about the clue o' this here old book?" he demanded. "Why ain't you bringing that forward? I'm the late Daniel Multenius's nearest male relative, and I say that clue's a deal more important nor what we've been hearing all the morning. What about that book, now, Mr. Ayscough? Come on!—what about it!—and its owner?"

"What is this?" demanded the Coroner. "If there is anything—"

"Anything, sir!" exclaimed Melky. "There's just this—between the time that my cousin there, Miss Zillah Wildrose left the old man alive, and the time when Mr. Lauriston found him dead, somebody came into the shop as left a valuable book behind him on the parlour table, which book, according to all the advertisements in the morning papers, is the property of Mr. Spencer Levendale, the Member of Parliament, as lives in Sussex Square. Why ain't that matter brought up? Why ain't Mr. Levendale brought here? I ask you, Mr. Coroner, to have it seen into! There's more behind it—"

The Coroner held up a hand and beckoned the police inspector and Mr. Parminter to approach his desk; a moment later, Ayscough was summoned. And Lauriston, watching the result of this conference, was quickly aware that the Coroner was not particularly pleased; he suddenly turned on the inspector with a question which was heard by every one in court.

"Why was not the matter of the book put before the Court at first?" he demanded. "It seems to me that there may be a most important clue in it. The fact of the book's having been found should most certainly have been mentioned, at once. I shall adjourn for a week, from today, and you will produce the book and bring Mr. Spencer Levendale here as a witness. This day week, gentlemen!"

Melky Rubinstein turned, whispered a hurried word to Zillah and Mrs. Goldmark, and then, seizing Lauriston by the elbow, drew him quickly away from the court.

## CHAPTER ELEVEN
## THE BACK DOOR

Once outside in the street, Melky turned down the nearest side-street, motioning Lauriston to follow him. Before they had gone many yards he edged himself close to his companion's side, at the same time throwing a cautious glance over his own shoulder.

"There's one o' them blooming detectives after us!" said Melky. "But that's just what's to be expected, mister!—they'll never let you out o' their sight until one of two things happen!"

"What things?" asked Lauriston.

"Either you'll have to prove, beyond all doubt, that them rings is yours, and was your poor mother's before you," answered Melky, "or we shall have to put a hand on the chap that scragged my uncle. That's a fact! Mister!—will you put your trust and confidence in me, and do what I tell you? It's for your own good."

"I don't know that I could do better," responded Lauriston, after a moment's thought. "You're a right good fellow, Melky—I'm sure of that! What do you want me to do?"

Melky pulled out a handsome gold watch and consulted it.

"It's dinner-time," he said. "Come round to Mrs. Goldmark's and get some grub. I'll tell you what to do while we're eating. I've been thinking things over while that there Parminter was badgering poor Zillah, and s'elp me, there only is one thing for you to do, and you'd best to do it sharp! But come on to Praed Street—don't matter if this here chap behind does shadow you—I can get the better of him as easy as I could sell this watch! It 'ud take all the detectives in London to beat me, if I put my mind to it."

They were at Mrs. Goldmark's eating-house in five minutes: Melky, who knew all the ins and outs of that establishment, conducted Lauriston into an inner room, and to a corner wherein there was comparative privacy, and summoned a waitress. Not until he and his companion were half way through their meal did he refer to the business which was in his thoughts: then he leaned close to Lauriston and began to talk.

"Mister!" he whispered. "Where do you come from?"

"Peebles," answered Lauriston. "You heard me tell them so, in that court."

"I'm no scholar," said Melky. "I ain't no idea where Peebles is, except that it's in Scotland. Is it far into that country, or where is it?"

"Not far across the Border," replied Lauriston.

"Get there in a few hours, I reckon?" asked Melky. "You could? Very well, then, mister, you take my tip—get there! Get there—quick!"

Lauriston laid down his knife and fork and stared.

"Whatever for?" he exclaimed.

"To find somebody—anybody—as can prove that those rings are yours!" answered Melky solemnly and emphatically. "Tain't no use denying it—you're in a dangerous position. The police always goes for the straightest and easiest line. Their line was clear enough, just now—Parminter give it away! They've a theory—they always have a theory—and when once

**45**

police gets a theory, nothing can drive it out o' their heads—their official heads, anyway. What they're saying, and what they'll try to establish, is this here. That you were hard up, down to less than your last penny. You went to Mr. Multenius's—you peeked and peered through the shop window and saw him alone, or, perhaps, saw the place empty. You went in—you grabbed a couple o' rings—he interrupted you—you scragged him! That's their line—and Zillah can't swear that those rings which you claim to be yours aren't her grandfather's, and up to now you can't prove that they're yours and were once your mother's! Mister!—be off to this here Peebles at once—immediate!—and find somebody, some old friend, as can swear that he or she—never mind which—knows them rings to be your property beyond a shadow of doubt! Bring that friend back—bring him if he has to come in an invalid carriage!"

Lauriston was so much struck by Melky's argument and advice that it needed no more explanations to convince him of its wisdom.

"But—how could I get away'" he asked. "There'll be that detective chap hanging about outside—I know I've been shadowed ever since last evening! They'll never let me get away from London, however much I wish. The probability is that if they saw me going to a railway station they'd arrest me."

"My own opinion, mister, after what's taken place this morning, is that if you stop here, you'll be arrested before night," remarked Melky coolly. "I'd lay a tenner on it! But you ain't going to stop—you must go! There must be somebody in the old spot as can swear that them two rings o' yours is family property, and you must find 'em and bring 'em, if you value your neck. As to slipping the police, I'll make that right for you, proper! Now, then, what money have you about you, Mr. Lauriston?"

"Plenty!" answered Lauriston. "Nearly forty pounds—the money I got last night."

"Will you do exactly what I tell you?" asked Melky, "And do it at once, without any hesitation, any hanging about, any going home to Mother Flitwick's, or anything o' that sort?"

"Yes!" replied Lauriston. "I'm so sure you're right, that I will."

"Then you listen to me—careful," said Melky. "See that door in the corner? As soon as you've finished that pudding, slip out o' that door. You'll find yourself in a little yard. Go out o' that yard, and you'll find yourself in a narrow passage. Go straight down the passage, and you'll come out in Market Street. Go straight down Southwick Street—you know it—to Oxford and Cambridge Terrace, and you'll see a cab-rank right in front of you. Get into a taxi, and tell the fellow to drive you to

Piccadilly Circus. Leave him there—take a turn round so's he won't see what you do—then get into another taxi, and drive to St. Pancras Church. Get out there—and foot it to King's Cross Station. You'll catch the 3.15 for the North easy—and after you're once in it, you're all right. Get to Peebles!—that's the thing! S'elp me, Mr. Lauriston, it's the only thing!"

Five minutes later, there being no one but themselves in the little room, Lauriston gave Melky a hearty grip of the hand, walked out of the door in the corner, and vanished. And Melky, left alone, pulled out his cigarette case, and began to smoke, calmly and quietly. When the waitress came back, he whispered a word or two to her; the waitress nodded with full comprehension—for everybody knew Melky at Goldmark's, and if the waitresses wanted a little jewellery now and then, he let them have it at cost price.

"So you can give me the checks for both," said Melky. "I'll pay 'em."

But Melky let three-quarters of an hour elapse before he went to the desk in the outer shop. He sipped a cup of coffee; he smoked several cigarettes; it was quite a long time before he emerged into Praed Street, buttoning his overcoat. And without appearing to see anything, he at once saw the man who had followed Lauriston and himself from the Coroner's Court. Being almost preternaturally observant, he also saw the man start with surprise—but Melky showed, and felt, no surprise, when the watcher came after him.

"You know me, Mr. Rubinstein," he said, almost apologetically. "You know, of course, we're keeping an eye on that young Scotch fellow—we've got to! He went in there, to Goldmark's, with you? Is he still there?"

"Strikes me you ain't up to your job!" remarked Melky, coolly. "He went out, three-quarters of an hour ago. Gone home, I should say."

The man turned away, evidently puzzled, but just as evidently taking Melky's word. He went off in the direction of Star Street, while Melky strolled along to the pawnbroker's shop. It was necessary that he should tell his cousin of what he had done.

Mrs. Goldmark was still with Zillah—Melky unfolded his story to the two of them. Zillah heard it with unfeigned relief; Mrs. Goldmark, who, being a young and pretty widow, was inclined to sentiment, regarded Melky with admiration.

"My!—if you ain't the cute one, Mr. Rubinstein!" she exclaimed, clapping her plump hands. "As for me, now, I wouldn't have thought of that in a hundred years! But it's you that's the quick mind."

Melky laid a finger to the side of his nose.

"Do you know what, Mrs. Goldmark?" he said. "I ain't going to let them police fellows put a hand on young Lauriston, not me! I've my own ideas about this here business—wait till I put my hand on somebody, see? Don't it all come out clear to you?—if I find the right man, then there ain't no more suspicion attaching to this young chap, ain't it? Oh, I'm no fool, Mrs. Goldmark; don't you make no mistake!"

"I'm sure!" asserted Mrs. Goldmark. "Yes, indeed—you don't carry your eyes in your head for nothing, Mr. Rubinstein!"

Zillah, who had listened abstractedly to these compliments suddenly turned on her cousin.

"What are you going to do then, Melky?" she demanded. "What's all this business about that book? And what steps are you thinking of taking?"

But Melky rose and, shaking his head, buttoned up his overcoat as if he were buttoning in a multitude of profound secrets.

"What you got to do, just now, Zillah—and Mrs. Goldmark too," he answered, "is to keep quiet tongues about what I done with young Lauriston. There ain't to be a word said! If any o' them police come round here, asking about him, you don't know nothing—see? You ain't seen him since he walked out o' that court with me—see? Which, of course—you ain't. And as for the rest, you leave that to yours truly!"

"Oh, what it is to have a mind!" exclaimed Mrs. Goldmark "I ain't no mind, beyond managing my business."

"Don't you show your mind in managing that?" said Melky, admiringly. "What do I always say of you, Mrs. Goldmark? Don't I always say you're the smartest business woman in all Paddington? Ain't that having a mind? Oh, I think you've the beautifullest mind, Mrs. Goldmark!"

With this compliment Melky left Mrs. Goldmark and Zillah, and went away to his lodgings. He was aware of a taxi-cab drawn up at Mrs. Flitwick's door as he went up the street; inside Mrs. Flitwick's shabby hall he found that good woman talking to a stranger—a well-dressed young gentleman, who was obviously asking questions. Mrs. Flitwick turned to Melky with an air of relief.

"Perhaps you can tell this gentleman where Mr. Lauriston is, Mr. Rubinstein?" she said. "I ain't seen him since he went out first thing this morning."

Melky looked the stranger over—narrowly. Then he silently beckoned him outside the house, and walked him out of earshot.

"You ain't the friend from Scotland?" asked Melky. "Him what sent the bank-note, last night?"

"Yes!" assented the stranger. "I see you're aware of that. My name is Purdie—John Purdie. Where is Lauriston? I particularly want to see him."

Melky tapped the side of his nose, and whispered.

"He's on his way to where you come from, mister!" he said. "Here!—I know who you are, and you'll know me in one minute. Come up to my sitting-room!"

## CHAPTER TWELVE
## THE FRIEND FROM PEEBLES

Melky, as principal lodger in Mrs. Flitwick's establishment, occupied what that lady was accustomed to describe as the front drawing-room floor—a couple of rooms opening one into the other. Into one of these, furnished as a sitting-room, he now led Lauriston's friend, hospitably invited him to a seat, and took a quiet look at him. He at once sized up Mr. John Purdie for what he was—a well-to-do, well-dressed, active-brained young business man, probably accustomed to controlling and dealing with important affairs. And well satisfied with this preliminary inspection, he immediately plunged into the affair of the moment.

"Mister," began Melky, pulling up a chair to Purdie's side, and assuming a tone and manner of implicit confidence. "I've heard of you. Me and Mr. Lauriston's close friends. My name's Mr. Rubinstein—Mr. Melchior Rubinstein, commonly called Melky. I know all about you—you're the friend that Lauriston asked for a bit of help to see him through, like—ain't it? Just so—and you sent him twenty pounds to be going on with—which he got, all right, last night. Also, same time, he got another twenty quid for two of his lit'ry works—stories, mister. Mister!—I wish he'd got your money and the other money just an hour before it come to hand! S'elp me!—if them there letters had only come in by one post earlier, it 'ud ha' saved a heap o' trouble!"

"I haven't the remotest notion of what you're talking about, you know," said Purdie good-naturedly. "You evidently know more than I do. I knew Andie Lauriston well enough up to the time he left Peebles, but I've never seen or heard of him since until he wrote to me the other week. What's it all about, and why has he gone back to Peebles? I told him I was coming up here any day now—and here I am, and he's gone!"

Melky edged his chair still nearer to his visitor, and with a cautious glance at the door, lowered his voice.

"I'm a-going to tell you all about it, mister," he said. "I know you Scotch gentlemen have got rare headpieces on you, and you'll pick it up sharp enough. Now you listen to me, Mr. Purdie, same as if I was one of them barrister chaps stating a case, and you'll get at it in no time."

John Purdie, who had already recognized his host as a character, as interesting as he was amusing, listened attentively while Melky told the story of Lauriston's doings and adventure from the moment of his setting out to pawn his watch at Multenius's pledge-office to that in which, on Melky's suggestion, he had made a secret and hurried departure for Peebles. Melky forgot no detail; he did full justice to every important point, and laid particular stress on the proceedings before the Coroner. And in the end he appealed confidently to his listener.

"And now I put it up to you, mister—straight!" concluded Melky. "Could I ha' done better for him than to give him the advice I did? Wasn't it best for him to go where he could get some evidence on his own behalf, than to run the risk of being arrested, and put where he couldn't do nothing for himself? What d'you say, now, Mr. Purdie?"

"Yes," agreed Purdie, after a moment's further thought. "I think you did well. He'll no doubt be able to find some old friends in Peebles who can surely remember that his mother did possess those two rings. But you must bear this in mind—the police, you say, have shadowed him since yesterday afternoon. Well, when they find he's flown, they'll take that as a strong presumptive evidence of guilt. They'll say he's flying from justice!"

"Don't matter, mister, if Lauriston comes back with proof of his innocence," replied Melky.

"Yes, but they'll not wait for that," said Purdie. "They'll set the hue-and-cry on to him—at once. He's not the sort to be easily mistaken or overlooked—unless he's changed a lot this late year or two—he was always a good-looking lad."

"Is so now, mister," remarked Melky, "is so now!"

"Very well," continued Purdie. "Then I want to make a suggestion to you. It seems to me that the wisest course is for you and me to go straight to the police authorities, and tell them frankly that Lauriston has gone to get evidence that those rings are really his property, and that he'll return in a day or two with that evidence. That will probably satisfy them—I think I can add a bit more that will help further. We don't want it to be thought that the lad's run away rather than face a possible charge of murder, you know!"

"I see your point, mister, I see your point!" agreed Melky. "I'm with you!—I ain't no objection to that. Of course, there ain't no need to tell the police precisely where he has gone—what?"

"Not a bit!" said Purdie. "But I'll make myself responsible to them for his re-appearance. Now—did you and he arrange anything about communicating with each other?"

"Yes," replied Melky. "If anything turns up this next day or two I'm to wire to him at the post-office, Peebles. If he finds what he wants, he'll wire to me, here, at once."

"Good!" said Purdie. "Now, here's another matter. You've mentioned Mr. Spencer Levendale and this book which was so strangely left at the pledge-office. I happen to know Mr. Levendale—pretty well."

"You do, mister!" exclaimed Melky. "Small world, ain't it, now?"

"I met Mr. Spencer Levendale last September—two months ago," continued Purdie. "He was staying at an hotel in the Highlands, with his children and their governess: I was at the same hotel, for a month—he and I used to go fishing together. We got pretty friendly, and he asked me to call on him next time I was in town. Here I am—and when we've been to the police, I'm going to Sussex Square—to tell him I'm a friend of Lauriston's, that Lauriston is in some danger over this business, and to ask him if he can tell me more about—that book!"

Melky jumped up and wrung his visitor's hand.

"Mister!—you're one o' the right sort," he said fervently. "That there book has something to do with it! My idea is that the man what carried that book into the shop is the man what scragged my poor old relative—fact, mister! Levendale, he wouldn't tell us anything much this morning—maybe he'll tell you more. Stand by Lauriston, mister!—we'll pull him through."

"You seem very well disposed towards him," remarked Purdie. "He's evidently taken your fancy."

"And my cousin Zillah's," answered Melky, with a confidential grin. "Zillah—loveliest girl in all Paddington, mister—she's clear gone on the young fellow! And—a word in your ear, mister!—Zillah's been educated like a lady, and now that the old man's gone, Zillah'll have—ah! a fortune that 'ud make a nigger turn white! And no error about it! See it through, mister!"

"I'll see it through," said Purdie. "Now, then—these police. Look here—is there a good hotel in this neighbourhood?—I've all my traps in that taxi-cab downstairs—I drove straight here from the station, because I wanted to see Andie Lauriston at once."

"Money's no object to you, I reckon, mister?" asked Melky, with a shrewd glance at the young Scotsman's evident signs of prosperity.

"Not in reason," answered Purdie.

"Then there's the Great Western Hotel, at the end o' Praed Street," said Melky. "That'll suit a young gentleman like you, mister, down to the ground. And you'll be right on the spot!"

"Come with me, then," said Purdie. "And then to the police."

Half-an-hour's private conversation with the police authorities enabled Purdie to put some different ideas into the official heads. They began to

look at matters in a new light. Here was a wealthy young Scottish manufacturer, a person of standing and position, who was able to vouch for Andrew Lauriston in more ways than one, who had known him from boyhood, had full faith in him and in his word, and was certain that all that Lauriston had said about the rings and about his finding of Daniel Multenius would be found to be absolutely true. They willingly agreed to move no further in the matter until Lauriston's return—and Purdie noticed, not without a smile, that they pointedly refrained from asking where he had gone to. He came out from that interview with Ayscough in attendance upon him—and Melky, waiting without, saw that things had gone all right.
"You might let me have your London address, sir," said Ayscough. "I might want to let you know something."
"Great Western Hotel," answered Purdie. "I shall stay there until Lauriston's return, and until this matter's entirely cleared up, as far as he's concerned. Come there, if you want me. All right," he continued, as he and Melky walked away from the police-station. "They took my word for it!—they'll do nothing until Lauriston comes back. Now then, you know this neighbourhood, and I don't—show me the way to Sussex Square—I'm going to call on Mr. Levendale at once."
John Purdie had a double object in calling on Mr. Spencer Levendale. He had mentioned to Melky that when he met Levendale in the Highlands, Levendale, who was a widower, had his children and their governess with him. But he had not mentioned that he, Purdie, had fallen in love with the governess, and that one of his objects in coming to London just then was to renew his acquaintance with her. It was chiefly of the governess that he was thinking as he stood on the steps of the big house in Sussex Square—perhaps, in a few minutes, he would see her again.
But Purdie was doomed to see neither Mr. Spencer Levendale nor the pretty governess that day. Mr. Levendale, said the butler, was on business in the city and was to dine out that evening: Miss Bennett had taken the two children to see a relative of theirs at Hounslow, and would not return until late. So Purdie, having pencilled his London address on them, left cards for Mr. Levendale and Miss Bennett, and, going back to his hotel, settled himself in his quarters to await developments. He spent the evening in reading the accounts of the inquest on Daniel Multenius— in more than one of the newspapers they were full and circumstantial, and it needed little of his shrewd perception to convince him that his old schoolmate stood in considerable danger if he failed to establish his ownership of the rings.
He had finished breakfast next morning and was thinking of strolling

round to Melky Rubinstein's lodgings, to hear if any news had come from Lauriston, when a waiter brought him Ayscough's card, saying that its presenter was waiting for him in the smoking-room. Purdie went there at once: the detective, who looked unusually grave and thoughtful, drew him aside into a quiet part of the room.

"There's a strange affair occurred during the night, Mr. Purdie," said Ayscough, when they were alone. "And it's my opinion it's connected with this Multenius affair."

"What is it?" asked Purdie.

"This," replied Ayscough. "A Praed Street tradesman—in a small way—was picked up, dying, in a quiet street off Maida Vale, at twelve o'clock last night, and he died soon afterwards. And—he'd been poisoned!—but how, the doctors can't yet tell."

## CHAPTER THIRTEEN
## THE CALL FOR HELP

Purdie, whose temperament inclined him to slowness and deliberation in face of any grave crisis, motioned the detective to take a seat in the quiet corner of the smoking-room, into which they had retreated, and sat down close by him.

"Now, to begin with," he said, "why do you think this affair is connected with the affair of the old pawn-broker? There must be some link."

"There is a link, sir," answered Ayscough. "The man was old Daniel Multenius's next door neighbour: name of Parslett—James Parslett, fruit and vegetable dealer. Smallish way of business, but well known enough in that quarter. Now, I'll explain something to you. I'm no hand at drawing," continued the detective, "but I think I can do a bit of a rough sketch on this scrap of paper which will make clear to you the lie of the land. These two lines represent Praed Street. Here, where I make this cross, is Daniel Multenius's pawnshop. The front part of it—the jeweller's shop—looks out on Praed Street. At the side is a narrow passage or entry: from that you get access to the pledge-office. Now then, Multenius's premises run down one side of this passage: Parslett's run down the other. Parslett's house has a side-door into it, exactly opposite the door into Multenius's pledge office. Is that clear, Mr. Purdie?"

"Quite!" answered Purdie. "I understand it exactly."

"Then my theory is, that Parslett saw the real murderer of Daniel Multenius come out of Multenius's side-door, while he, Parslett, was standing at his own; that he recognized him, that he tried to blackmail him yesterday, and that the man contrived to poison him, in such a fashion that Parslett died shortly after leaving him," said Ayscough, confidently. "It's but a theory—but I'll lay anything I'm not far out in it!"

"What reason have you for thinking that Parslett blackmailed the murderer?" asked Purdie.

"This!" answered the detective, with something of triumph in his tone. "I've been making some enquiries already this morning, early as it is. When Parslett was picked up and carried to the hospital—this St. Mary's Hospital, close by here—he was found to have fifty pounds in gold in his pocket. Now, according to Parslett's widow, whom I've seen this morning, Parslett was considerably hard up yesterday. Trade hasn't been very good with him of late, and she naturally knows his circumstances. He went out of the house last night about nine o'clock, saying he was going to have a stroll round, and the widow says she's certain he'd no fifty pounds on him when he left her—it would be a wonder, she says, if he'd as much as fifty shillings! Now then, Mr. Purdie, where did a man like that pick up fifty sovereigns between the time he went out, and the time he was picked up, dying?"

"He might have borrowed it from some friend," suggested Purdie.

"I thought of that, sir," said Ayscough. "It seems the natural thing to think of. But Mrs. Parslett says they haven't a friend from whom he could have borrowed such an amount—not one! No, sir!—my belief is that Parslett saw some man enter and leave Multenius's shop; that he knew the man; that he went and plumped him with the affair, and that the man gave him that gold to get rid of him at the moment—and contrived to poison him, too!"

Purdie considered the proposition for awhile in silence.

"Well," he remarked at last, "if that's so, it seems to establish two facts—first, that the murderer is some man who lives in this neighbourhood, and second, that he's an expert in poisons."

"Right, sir!" agreed Ayscough. "Quite right. And it would, of course, establish another—the innocence of your friend, Lauriston."

Purdie smiled.

"I never had any doubt of that," he said.

"Between ourselves, neither had I," remarked Ayscough heartily. "I told our people that I, personally, was convinced of the young fellow's complete innocence from the very first—and it was I who found him in the shop. It's a most unfortunate thing that he was there, and a sad coincidence that those rings of his were much of a muchness with the rings in the tray in the old man's parlour—but I've never doubted him. No, sir!—I believe all this business goes a lot deeper than that! It's no common affair—old Daniel Multenius was attacked by somebody—somebody!—for some special reason—and it's going to take a lot of getting at. And I'm convinced this Parslett affair is a development—Parslett's been poisoned because he knew too much."

"You say you don't know what particular poison was used?" asked Purdie. "It would be something of a clue to know that. Because, if it turned out to be one of a very subtle nature, that would prove that whoever administered it had made a special study of poisons."

"I don't know that—yet," answered Ayscough. "But," he continued, rising from his chair, "if you'd step round with me to the hospital, we might get to know, now. There's one or two of their specialists been making an examination. It's only a mere step along the street."

Purdie followed the detective out and along Praed Street. Before they reached the doors of the hospital, a man came up to Ayscough: a solid, substantial-looking person, of cautious manner and watchful eye, whose glance wandered speculatively from the detective to his companion. Evidently sizing Purdie up as some one in Ayscough's confidence, he spoke—in the fashion of one who has something as mysterious, as important, to communicate.

"Beg your pardon, Mr. Ayscough," he said. "A word with you sir. You know me, Mr. Ayscough?"

Ayscough looked sharply at his questioner.

"Mr. Goodyer, isn't it?" he asked. "Oh, yes, I remember. What is it? You can speak before this gentleman—it's all right."

"About this affair of last night—Parslett, you know," said Goodyer, drawing the detective aside, and lowering his voice, so that passers-by might not hear. "There's something I can tell you—I've heard all about the matter from Parslett's wife. But I've not told her what I can tell you, Mr. Ayscough."

"And—what's that?" enquired the detective.

"I'm Parslett's landlord, you know," continued Goodyer. "He's had that shop and dwelling-house of me for some years. Now, Parslett's not been doing very well of late, from one cause or another, and to put it in a nutshell, he owed me half a year's rent. I saw him yesterday, and told him I must have the money at once: in fact, I pressed him pretty hard about it.—I'd been at him for two or three weeks, and I could see it was no good going on. He'd been down in the mouth about it, the last week or so, but yesterday afternoon he was confident enough. 'Now, you needn't alarm yourself, Mr. Goodyer,' he said. 'There's a nice bit of money going to be paid to me tonight, and I'll settle up with you before I stick my head on the pillow,' he said. 'Tonight, for certain?' says I. 'Before even I go to bed!' he says. 'I can't fix it to a minute, but you can rely on me calling at your house in St. Mary's Terrace before eleven o'clock—with the money.' And he was so certain about it, Mr. Ayscough, that I said no more than that I should be much obliged, and I'd wait up for him. And," concluded Goodyer, "I did wait up—till half-past twelve—but he never came. So this morning, of course, I walked round here—and then I heard what happened—about him being picked up dying and since being dead—with fifty pounds in gold in his pocket. Of course, Mr. Ayscough, that was the money he referred to."

"You haven't mentioned this to anybody?" asked Ayscough.

"Neither to the widow nor to anybody—but you," replied Goodyer.

"Don't!" said Ayscough. "Keep it to yourself till I give you the word. You didn't hear anything from Parslett as to where the money was coming from?"

"Not one syllable!" answered Goodyer. "But I could see he was dead sure of having it."

"Well—keep quiet about it," continued Ayscough. "There'll be an inquest, you know, and what you have to tell'll come in handy, then. There's some mystery about all this affair, Mr. Goodyer, and it's going to take some unravelling."

"You're right!" said Goodyer. "I believe you!"

He went off along the street, and the detective turned to Purdie and motioned him towards the hospital.

"Queer, all that, sir!" he muttered. "Very queer! But it all tends to showing that my theory's the right one. Now if you'll just stop in the waiting-room a few minutes, I'll find out if these doctors have come to any conclusion about the precise nature of the poison."

Purdie waited for ten minutes, speculating on the curiosities of the mystery into which he had been so strangely plunged: at last the detective came back, shaking his head.

"Can't get a definite word out of 'em, yet," he said, as they went away. "There's two or three of 'em—big experts in—what do you call it—oh, yes, toxology—putting their heads together over the analysing business, and they won't say anything so far—they'll leave that to the inquest. But I gathered this much, Mr. Purdie, from the one I spoke to—this man Parslett was poisoned in some extremely clever fashion, and by some poison that's not generally known, which was administered to him probably half-an-hour before it took effect. What's that argue, sir, but that whoever gave him that poison is something of an expert? Deep game, Mr. Purdie, a very deep game indeed!—and now I don't think there's much need to be anxious about that young friend of yours. I'm certain, anyway, that the man who poisoned Parslett is the man who killed poor old Daniel Multenius. But—we shall see."

Purdie parted from Ayscough outside the hospital and walked along to Mrs. Flitwick's house in Star Street. He met Melky Rubinstein emerging from the door; Melky immediately pulled out a telegram which he thrust into Purdie's hand.

"Just come, mister!" exclaimed Melky. "There's a word for you in it—I was going to your hotel. Read what he says."

Purdie unfolded the pink paper and read.

"On the track all right understand Purdie is in town if he comes to Star Street explain all to him will wire again later in day."

"Good!" said Purdie. He handed back the telegram and looked meditatively at Melky. "Are you busy this morning?" he asked.

"Doing no business whatever, mister," lisped Melky, solemnly. "Not until this business is settled—not me!"

"Come to the hotel with me," continued Purdie. "I want to talk to you about something."

But when they reached the hotel, all thought of conversation was driven out of Purdie's mind for the moment. The hall-porter handed him a note, remarking that it had just come. Purdie's face flushed as he recognized the handwriting: he turned sharply away and tore open the envelope. Inside, on a half-sheet of notepaper, were a few lines—from the pretty governess at Mr. Spencer Levendale's.

"Can you come here at once and ask for me? There is something seriously wrong: I am much troubled and have no one in London I can consult."

With a hasty excuse to Melky, Purdie ran out of the hotel, and set off in quick response to the note.

## CHAPTER FOURTEEN
## THE PRIVATE LABORATORY

As he turned down Spring Street towards Sussex Square, Purdie hastily reviewed his knowledge of Mr. Spencer Levendale and his family. He had met them, only two months previously, at a remote and out-of-the-way place in the Highlands, in a hotel where he and they were almost the only guests. Under such circumstances, strangers are soon drawn together, and as Levendale and Purdie had a common interest in fishing they were quickly on good terms. But Purdie was thinking now as he made his way towards Levendale's London house that he really knew very little of this man who was evidently mixed up in some way with the mystery into which young Andie Lauriston had so unfortunately also become intermingled. He knew that Levendale was undoubtedly a very wealthy man: there were all the signs of wealth about him; he had brought several servants down to the Highlands with him: money appeared to be plentiful with him as pebbles are on a beach. Purdie learnt bit by bit that Levendale had made a great fortune in South Africa, that he had come home to England and gone into Parliament; that he was a widower and the father of two little girls—he learnt, too, that the children's governess, Miss Elsie Bennett, a pretty and taking girl of twenty-two or three, had come with them from Cape Town. But of Levendale's real character and self he knew no more than could be gained from holiday acquaintance. Certain circumstances told him by Melky about the rare book left in old Multenius's parlour inclined Purdie to be somewhat suspicious that Levendale was concealing something which he knew about that affair—and now here was Miss Bennett writing what, on the face of it, looked like an appealing letter to him, as if something had happened.

Purdie knew something had happened as soon as he was admitted to the house. Levendale's butler, who had accompanied his master to the Highlands, and had recognized Purdie on his calling the previous day, came hurrying to him in the hall, as soon as the footman opened the door. "You haven't seen Mr. Levendale since you were here yesterday, sir?" he asked, in a low, anxious voice.

"Seen Mr. Levendale? No!" answered Purdie. "Why—what do you mean?"

The butler looked round at a couple of footmen who hung about the door. "Don't want to make any fuss about it, Mr. Purdie," he whispered, "though it's pretty well known in the house already. The fact is, sir, Mr. Levendale's missing!"

"Missing?" exclaimed Purdie. "Since when?"

"Only since last night, sir," replied the butler, "but the circumstances are queer. He dined out with some City gentlemen, somewhere, last night, and he came home about ten o'clock. He wasn't in the house long. He went into his laboratory—he spends a lot of time in experimenting in chemistry, you know, sir—and he called me in there. 'I'm going out again for an hour, Grayson,' he says. 'I shall be in at eleven: don't go to bed, for I want to see you for a minute or two.' Of course, there was nothing in that, Mr. Purdie, and I waited for him. But he never came home—and no message came. He never came home at all—and this morning I've telephoned to his two clubs, and to one or two other places in the City—nobody's seen or heard anything of him. And I can't think what's happened—it's all so unlike his habits."

"He didn't tell you where he was going?" asked Purdie.

"No, sir, but he went on foot," answered the butler. "I let him out—he turned up Paddington way."

"You didn't notice anything out of the common about him?" suggested Purdie.

The butler hesitated for a moment.

"Well, sir," he said at last, "I did notice something. Come this way, Mr. Purdie."

Turning away from the hall, he led Purdie through the library in which Levendale had received Ayscough and his companions into a small room that opened out of it.

Purdie, looking round him, found that he was standing in a laboratory, furnished with chemical apparatus of the latest descriptions. Implements and appliances were on all sides; there were rows of bottles on the shelves; a library of technical books filled a large book-case; everything in the place betokened the pursuit of a scientific investigator. And Purdie's keen sense of smell immediately noted the prevalent atmosphere of drugs and chemicals.

"It was here that I saw Mr. Levendale last night, sir," said the butler. "He called me in. He was measuring something from one of those bottles into a small phial, Mr. Purdie—he put the phial in his waistcoat pocket. Look at those bottles, sir—you'll see they all contain poison!—you can tell that by the make of 'em."

Purdie glanced at the shelf which the butler indicated. The bottles ranged on it were all of blue glass, and all triangular in shape, and each bore a red label with the word *Poison* prominently displayed.

"Odd!" he said. "You've some idea?" he went on, looking closely at the butler. "Something on your mind about this? What is it?"

The butler shook his head.

"Well, sir," he answered, "when you see a gentleman measuring poison into a phial, which he carefully puts in his pocket, and when he goes out, and when he never comes back, and when you can't hear of him, anywhere! why, what are you to think? Looks strange, now, doesn't it, Mr. Purdie?"

"I don't know Mr. Levendale well enough to say," replied Purdie. "There may be some quite good reason for Mr. Levendale's absence. He'd no trouble of any sort, had he?"

"He seemed a bit upset, once or twice, yesterday—and the night before," said the butler. "I noticed it—in little things. Well!—I can't make it out, sir. You see, I've been with him ever since he came back to England—some years now—and I know his habits, thoroughly. However, we can only wait—I believe Miss Bennett sent for you, Mr. Purdie?"

"Yes," said Purdie. "She did."

"This way, sir," said the butler. "Miss Bennett's alone, now—the children have just gone out with their nurses."

He led Purdie through the house to a sitting-room looking out on the garden of the Square, and ushered him into the governess's presence.

"I've told Mr. Purdie all about it, miss," he said, confidentially. "Perhaps you'll talk it over with him! I can't think of anything more to do—until we hear something."

Left alone, Purdie and Elsie Bennett looked at each other as they shook hands. She was a fair, slender girl, naturally shy and retiring; she was manifestly shy at renewing her acquaintance with Purdie, and Purdie himself, conscious of his own feelings towards her, felt a certain embarrassment and awkwardness.

"You sent for me," he said brusquely. "I came the instant I got your note. Grayson kept me talking downstairs. You're bothered—about Mr. Levendale?"

"Yes," she answered. Then she pointed to a chair. "Won't you sit down?" she said, and took a chair close by. "I sent for you, because—it may seem strange, but it's a fact!—I couldn't think of anybody else! It seemed so fortunate that you were in London—and close by. I felt that—that I could depend on you."

"Thank you," said Purdie. "Well—you can! And what is it?"

"Grayson's told you about Mr. Levendale's going out last night, and never coming back, nor sending any message?" she continued. "As Grayson says, considering Mr. Levendale's habits, that is certainly very strange! But—I want to tell you something beyond that—I must tell somebody! And I know that if I tell you you'll keep it secret—until, or unless you think you ought to tell it to—the police!"

Purdie started.

"The police!" he exclaimed. "What is it?"

Elsie Bennett turned to a table, and picked up a couple of newspapers.

"Have you read this Praed Street mystery affair?" she asked. "I mean the account of the inquest?"

"Every word—and heard more, besides," answered Purdie. "That young fellow, Andie Lauriston, is an old schoolmate and friend of mine. I came here yesterday to see him, and found him plunged into this business. Of course, he's absolutely innocent."

"Has he been arrested?" asked Elsie, almost eagerly.

"No!" replied Purdie. "He's gone away—to get evidence that those rings which are such a feature of the case are really his and were his mother's."

"Have you noticed these particulars, at the end of the inquest, about the book which was found in the pawnbroker's parlour?" she went on. "The Spanish manuscript?"

"Said to have been lost by Mr. Levendale in an omnibus," answered Purdie. "Yes! What of it?"

The girl bent nearer to him.

"It seems a dreadful thing to say," she whispered, "but I must tell somebody—I can't, I daren't keep it to myself any longer! Mr. Levendale isn't telling the truth about that book!"

Purdie involuntarily glanced at the door—and drew his chair nearer to Elsie's.

"You're sure of that?" he whispered. "Just so! Now—in what way?"

"It says here," answered Elsie, tapping the newspapers with her finger, "that Mr. Levendale lost this book in a 'bus, which he left at the corner of Chapel Street, and that he was so concerned about the loss that he immediately sent advertisements off to every morning newspaper in London. The last part of that is true—the first part is not true! Mr. Levendale did not lose his book—he did not leave it in the 'bus! I'm sorry to have to say it—but all that is invention on his part—why, I don't know."

Purdie had listened to this with a growing feeling of uneasiness and suspicion. The clouds centring round Levendale were certainly thickening.

"Now, just tell me—how do you know all this?" he asked. "Rely on me—to the full!"

"I'll tell you," replied Elsie, readily. "Because, about four o'clock on the afternoon of the old man's death, I happened to be at the corner of Chapel Street. I saw Mr. Levendale get out of the 'bus. He did not see me. He crossed Edgware Road and walked rapidly down Praed Street. And—he was carrying that book in his hand!"

"You're sure it was that book?" asked Purdie.

"According to the description given in this account and in the advertisement—yes," she answered. "I noticed the fine binding. Although Mr. Levendale didn't see me—there were a lot of people about—I was close to him. I am sure it was the book described here."

"And—he went in the direction of the pawnshop?" said Purdie. "What on earth does it all mean? What did he mean by advertising for the book, when—"

Before he could say more, a knock came at the door, and the butler entered, bearing an open telegram in his hand. His face wore an expression of relief.

"Here's a wire from Mr. Levendale, Miss Bennett," he said. "It's addressed to me. He says, 'Shall be away from home, on business, for a few days. Let all go on as usual.' That's better, miss! But," continued Grayson, glancing at Purdie, "it's still odd—for do you see, sir, where that wire has been sent from? Spring Street—close by!"

61

## CHAPTER FIFTEEN
## CONFERENCE

Purdie was already sufficiently acquainted with the geography of the Paddington district to be aware of the significance of Grayson's remark. The Spring Street Post Office, at which Levendale's wire had been handed in, was only a few minutes' walk from the house. It stood, in fact, between Purdie's hotel and Sussex Square, and he had passed it on his way to Levendale's. It was certainly odd that a man who was within five minutes' walk of his own house should send a telegram there, when he had nothing to do but walk down one street and turn the corner of another to give his message in person.

"Sent off, do you see, sir, twenty minutes ago," observed the butler, pointing to some figures in the telegram form. "So—Mr. Levendale must have been close by—then!"

"Not necessarily," remarked Purdie. "He may have sent a messenger with that wire—perhaps he himself was catching a train at Paddington."

Grayson shook his head knowingly.

"There's a telegraph office on the platform there, sir," he answered.

"However—there it is, and I suppose there's no more to be done."

He left the room again, and Purdie looked at the governess. She, too, looked at him: there was a question in the eyes of both.

"What do you make of that?" asked Purdie after a pause.

"What do you make of it?" she asked in her turn.

"It looks odd—but there may be a reason for it," he answered. "Look here!—I'm going to ask you a question. What do you know of Mr. Levendale? You've been governess to his children for some time, haven't you?"

"For six months before he left Cape Town, and ever since we all came to England, three years ago," she answered. "I know that he's very rich, and a very busy man, and a member of Parliament, and that he goes to the City a great deal—and that's all! He's a very reserved man, too—of course, he never tells me anything. I've never had any conversation with him excepting about the children."

"You're upset about this book affair?" suggested Purdie.

"Why should Mr. Levendale say that he left that book in the omnibus, when I myself saw him leave the 'bus with it in his hand, and go down Praed Street with it?" she asked. "Doesn't it look as if he were the person who left it in that room—where the old man was found lying dead?"

"That, perhaps, is the very reason why he doesn't want people to know that he did leave it there," remarked Purdie, quietly. "There's more in all this than lies on the surface. You wanted my advice? Very well don't say

62

anything to anybody till you see me again. I must go now—there's a man waiting for me at my hotel. I may call again, mayn't I?"

"Do!" she said, giving him her hand. "I am bothered about this—it's useless to deny it—and I've no one to talk to about it. Come—any time."

Purdie repressed a strong desire to stay longer, and to turn the conversation to more personal matters. But he was essentially a business man, and the matters of the moment seemed to be critical. So he promised to return, and then hurried back to his hotel—to find Melky Rubinstein pacing up and down outside the entrance.

Purdie tapped Melky's shoulder and motioned him to walk along Praed Street.

"Look here!" he said. "I want you to take me to see your cousin—and the pawnshop. We must have a talk—you said your cousin's a good business woman. She's the sort we can discuss business with, eh?"

"My cousin Zillah Wildrose, mister," answered Melky, solemnly, "is one of the best! She's a better headpiece on her than what I have—and that's saying a good deal. I was going to suggest you should come there. Talk!—s'elp me, Mr. Purdie, it strikes me there'll be a lot of that before we've done. What about this here affair of last night?—I've just seen Mr. Ayscough, passing along—he's told me all about it. Do you think it's anything to do with our business?"

"Can't say," answered Purdie. "Wait till we can discuss matters with your cousin."

Melky led the way to the side-door of the pawnshop. Since the old man's death, the whole establishment had been closed—Zillah had refused to do any business until her grandfather's funeral was over. She received her visitors in the parlour where old Daniel had been found dead: after a moment's inspection of her, and the exchange of a few remarks about Lauriston, Purdie suggested that they should all sit down and talk matters over.

"Half-a-mo!" said Melky. "If we're going to have a cabinet council, mister, there's a lady that I want to bring into it—Mrs. Goldmark. I know something that Mrs. Goldmark can speak to—I've just been considering matters while I was waiting for you, Mr. Purdie, and I'm going to tell you and Zillah, and Mrs. Goldmark, of a curious fact that I know of. I'll fetch her—and while I'm away Zillah'll show you that there book what was found there."

Purdie looked with interest at the Spanish manuscript which seemed to be a factor of such importance.

"I suppose you never saw this before?" he asked, as Zillah laid it on the table before him. "And you're certain it wasn't in the place when you went out that afternoon, leaving your grandfather alone?"

"That I'm positive of," answered Zillah. "I never saw it in my life until my attention was drawn to it after he was dead. That book was brought in here during my absence, and it was neither bought nor pawned—that's absolutely certain! Of course, you know whose book it is?"

"Mr. Spencer Levendale's," answered Purdie. "Yes I know all those particulars—and about his advertisements for it, and a little more.

And I want to discuss all that with you and your cousin. This Mrs. Goldmark—she's to be fully trusted?"

Zillah replied that Mrs. Goldmark was worthy of entire confidence, and an old friend, and Melky presently returning with her, Purdie suggested they should all sit down and talk—informally and in strict privacy.

"You know why I'm concerning myself in this?" he said, looking round at his three companions. "I'm anxious that Andie Lauriston should be fully and entirely cleared! I've great faith in him—he's beginning what I believe will be a successful career, and it would be a terrible thing if any suspicion rested on him. So I want, for his sake, to thoroughly clear up this mystery about your relative's death."

"Mister!" said Melky, in his most solemn tones. "Speaking for my cousin there, and myself, there ain't nothing what we wouldn't do to clear Mr. Lauriston! We ain't never had one moment's suspicion of him from the first, knowing the young fellow as we do. So we're with you in that matter, ain't we, Zillah?"

"Mr. Purdie feels sure of that," agreed Zillah, with a glance at Lauriston's old schoolmate. "There's no need to answer him, Melky."

"I am sure!" said Purdie. "So—let's put our wits together—we'll consider the question of approaching the police when we've talked amongst ourselves. Now—I want to ask you some very private questions. They spring out of that rare book there. There's no doubt that book belongs to Mr. Levendale. Do either of you know if Mr. Levendale had any business relations with the late Mr. Rubinstein?"

Zillah shook her head.

"None!—that I know of," she answered. "I've helped my grandfather in this business for some time. I never heard him mention Mr. Levendale. Mr. Levendale never came here, certainly."

Melky shook his head, too.

"When Mr. Ayscough, and Mr. Lauriston, and me went round to Sussex Square, to see Mr. Levendale about that advertisement for his book," he remarked, "he said he'd never heard of Daniel Multenius. That's a fact, mister!"

"Had Mr. Multenius any private business relations of which he didn't tell you?" asked Purdie, turning to Zillah.

"He might have had," admitted Zillah. "He was out a good deal. I don't know what he might do when he went out. He was—close. We—it's no use denying it—we don't know all about it. His solicitor's making some enquiries—I expect him here, any time, today."

"It comes to this," observed Purdie. "Your grandfather met his death by violence, the man who attacked him came in here during your absence. The question I want to get solved is—was the man who undoubtedly left that book here the guilty man? If so—who is he?"

Melky suddenly broke the silence which followed upon this question.

"I'm going to tell something that I ain't told to nobody as yet!" he said. "Not even to Zillah. After this here parlour had been cleared, I took a look round. I've very sharp eyes, Mr. Purdie. I found this here—half-hidden under the rug there, where the poor old man had been lying." He pulled out the platinum solitaire, laid it on the palm of one hand, and extended the hand to Mrs. Goldmark. "You've seen the like of that before, ain't you?" asked Melky.

"Mercy be upon us!" gasped Mrs. Goldmark, starting in her seat. "I've the fellow to it lying in my desk!"

"And it was left on a table in your restaurant," continued Melky, "by a man what looked like a Colonial party—I know!—I saw it by accident in your place the other night, and one o' your girls told me. Now then, Mr. Purdie, here's a bit more of puzzlement—and perhaps a clue. These here platinum solitaire cuff-links are valuable—they're worth—well, I'd give a good few pounds for the pair. Now who's the man who lost one in this here parlour—right there!—and the other in Mrs. Goldmark's restaurant? For—it's a pair! There's no doubt about that, mister!—there's that same curious and unusual device on each. Mister!—them studs has at some time or other been made to special order!"

Purdie turned the solitaire over, and looked at Zillah.

"Have you ever seen anything like this before?" he asked.

"Never!" said Zillah. "It's as Melky says—specially made."

"And you have its fellow—lost in your restaurant?" continued Purdie, turning to Mrs. Goldmark.

"Its very marrow," assented Mrs. Goldmark, fervently, "is in my desk! It was dropped on one of our tables a few afternoons ago by a man who, as Mr. Rubinstein says, looked like one of those Colonials. Leastways, my waitress, Rosa, she picked it up exactly where he'd been sitting. So I put it away till he comes in again, you see. Oh, yes!"

"Has he been in again?" asked Purdie.

"Never was he inside my door before!" answered Mrs. Goldmark dramatically. "Never has he been inside it since! But—I keep his property, just so. In my desk it is!"

Purdie considered this new evidence in silence for a moment.

"The question now is—this," he said presently. "Is the man who seems undoubtedly to have dropped those studs the same man who brought that book in here? Or, had Mr. Multenius two callers here during your absence, Miss Wildrose? And—who is this mysterious man who dropped the studs—valuable things, with a special device on them? He'll have to be traced! Mrs. Goldmark—can you describe him, particularly?"

Before Mrs. Goldmark could reply, a knock came at the side-door, and Zillah, going to answer it, returned presently with a middle-aged, quiet-looking, gold-spectacled gentleman whom she introduced to Purdie as Mr. Penniket, solicitor to the late Daniel Multenius.

## CHAPTER SIXTEEN
## THE DETECTIVE CALLS

Mr. Penniket, to whom the two cousins and Mrs. Goldmark were evidently very well known, looked a polite enquiry at the stranger as he took the chair which Melky drew forward for him.

"As Mr. Purdie is presumably discussing this affair with you," he observed, "I take it that you intend him to hear anything I have to tell?"

"That's so, Mr. Penniket," answered Melky. "Mr. Purdie's one of us, so to speak—you can tell us anything you like, before him. We were going into details when you come—there's some strange business on, Mr. Penniket! And we want to get a bit clear about it before we tell the police what we know."

"You know something that they don't know?" asked Mr. Penniket.

"More than a bit!" replied Melky, laconically. "This here affair's revolving itself into a network, mister, out of which somebody's going to find it hard work to break through!"

The solicitor, who had been quietly inspecting Purdie, gave him a sly smile.

"Then before I tell you what I have just found out," he said, turning to Melky, "I think you had better tell me all you know, and what you have been discussing. Possibly, I may have something to tell which bears on our knowledge. Let us be clear!"

He listened carefully while Purdie, at Zillah's request, told him briefly what had been said before his arrival, and Purdie saw at once that none of the facts surprised him. He asked Mrs. Goldmark one or two questions about the man who was believed to have dropped one of his cuff-links in her restaurant; he asked Melky a question as to his discovery of the other; he made no comment on the answers which they gave him. Finally, he drew his chair nearer to the table at which they were sitting, and invited their attention with a glance.

"There is no doubt," he said, "that the circumstances centring round the death of my late client are remarkably mysterious! What we want to get at, put into a nut-shell, is just this—what happened in this parlour between half-past four and half-past five on Monday afternoon? We might even narrow that down to—what happened between ten minutes to five and ten minutes past five? Daniel Multenius was left alone—we know that. Some person undoubtedly came in here—perhaps more than one person came. Who was the person? Were there two persons? If there were two, did they come together—or singly, separately? All that will have to be solved before we find out who it was that assaulted my late client, and so injured him that he died under the shock. Now, Miss Wildrose, and Mr. Rubinstein, there's one fact which you may as well get into your minds at once. Your deceased relative had his secrets!"

Neither Zillah nor Purdie made any comment on this, and the solicitor, with a meaning look at Purdie, went on. "Not that Daniel Multenius revealed any of them to me!" he continued. "I have acted for him in legal matters for some years, but only in quite an ordinary way. He was a well-to-do man, Mr. Purdie—a rich man, in fact, and a considerable property owner—I did all his work of that sort. But as regards his secrets, I know nothing—except that since yesterday, I have discovered that he certainly had them. I have, as Miss Wildrose knows—and by her instructions—been making some enquiries at the bank where Mr. Multenius kept his account—the Empire and Universal, in Lombard Street—and I have made some curious unearthings in the course of them. Now then, between ourselves—Mr. Purdie being represented to me as in your entire confidence—I may as well tell you that Daniel Multenius most certainly had dealings of a business nature completely outside his business as jeweller and pawnbroker in this shop. That's positively certain. And what is also certain is that in some of those dealings he was, in some way or another, intimately associated with the man whose name has already come up a good deal since Monday—Mr. Spencer Levendale!"

"S'elp me!" muttered Melky. "I heard Levendale, with my own two ears, say that he didn't know the poor old fellow!"

"Very likely," said Mr. Penniket, drily. "It was not convenient to him—we will assume—to admit that he did, just then. But I have discovered—

from the bankers—that precisely two years ago, Mr. Spencer Levendale paid to Daniel Multenius a sum of ten thousand pounds. That's a fact!"

"For what, mister?" demanded Melky.

"Can't say—nobody can say," answered the solicitor. "All the same, he did—paid it in, himself, to Daniel Multenius's credit, at the Empire and Universal. It went into the ordinary account, in the ordinary way, and was used by Mr. Multenius as part of his own effects—as no doubt it was. Now," continued Mr. Penniket, turning to Zillah, "I want to ask you a particular question. I know you had assisted your grandfather a great deal of late years. Had you anything to do with his banking account?"

"No!" replied Zillah, promptly. "That's the one thing I never had anything to do with. I never saw his pass-book, nor his deposit-book, nor even his cheque-book. He kept all that to himself."

"Just so," said Mr. Penniket. "Then, of course, you don't know that he dealt with considerable sums—evidently quite outside this business. He made large—sometimes very heavy—payments. And—this, I am convinced, is of great importance to the question we are trying to solve—most of these payments were sent to South Africa."

The solicitor glanced round his audience as if anxious to see that its various members grasped the significance of this announcement. And Melky at once voiced the first impression of, at any rate, three of them.

"Levendale comes from those parts!" he muttered. "Came here some two or three years ago—by all I can gather."

"Just so," said Mr. Penniket. "Therefore, possibly this South African business, in which my late client was undoubtedly engaged, is connected with Mr. Levendale. That can be found out. But I have still more to tell you—perhaps, considering everything, the most important matter of the whole lot. On Monday morning last—that would be a few hours before his death—Mr. Multenius called at the bank and took from it a small packet which he had entrusted to his banker's keeping only a fortnight previously. The bankers do not know what was in that packet—he had more than once got them to take care of similar packets at one time or another. But they described it to me just now. A packet, evidently enclosing a small, hard box, some four or five inches square in all directions, wrapped in strong cartridge paper, and heavily sealed with red wax. It bore Mr. Multenius's name and address—written by himself. Now, then, Miss Wildrose—he took that packet away from the bank at about twelve-thirty on Monday noon. Have you seen anything of it?"

"Nothing!" answered Zillah with certainty. "There's no such packet here, Mr. Penniket. I've been through everything—safes, drawers, chests, since my grandfather died, and I've not found anything that I didn't know of. I remember that he went out last Monday morning—he was away two hours, and came in again about a quarter past one, but I never saw such a packet in his possession as that you describe. I know nothing of it."

"Well," said the solicitor, after a pause, "there are the facts. And the question now is—ought we not to tell all this to the police, at once? This connection of Levendale with my late client—as undoubted as it seems to have been secret—needs investigation. According to Mr. Purdie here—Levendale has suddenly disappeared—or, at any rate, left home under mysterious circumstances. Has that disappearance anything to do with Multenius's death? Has it anything to do with the death of this next door man, Parslett, last night? And has Levendale any connections with the strange man who dropped one platinum solitaire stud in Mrs. Goldmark's restaurant, and another in this parlour?"

No one attempted to answer these questions for a moment; then, Melky, as if seized with a sudden inspiration, smote the table and leaned over it towards the solicitor.

"Mr. Penniket!" he said, glancing around him as if to invite approval of what he was about to say. "You're a lawyer, mister!—you can put things in order and present 'em as if they was in a catalogue! Take the whole business to New Scotland Yard, sir!—let the big men at headquarters have a go at it. That's what I say! There's some queer mystery at the bottom of all this, Mr. Penniket, and it ain't a one-man job. Go to the Yard, mister—let 'em try their brains on it!"

Zillah made a murmured remark which seemed to second her cousin's proposal, and Mr. Penniket turned to Purdie.

"I understand you to be a business man," he remarked. "What do you say?"

"As far as I can put things together," answered Purdie, "I fully agree that there is some extraordinary mystery round and about Mr. Multenius's death. And as the detective force at New Scotland Yard exists for the solution of such problems—why, I should certainly tell the authorities there everything that is known. Why not?"

"Very good," said Mr. Penniket. "Then it will be well if you two come with me. The more information we can give to the heads of the Criminal Investigation Department, the better. We'll go there at once."

In a few moments, the three men had gone, and Zillah and Mrs. Goldmark, left alone, looked at each other.

"Mrs. Goldmark!" said Zillah, after a long silence. "Did you see that man, yourself, who's supposed to have dropped that platinum solitaire in your restaurant?"

"Did I see him?" exclaimed Mrs. Goldmark. "Do I see you, Zillah? See him I did!—though never before, and never since! And ain't I the good memory for faces—and won't I know him again if he comes my way? Do you know what?—I ain't never forgotten a face what I've once looked at! Comes from keeping an eye on customers who looks as if they might have forgot to bring their moneys with 'em!"

"Well, I hope you'll see this man again," remarked Zillah. "I'd give a lot to get all the mystery cleared up."

Mrs. Goldmark observed that mysteries were not cleared up in a day, and presently went away to see that her business was being conducted properly. She was devoting herself to Zillah in very neighbourly fashion just then, but she had to keep running into the restaurant every hour or two to keep an eye on things. And during one of her absences, later in the early evening of that day, Zillah, alone in the house, answered a knock at the door, and opening it found Ayscough outside. His look betokened news, and Zillah led him into the parlour.

"Alone?" asked Ayscough. "Aye, well, I've something to tell you that I want you to keep to yourself—for a bit, anyway. Those rings, you know, that the young fellow, Lauriston, says are his, and had been his mother's?"

"Well?" said Zillah, faintly, and half-conscious of some coming bad news. "What of them?"

"Our people," continued the detective, "have had some expert chap—jeweller, or something of that sort, examining those rings, and comparing them with the rings that are in your tray. And in that tray there are several rings which have a private mark inside them. Now, then!—those two rings which Lauriston claims are marked in exactly the same fashion!"

## CHAPTER SEVENTEEN
### WHAT THE LAMPS SHONE ON

Zillah leaned suddenly back against the table by which she was standing, and Ayscough, who was narrowly watching the effect of his news, saw her turn very pale. She stood staring at him during a moment's silence; then she let a sharp exclamation escape her lips, and in the same instant her colour came back—heightened from surprise and indignation.

"Impossible!" she said. "I can't believe it; There may be marks inside our rings—that's likely enough. But how could those marks correspond with the marks in his rings?"

"I tell you it is so!" answered Ayscough. "I've seen the marks in both—with my own eyes. It occurred to one of our bosses this evening to have all the rings carefully examined by an expert—he got a man from one of the jeweller's shops in Edgware Road. This chap very soon pointed out that inside the two rings which young Lauriston says are his, and come to him from his mother, are certain private marks—jewellers' marks, this man called 'em—which are absolutely identical with similar marks which are inside some of the rings in the tray which was found on this table. That's a fact!—I tell you I've seen 'em—all! And—you see the significance of it! Of course, our people are now dead certain that young Lauriston's story is false, and that he grabbed those two rings out of that tray. See?"

"Are you certain of it—yourself?" demanded Zillah.

Ayscough hesitated and finally shook his head.

"Well, between ourselves, I'm not!" he answered. "I've a feeling from the first, that the lad's innocent enough. But it's a queer thing—and it's terribly against him. And—what possible explanation can there be?"

"You say you've seen those marks," said Zillah. "Would you know them again—on other goods?"

"I should!" replied Ayscough. "I can tell you what they are. There's the letter M. and then two crosses—one on each side of the letter. Very small, you know, and worn, too—this man I'm talking of used some sort of a magnifying glass."

Zillah turned away and went into the shop, which was all in darkness. Ayscough, waiting, heard the sound of a key being turned, then of a metallic tinkling; presently the girl came back, carrying a velvet-lined tray in one hand, and a jeweller's magnifying glass in the other.

"The rings in that tray you're talking about—the one you took away—are all very old stock," she remarked. "I've heard my grandfather say he'd had some of them thirty years or more. Here are some similar ones—we'll see if they're marked in the same fashion."

Five minutes later, Zillah had laid aside several rings marked in the way Ayscough had indicated, and she turned from them to him with a look of alarm.

"I can't understand it!" she exclaimed. "I know that these rings, and those in that tray at the police-station, are part of old stock that my grandfather had when he came here. He used to have a shop, years ago, in the City—I'm not quite sure where, exactly—and this is part of the stock he brought from it. But, how could Mr. Lauriston's rings bear those marks? Because, from what I know of the trade, those are private marks—my grandfather's private marks!"

"Well, just so—and you can imagine what our people are inclined to say

about it," said the detective. "They say now that the two rings which Lauriston claims never were his nor his mother's, but that he stole them out of your grandfather's tray. They're fixed on that, now."
"What will they do?" asked Zillah, anxiously. "Is he in danger?"
Ayscough gave her a knowing look.
"Between you and me," he said, lowering his voice to a whisper, "I came around here privately—on my own hook, you know. I should be sorry if this really is fixed on the young fellow—there's a mystery, but it may be cleared up. Now, he's gone off to find somebody who can prove that those rings really were his mother's. You, no doubt, know where he's gone?"
"Yes—but I'm not going to tell," said Zillah firmly. "Don't ask me!"
"Quite right—I don't want to know myself," answered Ayscough. "And you'll probably have an idea when he's coming back? All right—take a tip from me. Keep him out of the way a bit—stop him from coming into this district. Let him know all about those marks—and if he can clear that up, well and good. You understand?—and of course, all this is between you and me."
"You're very good, Mr. Ayscough," replied Zillah, warmly. "I won't forget your kindness. And I'm certain this about the marks can be cleared up—but I don't know how!"
"Well—do as I say," said the detective. "Just give the tip to your cousin Melky, and to that young Scotch gentleman—let 'em keep Lauriston out of the way for a few days. In the meantime—this is a very queer case!—something may happen that'll fix the guilt on somebody else—conclusively. I've my own ideas and opinions—but we shall see. Maybe we shall see a lot—and everybody'll be more astonished than they're thinking for."
With this dark and sinister hint, Ayscough went away, and Zillah took the rings back to the shop, and locked them up again. And then she sat down to wait for Mrs. Goldmark—and to think. She had never doubted Lauriston's story for one moment, and she did not doubt it now. But she was quick to see the serious significance of what the detective had just told her and she realized that action must be taken on the lines he had suggested. And so, having made herself ready for going out, she excused herself to Mrs. Goldmark when that good lady returned, and without saying anything to her as to the nature of her errand, hurried round to Star Street, to find Melky Rubinstein and tell him of the new development.
Mrs. Flitwick herself opened the door to Zillah and led her into the

narrow passage. But at the mention of Melky she shook her head.

"I ain't set eyes on Mr. Rubinstein not since this morning, miss," said she. "He went out with that young Scotch gentleman what come here yesterday asking for Mr. Lauriston, and he's never been in again—not even to put his nose inside the door. And at twelve o'clock there come a telegram for him—which it was the second that come this morning. The first, of course, he got before he went out; the one that come at noon's awaiting him. No—I ain't seen him all day!"

Zillah's quick wits were instantly at work as soon as she heard of the telegram.

"Oh, I know all about that wire, Mrs. Flitwick!" she exclaimed. "It's as much for me as for my cousin. Give it to me—and if Mr. Rubinstein comes in soon—or when he comes—tell him I've got it, and ask him to come round to me immediately—it's important."

Mrs. Flitwick produced the telegram at once, and Zillah, repeating her commands about Melky, hurried away with it. But at the first street lamp she paused, and tore open the envelope, and pulled out the message. As she supposed, it was from Lauriston, and had been handed in at Peebles at eleven o'clock that morning.

"Got necessary information returning at once meet me at King's Cross at nine-twenty this evening. L."

Zillah looked at her watch. It was then ten minutes to nine. There was just half an hour before Lauriston's train was due. Without a moment's hesitation, she turned back along Star Street, hurried into Edgware Road and hailing the first taxi-cab she saw, bade its driver to get to the Great Northern as fast as possible. Whatever else happened, Lauriston must be met and warned.

The taxi-cab made good headway along the Marylebone and Euston Roads, and the hands of the clock over the entrance to King's Cross had not yet indicated a quarter past nine when Zillah was set down close by. She hurried into the station, and to the arrival platform. All the way along in the cab she had been wondering what to do when she met Lauriston—not as to what she should tell him, for that was already settled, but as to what to advise him to do about following Ayscough's suggestion and keeping out of the way, for awhile. She had already seen enough of him to know that he was naturally of high spirit and courage, and that he would hate the very idea of hiding, or of seeming to run away. Yet, what other course was open if he wished to avoid arrest? Zillah, during her short business experience had been brought in contact with the police authorities and their methods more than once, and she knew that there is nothing the professional detective likes so much as to follow the obvious—as the easiest and safest. She had been quick to appreciate all that Ayscough told her—she knew how the police mind would reason about it: it would be quite enough for it to know that on the rings which Andy Lauriston said were his there were marks which were certainly identical with those on her grandfather's property: now that the police authorities were in possession of that fact, they would go for Lauriston without demur or hesitation, leaving all the other mysteries and ramifications of the Multenius affair to be sorted, or to sort themselves, at leisure. One thing was certain—Andie Lauriston was in greater danger now than at any moment since Ayscough found him leaving the shop, and she must save him—against his own inclinations if need be.

But before the train from the North was due, Zillah was fated to have yet another experience. She had taken up a position directly beneath a powerful lamp at the end of the arrival platform, so that Lauriston, who would be obliged to pass that way, could not fail to see her. Suddenly turning, to glance at the clock in the roof behind her, she was aware of a man, young, tall, athletic, deeply bronzed, as from long contact with the Southern sun, who stood just behind a knot of loungers, his heavy overcoat and the jacket beneath it thrown open, feeling in his waistcoat pockets as if for his match-box—an unlighted cigar protruded from the corner of his rather grim, determined lips. But it was not at lips, nor at the cigar, nor at the searching fingers that Zillah looked, after that first comprehensive glance—her eyes went straight to an object which shone in the full glare of the lamp above her head. The man wore an old-fashioned, double-breasted fancy waistcoat, but so low as to reveal a good deal of his shirt-front. And in that space, beneath his bird's-eye blue tie, loosely knotted in a bow, Zillah saw a stud, which her experienced eyes knew to be of platinum, and on it was engraved the same curious device which she had seen once before that day—on the solitaire exhibited by Melky.

The girl was instantly certain that here was the man who had visited Mrs. Goldmark's eating-house. Her first instinct was to challenge him with the fact—but as she half moved towards him, he found his match-box, struck a match, and began to light his cigar. And just then came the great engine of the express, panting its way to a halt beside them, and with it the folk on the platform began to stir, and Zillah was elbowed aside. Her situation was perplexing—was she to watch the man and perhaps lose Lauriston in the crowd already passing from the train, or—

The man was still leisurely busy with his cigar, and Zillah turned and went a few steps up the platform. She suddenly caught sight of Lauriston, and running towards him gripped his arm, and drew him to the lamp. But

74

in that moment of indecision, the man had vanished.
## CHAPTER EIGHTEEN
## MR. STUYVESANT GUYLER
Lauriston, surprised beyond a little at seeing Zillah, found his surprise turned into amazement as she seized his arm and forced him along the platform, careless of the groups of passengers and the porters, crowding about the baggage vans.

"What is it?" he demanded. "Has something happened? Where are we going?"

But Zillah held on determinedly, her eyes fixed ahead.

"Quick!" she said, pantingly. "A man I saw just now! He was there—he's gone—while I looked for you. We must find him! He must have gone this way. Andie!—look for him! A tall, clean-shaven man in a slouched hat and a heavy travelling coat—a foreigner of some sort. Oh, look!"

It was the first time she had called Lauriston by his name, and he gave her arm an involuntary pressure as they hastened along.

"But why?" he asked. "Who is he—what do you want with him? What's it all about?"

"Oh, find him!" she exclaimed. "You don't know how important it is! If I lose sight of him now, I'll very likely never see him again. And he must be found—and stopped—for your sake!"

They had come to the end of the platform, by that time, and Lauriston looked left and right in search of the man described. Suddenly he twisted Zillah round.

"Is that he—that fellow talking to another man?" he asked. "See him—there?"

"Yes!" said Zillah. She saw the man of the platinum stud again, and on seeing him, stopped dead where she was, holding Lauriston back. The man, leisurely smoking his cigar, was chatting to another man, who, from the fact that he was carrying a small suit-case in one hand and a rug over the other arm, had evidently come in by the just-arrived express. "Yes!" she continued. "That's the man! And—we've just got to follow him wherever he goes!"

"What on earth for?" asked Lauriston. "What mystery's this? Who is he?"

At that moment the two men parted, with a cordial handshake; the man of the suit-case and the rug turned towards the stairs which led to the underground railway; the other man walked slowly away through the front of the station in the direction of the Great Northern Hotel. And Zillah immediately dragged Lauriston after him, keeping a few yards' distance, but going persistently forward. The man in front crossed the road, and strode towards the portico of the hotel—and Zillah suddenly made up her mind.

"We've got to speak to that man!" she said. "Don't ask why, now—you'll know in a few minutes. Ask him if he'll speak to me?"

Lauriston caught up the stranger as he set foot on the steps leading to the hotel door. He felt uncomfortable and foolish—but Zillah's tone left him no option but to obey.

"I beg your pardon," said Lauriston, as politely as possible, "but—this lady is very anxious to speak to you."

The man turned, glanced at Zillah, who had hurried up, and lifted his slouched hat with a touch of old-fashioned courtesy. There was a strong light burning just above them: in its glare all three looked at each other. The stranger smiled—a little wonderingly.

"Why, sure!" he said in accents that left no doubt of his American origin. "I'd be most happy. You're not mistaking me for somebody else?"

Zillah was already flushed with embarrassment. Now that she had run her quarry to earth, and so easily, she scarcely knew what to do with it.

"You'll think this very strange," she said, stammeringly, "but if you don't mind telling me something?—you see, I saw you just now in the station, when you were feeling for your match-box, and I noticed that you wore a platinum stud—with an unusual device on it."

The American laughed—a good-natured, genial laugh—and threw open his coat. At the same moment he thrust his wrists forward.

"This stud!" he said. "That's so!—it is platinum, and the device is curious. And the device is right there, too, see—on those solitaire cuff-studs! But—"

He paused looking at Zillah, whose eyes were now fastened on the cuff-studs, and who was obviously so astonished as to have lost her tongue.

"You seemed mighty amazed at my studs!" said the stranger, with another laugh. "Now, you'll just excuse me if I ask—why?"

Zillah regained her wits with an effort, and became as business-like as usual.

"Don't, please, think I'm asking idle and purposeless questions," she said. "Have you been long in London?"

"A few days only," answered the stranger, readily enough.

"Have you read of what's already called the Praed Street Murder in the papers?" continued Zillah.

"Yes—I read that," the stranger said, his face growing serious. "The affair of the old man—the pawnbroker with the odd name. Yes!"

"I'm the old man's granddaughter," said Zillah, brusquely. "Now, I'll tell you why I was upset by seeing your platinum stud. A solitaire stud, made of platinum, and ornamented with exactly the same device as yours, was found in our parlour after my grandfather's death—and another, evidently the fellow to it, was found in an eating-house, close by. Now, do you understand why I wished to speak to you?"

While Zillah spoke, the American's face had been growing graver and graver, and when she made an end, he glanced at Lauriston and shook his head.

"Say!" he said. "That's a very serious matter! You're sure the device was the same, and the material platinum?"

"I've been reared in the jewellery trade," replied Zillah. "The things I'm talking of are of platinum—and the device is precisely the same as that on your stud."

"Well!—that's mighty queer!" remarked the American. "I can't tell you why it's queer, all in a minute, but I do assure you it's just about the queerest thing I ever heard of in my life—and I've known a lot of queerness. Look here!—I'm stopping at this hotel—will you come in with me, and we'll just get a quiet corner and talk some? Come right in, then."

He led the way into the hotel, through the hall, and down a corridor from which several reception rooms opened. Looking into one, a small smoking lounge, and finding it empty, he ushered them aside. But on the threshold Zillah paused. Her business instincts were by this time fully aroused. She felt certain that whoever this stranger might he, he had nothing to do with the affair in Praed Street, and yet might be able to throw extraordinary light on it, and she wanted to take a great step towards clearing it up. She turned to the American.

"Look here!" she said. "I've told you what I'm after, and who I am. This gentleman is Mr. Andrew Lauriston. Did you read his name in the paper's account of that inquest?"

The American glanced at Lauriston with some curiosity.

"Sure!" he answered. "The man that found the old gentleman dead."

"Just so," said Zillah. "There are two friends of ours making enquiries on Mr. Lauriston's behalf at this moment. One of them's my cousin, Mr. Rubinstein; the other's Mr. Purdie, an old friend of Mr. Lauriston's. I've an idea where'll they'll be, just now—do you mind if I telephone them to come here, at once, so that they can hear what you have to tell us?"

"Not in the least!" assented the American heartily. "I'll be glad to help in any way I can—I'm interested. Here!—there's a telephone box right there—you go in now, and call those fellows up and tell 'em to come right along, quick!"

He and Lauriston waited while Zillah went into the telephone box: she felt sure that Melky and Purdie would have returned to Praed Street by that time, and she rang up Mrs. Goldmark at the Pawnshop to enquire. Within a minute or two she had rejoined Lauriston and the American—during her absence the stranger had been speaking to a waiter, and he now led his two guests to a private sitting-room.

"We'll be more private in this apartment," he observed. "No fear of interruption or being overheard. I've told the waiter man there's two gentlemen coming along, and they're to be brought in here as soon as they land. Will they be long?"

"They'll be here within twenty minutes," answered Zillah. "It's very kind of you to take so much trouble!"

The American drew an easy chair to the fire, and pointed Zillah to it.

"Well," he remarked, "I guess that in a fix of this sort, you can't take too much trouble! I'm interested in this case—and a good deal more than interested now that you tell me about these platinum studs. I reckon I can throw some light on that, anyway! But we'll keep it till your friends come. And I haven't introduced myself—my name's Stuyvesant Guyler. I'm a New York man—but I've knocked around some—pretty considerable, in fact. Say!—have you got any idea that this mystery of yours is at all connected with South Africa? And—incidentally—with diamonds?"

Zillah started and glanced at Lauriston.

"What makes you think of South Africa—and of diamonds?" she asked.

"Oh, well—but that comes into my tale," answered Guyler. "You'll see in due course. But—had it?"

"I hadn't thought of diamonds, but I certainly had of South Africa," admitted Zillah.

"Seems to be working in both directions," said Guyler, meditatively.

"But you'll see that when I tell you what I know."

Purdie and Melky Rubinstein entered the room within the twenty minutes which Zillah had predicted—full of wonder to find her and Lauriston in company with a total stranger. But Zillah explained matters in a few words, and forbade any questioning until Mr. Stuyvesant Guyler had told his story.

"And before I get on to that," said Guyler, who had been quietly scrutinizing his two new visitors while Zillah explained the situation, "I'd just like to see that platinum solitaire that Mr. Rubinstein picked up—if he's got it about him?"

Melky thrust a hand into a pocket.

"It ain't never been off me, mister, since I found it!" he said, producing a little packet wrapped in tissue paper. "There you are!"

Guyler took the stud which Melky handed to him and laid it on the table around which they were all sitting. After glancing at it for a moment, he withdrew the studs from his own wrist-bands and laid them by its side.

"Yes, that's sure one of the lot!" he observed musingly. "I guess there's no possible doubt at all on that point. Well!—this is indeed mighty queer! Now, I'll tell you straight out. These studs—all of 'em—are parts of six sets of similar things, all made of that very expensive metal, platinum, in precisely the same fashion, and ornamented with the same specially invented device, and given to six men who had been of assistance to him in a big deal, as a little mark of his appreciation, by a man that some few years ago made a fortune in South Africa. That's so!"

Zillah turned on the American with a sharp look of enquiry.

"Who was he?" she demanded. "Tell us his name!"

"His name," replied Guyler, "was Spencer Levendale—dealer in diamonds."

## CHAPTER NINETEEN
## PURDIE STANDS FIRM

The effect produced by this announcement was evidently exactly that which the American expected, and he smiled, a little grimly, as he looked from one face to another. As for his hearers, they first looked at each other and then at him, and Guyler laughed and went on.

"That makes you jump!" he said. "Well, now, at the end of that inquest business in the papers the other day I noticed Spencer Levendale's name mentioned in connection with some old book that was left, or found in Mr. Daniel Multenius's back-parlour. Of course, I concluded that he was the same Spencer Levendale I'd known out there in South Africa, five years ago. And to tell you the truth, I've been watching your papers, morning and evening, since, to see if there was any more news of him. But so far I haven't seen any."

Purdie and Melky exchanged glances, and in response to an obvious hint from Melky, Purdie spoke.

"We can give you some news, then," he said. "It'll be common property tomorrow morning. Levendale has mysteriously disappeared from his house, and from his usual haunts!—and nobody knows where he is. And it's considered that this disappearance has something to do with the Praed Street affair."

"Sure!" assented Guyler. "That's just about a dead certainty. And in the Praed Street affair, these platinum stud things are going to play a good part, and when you and your police have got to the bottom of it, you'll sure find that something else has a big part, too!"

"What?" asked Purdie.

"Why, diamonds!" answered the American, with a quiet smile. "Just diamonds! Diamonds'll be at the bottom of the bag—sure!"

There was a moment of surprised silence, and then Melky turned eagerly to the American.

"Mister!" he said. "Let's be getting at something! What do you know, now, about this here Levendale?"

"Not much," replied Guyler. "But I'm open to tell what I do know. I've been a bit of a rolling stone, do you see—knocked about the world, pretty considerable, doing one thing and another, and I've falsified the old saying, for I've contrived to gather a good bit of moss in my rollings. Well, now, I was located in Cape Town for a while, some five years ago, and I met Spencer Levendale there. He was then a dealer in diamonds—can't say in what way exactly—for I never exactly knew—but it was well known that he'd made a big pile, buying and selling these goods, and he was a very rich man. Now I and five other men—all of different nationalities—were very useful to Levendale in a big deal that he was anxious to carry through—never mind what it was—and he felt pretty grateful to us, I reckon. And as we were all warmish men so far as money was concerned, it wasn't the sort of thing that he could hand out cheques for, so he hit on the notion of having sets of studs made of platinum—which is, as you're aware, the most valuable metal known, and on every stud he had a device of his own invention carefully engraved. Here's my set!—and what Mr. Rubinstein's got there is part of another. Now, then, who's the man who's been dropping his cuff-links about?"

Purdie, who had listened with deep attention to the American's statement, immediately put a question.

"That's but answered by asking you something," he said. "You no doubt know the names of the men to whom those sets of studs were given?"

But to Purdie's disappointment, the American shook his head.

"Well, now, I just don't!" he replied. "The fact is—as you would understand if you knew the circumstances—this was a queer sort of a secret deal, in which the assistance of various men of different nationality was wanted, and none of us knew any of the rest. However, I did come across the Englishman who was in it—afterwards. Recognized him, as a matter of fact, by his being in possession of those studs."

"And who was he?" asked Purdie.

"A man named Purvis—Stephen Purvis," answered Guyler. "Sort of man like myself—knocked around, taking up this and that, as long as there was money in it. I came across him in Johannesburg, maybe a year after that deal I was telling of. He didn't know who the other fellows were, neither."

"You've never seen him since?" suggested Purdie. "You don't know where he is?"

"Not a ghost of a notion!" said Guyler. "Didn't talk with him more than once, and then only for an hour or so."

"Mister!" exclaimed Melky, eagerly. "Could you describe this here Purvis, now? Just a bit of a description, like?"

"Sure!" answered the American. "That is—as I remember him. Biggish, raw-boned, hard-bitten sort of a man—about my age—clean-shaven—looked more of a Colonial than an Englishman—he'd been out in South Africa, doing one thing and another, since he was a boy."

"S'elp me if that doesn't sound like the man who was in Mrs. Goldmark's restaurant!" said Melky. "Just what she describes, anyhow!"

"Why, certainly—I reckon that is the man," remarked Guyler. "That's what I've been figuring on, all through. I tell you all this mystery is around some diamond affair in which this lady's grandfather, and Mr. Spencer Levendale, and this man Purvis have been mixed up—sure! And the thing—in my humble opinion—is to find both of them! Now, then, what's been done, and what's being done, in that way?"

Melky nodded at Purdie, as much as to invite him to speak.

"The authorities at New Scotland Yard have the Levendale affair in hand," said Purdie. "We've been in and out there, with Mr. Multenius's solicitor, all the afternoon and evening. But, of course, we couldn't tell anything about this other man because we didn't know anything, till now. You'll have no objection to going there tomorrow?"

"Not at all!" replied Guyler, cheerfully. "I'm located at this hotel for a week or two. I struck it when I came here from the North, a few days back, and it suits me very well, and I guess I'll just stop here while I'm in London this journey. No, I've no objection to take a hand. But—it seems to me—there's still a lot of difficulty about this young gentleman here—Mr. Lauriston. I read all the papers carefully, and sized up his predicament. Those rings, now?"

Zillah suddenly remembered all that Ayscough had told her that evening. She had forgotten the real motive of her visit to King's Cross in her excitement in listening to the American's story. She now turned to Purdie and the other two.

"I'd forgotten!" she exclaimed. "The danger's still there. Ayscough's been at the shop tonight. The police have had an expert examining those rings, and the rings in the tray. He says there are marks—private, jewellers' marks in the two rings which correspond with marks in our rings. In fact,

there's no doubt of it. And now, the police are certain that the two rings did belong to our tray—and—and they're bent on arresting—Andie!"
Lauriston flushed hotly with sheer indignation.
"That's all nonsense—what the police say!" he exclaimed. "I've found out who gave those two rings to my mother! I can prove it! I don't care a hang for the police and their marks—those rings are mine!"
Purdie laid a quiet hand on Lauriston's arm.
"None of us know yet what you've done or found out at Peebles about the rings," he said. "Tell us! Just give us the brief facts."
"I'm going to," answered Lauriston, still indignant. "I thought the whole thing over as I went down in the train. I remembered that if there was one person living in Peebles who would be likely to know about my mother and those rings, it would be an old friend of hers, Mrs. Taggart—you know her, John."
"I know Mrs. Taggart—go on," said Purdie.
"I didn't know if Mrs. Taggart was still living," continued Lauriston. "But I was out early this morning and I found her. She remembers the rings well enough: she described them accurately—what's more she told me what I didn't know—how they came into my mother's possession. You know as well as I do, John, that my father and mother weren't over well off—and my mother used to make a bit of extra money by letting her rooms to summer visitors. One summer she had a London solicitor, a Mr. Killick, staying there for a month—at least he came for a month, but he was taken ill, and he was there more than two months. My mother nursed him through his illness—and after he'd returned to London, he sent her those rings. And—if there are marks on them," concluded Lauriston, "that correspond with marks on the rings in that tray, all I have to say is that those marks must have been there when Mr. Killick bought them!—for they've never been out of our possession—my mother's and mine—until I took them to pawn."
Zillah suddenly clapped her hands—and she and Melky exchanged significant glances which the others did not understand.
"That's it!" she exclaimed. "That's what puzzled me at first. Now I'm not puzzled any more. Melky knows what I mean."
"What she means, mister," assented Melky, tapping Purdie's arm, "is precisely what struck me at once. It's just as Mr. Lauriston here says—them private marks were on the rings when Mr. Killick bought them. Them two rings, and some of the rings in the tray what's been mentioned all come from the same maker! There ain't nothing wonderful in all that to me and my cousin Zillah there!—we've been brought up in the trade,

d'ye see? But the police!—they're that suspicious that—well, the thing to do, gentlemen, is to find this here Mr. Killick."

"Just so," agreed Purdie. "Where is he to be found, Andie?"

But Lauriston shook his head, disappointedly.

"That's just what I don't know!" he answered. "It's five and twenty years since he gave my mother those rings, and according to Mrs. Taggart, he was then a middle-aged man, so he's now getting on in years. But—if he's alive, I can find him."

"We've got to find him," said Purdie, firmly. "In my opinion, he can give some evidence that'll be of more importance than the mere identifying of those rings—never mind what it is I'm thinking of, now. We must see to that tomorrow."

"But in the meantime," broke in Zillah. "Andie must not go home—to Mrs. Flitwick's! I know what Ayscough meant tonight—and remember, all of you, it was private between him and myself. If he goes home, he may be arrested, any minute. He must be kept out of the way of the police for a bit, and—"

Purdie rose from the table and shook his head determinedly.

"No," he said. "None of that! We're going to have no running away, no hiding! Andie Lauriston's not going to show the least fear of the police, or of any of their theories. He's just going to follow my orders—and I'm going to take him to my hotel for the night—leave him to me! I'm going to see this thing right through to the finish—however it ends. Now, let's separate. Mr. Guyler!"

"Sir?" answered the American. "At your service."

"Then meet me at my hotel tomorrow morning at ten," said Purdie. "There's a new chapter to open."

## CHAPTER TWENTY
## THE PARSLETT AFFAIR

At a quarter past ten o'clock on the morning following Ayscough's revelation to Zillah, the detective was closeted with a man from the Criminal Investigation Department at New Scotland Yard in a private room at the local police station, and with them was the superior official who had been fetched to the pawnshop in Praed Street immediately after the discovery of Daniel Multenius's body by Andie Lauriston. And this official was stating his view of the case to the two detectives—conscious that neither agreed with him.

"You can't get over the similarity of the markings of those rings!" he said confidently. "To my mind the whole thing's as plain as a pikestaff—the young fellow was hard up—he confessed he hadn't a penny on him!—he went in there, found the shop empty, saw those rings, grabbed a couple, was interrupted by the old man—and finished him off by scragging him! That's my opinion! And I advise getting a warrant for him and getting on with the work—all the rest of this business belongs to something else."

Ayscough silently glanced at the man from New Scotland Yard—who shook his head in a decided negative.

"That's not my opinion!" he said with decision. "And it's not the opinion of the people at headquarters. We were at this affair nearly all yesterday afternoon with that little Jew fellow, Rubinstein, and the young Scotch gentleman, Mr. Purdie, and our conclusion is that there's something of a big sort behind old Multenius's death. There's a regular web of mystery! The old man's death—that book, which Levendale did not leave in the 'bus, in spite of all he says, and of his advertisements!—Levendale's unexplained disappearance—the strange death of this man Parslett—the mystery of those platinum studs dropped in the pawnbroker's parlour and in Mrs. Goldmark's eating house—no!—the whole affair's a highly complicated one. That's my view of it."

"And mine," said Ayscough. He looked at the unbelieving official, and turned away from him to glance out of the window into the street. "May I never!" he suddenly exclaimed. "There's young Lauriston coming here, and Purdie with him—and a fellow who looks like an American. I should say Lauriston's got proof about his title to those rings—anyway, he seems to have no fear about showing himself here—case of walking straight into the lions' den, eh?"

"Bring 'em all in!" ordered the superior official, a little surlily. "Let's hear what it's all about!"

Purdie presently appeared in Ayscough's rear, preceding his two companions. He and the detective from New Scotland Yard exchanged nods; they had seen a good deal of each other the previous day. He nodded also to the superior official—but the superior official looked at Lauriston.

"Got that proof about those rings?" he enquired. "Of course, if you have—"

"Before Mr. Lauriston says anything about that," interrupted Purdie, "I want you to hear a story which this gentleman, Mr. Stuyvesant Guyler, of New York, can tell you. It's important—it bears right on this affair. If you just listen to what he can tell—"

The two detectives listened to Guyler's story about the platinum studs with eager, if silent interest: in the end they glanced at each other and then at the local official, who seemed to be going through a process of being convinced against his will.

"Just what I said a few minutes ago," muttered the New Scotland Yard man. "A highly complicated affair! Not going to be got at in five minutes."

"Nor in ten!" said Ayscough laconically. He glanced at Guyler. "You could identify this man Purvis if you saw him?" he asked.

"Why, certainly!" answered the American. "I guess if he's the man who was seen in that eating-house the other day he's not altered any—or not much."

The man at the desk turned to Purdie, glancing at Lauriston.

"About those rings?" he asked. "What's Mr. Lauriston got to say?"

"Let me tell," said Purdie, as Lauriston was about to speak. "Mr. Lauriston," he went on, "has been to Peebles, where his father and mother lived. He has seen an old friend of theirs, Mrs. Taggart, who remembers the rings perfectly. Moreover, she knows that they were given to the late Mrs. Lauriston by a Mr. Edward Killick, a London solicitor, who, of course, will be able to identify them. As to the marks, I think you'll find a trade explanation of that—those rings and the rings in Multenius's tray probably came from the same maker. Now, I find, on looking through the directory, that this Mr. Edward Killick has retired from practice, but I've also found out where he now lives, and I propose to bring him here. In the meantime—I want to know what you're going to do about Mr. Lauriston? Here he is!"

The superior official glanced at the New Scotland Yard man.

"I suppose your people have taken this job entirely in hand, now?" he asked.

"Entirely!" answered the detective.

"Got any instructions about Mr. Lauriston?" asked the official. "You haven't? Mr. Lauriston's free to go where he likes, then, as far as we're concerned, here," he added, turning to Purdie. "But—he'd far better stay at hand till all this is cleared up."

"That's our intention," said Purdie. "Whenever you want Mr. Lauriston, come to me at my hotel—he's my guest there, and I'll produce him. Now we're going to find Mr. Killick."

He and Lauriston and Guyler walked out together; on the steps of the police-station Ayscough called him back.

"I say!" he said, confidentially. "Leave that Mr. Killick business alone for an hour or two. I can tell you of something much more interesting than that, and possibly of more importance. Go round to the Coroner's Court—Mr. Lauriston knows where it is."

"What's on?" asked Lauriston.

"Inquest on that man Parslett," replied Ayscough with a meaning nod. "You'll hear some queer evidence if I'm not mistaken. I'm going there myself, presently."

He turned in again, and the three young men looked at each other.

"Say!" remarked Guyler, "I reckon that's good advice. Let's go to this court."

Lauriston led them to the scene of his own recent examination by Mr. Parminter. But on this occasion the court was crowded; it was with great difficulty that they contrived to squeeze themselves into a corner of it. In another corner, but far away from their own, Lauriston saw Melky Rubinstein; Melky, wedged in, and finding it impossible to move, made a grimace at Lauriston and jerked his thumb in the direction of the door, as a signal that he would meet him there when the proceedings were over. The inquest had already begun when Purdie and his companions forced their way into the court. In the witness-box was the dead man's widow—a pathetic figure in heavy mourning, who was telling the Coroner that on the night of her husband's death he went out late in the evening—just to take a walk round, as he expressed it. No—she had no idea whatever of where he was going, nor if he had any particular object in going out at all. He had not said one word to her about going out to get money from any one. After he went out she never saw him again until she was fetched to St. Mary's Hospital, where she found him in the hands of the doctors. He died, without having regained consciousness, just after she reached the hospital.

Nothing very startling so far, thought Purdie, at the end of the widow's evidence, and he wondered why Ayscough had sent them round. But more interest came with the next witness—a smart, bustling, middle-aged man, evidently a well-to-do business man, who entered the box pretty much as if he had been sitting down in his own office, to ring his bell and ask for the day's letters. A whisper running round the court informed the onlookers that this was the gentleman who picked Parslett up in the street. Purdie and his two companions pricked their ears.

Martin James Gardiner—turf commission agent—resident in Portsdown Road, Maida Vale. Had lived there several years—knew the district well—did not know the dead man by sight at all—had never seen him, that he knew of, until the evening in question.

"Tell us exactly what happened, Mr. Gardiner—in your own way," said the Coroner.

Mr. Gardiner leaned over the front of the witness-box, and took the court and the public into his confidence—genially.

"I was writing letters until pretty late that night," he said. "A little after eleven o'clock I went out to post them at the nearest pillar-box. As I went down the steps of my house, the deceased passed by. He was walking down Portsdown Road in the direction of Clifton Road. As he passed me, he was chuckling—laughing in a low tone. I thought he was—well, a bit intoxicated when I heard that, but as I was following him pretty closely, I soon saw that he walked straight enough. He kept perhaps six or eight yards in front of me until we had come to within twenty yards or so of the corner of Clifton Road. Then, all of a sudden—so suddenly that it's difficult for me to describe it!—he seemed to—well, there's no other word for it than—collapse. He seemed to give, you understand—shrank up, like—like a concertina being suddenly shut up! His knees gave—his whole body seemed to shrink—and he fell in a heap on the pavement!"

"Did he cry out—scream, as if in sudden pain—anything of that sort?" asked the Coroner.

"There was a sort of gurgling sound—I'm not sure that he didn't say a word or two, as he collapsed," answered the witness. "But it was so sudden that I couldn't catch anything definite. He certainly never made the slightest sound, except a queer sort of moaning, very low, from the time he fell. Of course, I thought the man had fallen in a fit. I rushed to him; he was lying, sort of crumpled up, where he had fallen. There was a street-lamp close by—I saw that his face had turned a queer colour, and his eyes were already closed—tightly. I noticed, too, that his teeth were clenched, and his fingers twisted into the palms of his hands."

"Was he writhing at all—making any movement?" enquired the Coroner.

"Not a movement! He was as still as the stones he was lying on!" said the witness. "I'm dead certain he never moved after he fell. There was nobody about, just then, and I was just going to ring the bell of the nearest house when a policeman came round the corner. I shouted to him—he came up. We examined the man for a minute; then I ran to fetch Dr. Mirandolet, whose surgery is close by there. I found him in; he came at once, and immediately ordered the man's removal to the hospital. The policeman got help, and the man was taken off. Dr. Mirandolet went with him. I returned home."

No questions of any importance were asked of Mr. Gardiner, and the Coroner, after a short interchange of whispers with his officer, glanced at a group of professional-looking men behind the witness-box.

"Call Dr. Mirandolet!" he directed.

Purdie at that moment caught Ayscough's eye. And the detective winked at him significantly as a strange and curious figure came out from the crowd and stepped into the witness-box.

## CHAPTER TWENTY-ONE
## WHAT MANNER OF DEATH?

One of the three companions who stood curiously gazing at the new witness as he came into full view of the court had seen him before. Lauriston, who, during his residence in Paddington, had wandered a good deal about Maida Vale and St. John's Wood, instantly recognized Dr. Mirandolet as a man whom he had often met or passed in those excursions and about whom he had just as often wondered. He was a notable and somewhat queer figure—a tall, spare man, of striking presence and distinctive personality—the sort of man who would inevitably attract attention wherever he was, and at whom people would turn to look in the most crowded street. His aquiline features, almost cadaverous complexion, and flashing, deep-set eyes, were framed in a mass of raven-black hair which fell in masses over a loosely fitting, unstarched collar, kept in its place by a voluminous black silk cravat; his thin figure, all the sparer in appearance because of his broad shoulders and big head, was wrapped from head to foot in a mighty cloak, raven-black as his hair, from the neck of which depended a hood-like cape. Not a man in that court would have taken Dr. Mirandolet for anything but a foreigner, and for a foreigner who knew next to nothing of England and the English, and John Purdie, whose interest was now thoroughly aroused, was surprised as he heard the witness's answer to the necessary preliminary questions.

Nicholas Mirandolet—British subject—born in Malta—educated in England—a licentiate of the Royal College of Surgeons and of the Royal College of Physicians—in private practice at Portsdown Road, Maida Vale, for the last ten years.

"I believe you were called to the deceased by the last witness, Dr. Mirandolet?" asked the Coroner. "Just so! Will you tell us what you found?"

"I found the deceased lying on the pavement, about a dozen yards from my house," answered Dr. Mirandolet, in a sharp, staccato voice. "A policeman was bending over him. Mr. Gardiner hurriedly told us what he had seen. My first thought was that the man was in what is commonly termed a fit—some form of epileptic seizure, you know. I hastily examined him—and found that my first impression was utterly wrong."

"What did you think—then?" enquired the Coroner.

Dr. Mirandolet paused and began to drum the edge of the witness-box with the tips of his long, slender white fingers. He pursed his clean-shaven lips and looked meditatively around him—leisurely surveying the faces turned on him. Finally he glanced at the Coroner, and snapped out a reply.

"I do not know what I thought!"

The Coroner looked up from his notes—in surprise.

"You—don't know what you thought?" he asked.

"No!" said Dr. Mirandolet. "I don't. And I will tell you why. Because I realized—more quickly than it takes me to tell it—that here was something that was utterly beyond my comprehension!"

"Do you mean—beyond your skill?" suggested the Coroner.

"Skill?" retorted the witness, with a queer, twisting grimace. "Beyond my understanding! I am a quick observer—I saw within a few seconds that here was a man who had literally been struck down in the very flush of life as if—well, to put it plainly, as if some extraordinary power had laid a blasting finger on the very life-centre within him. I was—dumfounded!"

The Coroner sat up and laid aside his pen.

"What did you do?" he asked quietly.

"Bade the policeman get help, and an ambulance, and hurry the man to St. Mary's Hospital, all as quickly as possible," answered Dr. Mirandolet. "While the policeman was away, I examined the man more closely. He was dying then—and I knew very well that nothing known to medical science could save him. By that time he had become perfectly quiet; his body had relaxed into a normal position; his face, curiously coloured when I first saw it, had become placid and pale; he breathed regularly, though very faintly—and he was steadily dying. I knew quite well what was happening, and I remarked to Mr. Gardiner that the man would be dead within half-an-hour."

"I believe you got him to the hospital within that time?" asked the Coroner.

"Yes—within twenty-five minutes of my first seeing him," said the witness. "I went with the ambulance. The man died very soon after admission, just as I knew he would. No medical power on earth could have saved him!"

The Coroner glanced at the little knot of professional men in the rear of the witness-box and seemed to be debating within himself as to whether he wanted to ask Dr. Mirandolet any more questions. Eventually he turned again to him.

"What your evidence amounts to, Dr. Mirandolet, is this," he said. "You were called to the man and you saw at once that you yourself could do nothing for him, so you got him away to the hospital as quickly as you possibly could. Just so!—now, why did you think you could do nothing for him?"

"I will tell you—in plain words," answered Dr. Mirandolet. "Because I did not recognize or understand one single symptom that I saw! Because, frankly, I knew very well that I did not know what was the matter! And so—I hurried him to people who ought to know more than I do and are reputedly cleverer than I am. In short—I recognized that I was in the presence of something—something!—utterly beyond my skill and comprehension!"

"Let me ask you one or two further questions," said the Coroner. "Have you formed any opinion of your own as to the cause of this man's death?"

"Yes!" agreed the witness, unhesitatingly. "I have! I believe him to have been poisoned—in a most subtle and cunning fashion. And"—here Dr. Mirandolet cast a side-glance at the knot of men behind him—"I shall be intensely surprised if that opinion is not corroborated. But—I shall be ten thousand times more surprised if there is any expert in Europe who can say what that poison was!"

"You think it was a secret poison?" suggested the Coroner.

"Secret!" exclaimed Dr. Mirandolet. "Aye—secret is the word. Secret—yes! And—sure!"

"Is there anything else you can tell us?" asked the Coroner.

"Only this," replied the witness, after a pause. "It may be material. As I bent over this man as he lay there on the pavement I detected a certain curious aromatic odour about his clothes. It was strong at first; it gradually wore off. But I directed the attention of the policeman and Mr. Gardiner to it; it was still hanging about him, very faintly, when we got him to the hospital: I drew attention to it there."

"It evidently struck you—that curious odour?" said the Coroner.

"Yes," answered Dr. Mirandolet. "It did. It reminded me of the East—I have lived in the East—India, Burmah, China. It seemed to me that this man had got hold of some Eastern scent, and possibly spilt some on his clothes. The matter is worth noting. Because—I have heard—I cannot say I have known—of men being poisoned in inhalation."

The Coroner made no remark—it was very evident from his manner that he considered Dr. Mirandolet's evidence somewhat mystifying. And Dr. Mirandolet stepped down—and in response to the official invitation Dr. John Sperling-Lawson walked into the vacated witness-box.

"One of the greatest authorities on poisons living," whispered Lauriston to Purdie, while Dr. Sperling-Lawson was taking the oath and answering the formal questions. "He's principal pathologist at that hospital they're talking about, and he constantly figures in cases of this sort. He's employed by the Home Office too—it was he who gave such important evidence in that Barnsbury murder case not so long since—don't you remember it?"

Purdie did remember, and he looked at the famous expert with great interest. There was, however, nothing at all remarkable about Dr. Sperling-Lawson's appearance—he was a quiet, self-possessed, plain-faced gentleman who might have been a barrister or a banker for all that any one could tell to the contrary. He gave his evidence in a matter-of-fact tone—strongly in contrast to Dr. Mirandolet's somewhat excited answers—but Purdie noticed that the people in court listened eagerly for every word.

He happened to be at the hospital, said Dr. Sperling-Lawson, when the man Parslett was brought in, and he saw him die. He fully agreed with Dr. Mirandolet that it was impossible to do anything to save the man's life when he was brought to the hospital, and he was quite prepared to say that the impossibility had existed from the moment in which Gardiner had seen Parslett collapse. In other words, when Parslett did collapse, death was on him.

"And—the cause of death?" asked the Coroner.

"Heart failure," replied the witness.

"Resulting from—what?" continued the Coroner.

Dr. Sperling-Lawson hesitated a moment—amidst a deep silence.

"I cannot answer that question," he said at last. "I can only offer an opinion. I believe—in fact, I am sure!—the man was poisoned. I am convinced he was poisoned. But I am forced to admit that I do not know what poison was used, and that after a most careful search I have not yet been able to come across any trace or sign of any poison known to me. All the same, I am sure he died from the effects of poison, but what it was, or how administered, frankly, I do not know!"

"You made a post-mortem examination?" asked the Coroner.

"Yes," replied the specialist, "in company with Dr. Seracold. The deceased was a thoroughly healthy, well-nourished man. There was not a trace of disease in any of the organs—he was evidently a temperate man, and likely to live to over the seventy years' period. And, as I have said, there was not a trace of poison. That is, not a trace of any poison known to me."

"I want to ask you a particularly important question," said the Coroner. "Are there poisons, the nature of which you are unacquainted with?"

"Yes!" answered the specialist frankly. "There are. But—I should not expect to hear of their use in London."

"Is there any European expert who might throw some light on this case?" asked the Coroner.

"Yes," said Dr. Sperling-Lawson. "One man—Professor Gagnard, of

Paris. As a matter of fact, I have already sent certain portions of certain organs to him—by a special messenger. If he cannot trace this poison, then no European nor American specialist can. I am sure of this—the secret is an Eastern one."

"Gentlemen," said the Coroner, "we will adjourn for a week. By that time there may be a report from Paris."

The crowd surged out into the damp November morning, eagerly discussing the evidence just given. Purdie, Lauriston, and Guyler, all equally mystified, followed, already beginning to speculate and to theorize. Suddenly Melky Rubinstein hurried up to them, waving a note.

"There was a fellow waiting outside with this from Zillah," said Melky. "She'd heard you were all here, and she knew I was. We're to go there at once—she's found some letters to her grandfather from that man Purvis! Come on!—it's another step forward!"

## CHAPTER TWENTY-TWO
## MR. KILLICK GOES BACK

Ayscough and the man from New Scotland Yard came out of the court at that moment in close and serious conversation: Melky Rubinstein left the other three, and hurried to the two detectives with his news; together, the six men set off for Praed Street. And Purdie, who by this time was developing as much excited interest as his temperament and business habits permitted, buttonholed the Scotland Yard man and walked alongside him.

"What's your professional opinion about what we've just heard in there?" he asked. "Between ourselves, of course."

The detective, who had already had several long conversations with Purdie at headquarters during the previous afternoon and evening, and knew him for a well-to-do young gentleman who was anxious to clear his friend Lauriston of all suspicion, shook his head. He was a quiet, sagacious, middle-aged man who evidently thought deeply about whatever he had in hand.

"It's difficult to say, Mr. Purdie," he answered. "I've no doubt that when we get to the bottom of this case it'll turn out to be a very simple one—but the thing is to get to the bottom. The ways are complicated, sir—uncommonly so! At present we're in a maze—seeking the right path."

"Do you think that this Parslett affair has anything to do with the Multenius affair?" asked Purdie.

"Yes—undoubtedly!" answered the detective. "There's no doubt whatever in my own mind that the man who poisoned Parslett is the man who caused the old pawnbroker's death—none! I figure it in this way. Parslett somehow, caught a glimpse of that man leaving Multenius's shop—by the side-door, no doubt—and knew him—knew him very well, mind you! When Parslett heard of what had happened in Multenius's back-parlour, he kept his knowledge to himself, and went and blackmailed the man. The man gave him that fifty pounds in gold to keep his tongue quiet—no doubt arranging to give him more, later on—and at the same time he cleverly poisoned him. That's my theory, Mr. Purdie."

"Then—the only question now is—who's the man?" suggested Purdie.

"That's it, sir—who's the man?" agreed the detective. "One thing's quite certain—if my theory's correct. He's a clever man—and an expert in the use of poisons."

Purdie walked on a minute or two in silence, thinking.

"It's no use beating about the bush," he said at last. "Do you suspect Mr. Levendale—after all you've collected in information—and after what I told you about what his butler saw—that bottle and phial?"

"I think that Levendale's in it," replied the detective, cautiously. "I'm sure he's in it—in some fashion. Our people are making no end of enquiries about him this morning, in various quarters—there's half-a-dozen of our best men at work in the City and the West End, Mr. Purdie. He's got to be found! So, too, has this man Stephen Purvis—whoever he is. We must find him, too."

"Perhaps these letters that Melky Rubinstein speaks of may throw some light on that," said Purdie. "There must be some way of tracing him, somewhere."

They were at the pawnshop by that time, and all six trooped in at the side-entrance. Old Daniel Multenius, unconscious of all the fuss and bother which his death had caused, was to be quietly interred that afternoon, and Zillah and Melky were already in their mourning garments. But Zillah had lost none of her business habits and instincts, and while the faithful Mrs. Goldmark attended to the funeral guests in the upstairs regions, she herself was waiting in the back-parlour for these other visitors. On the table before her, evidently placed there for inspection, lay three objects to which she at once drew attention—one, an old-fashioned, double-breasted fancy waistcoat, evidently of considerable age, and much worn, the others, two letters written on foreign notepaper.

"It never occurred to me," said Zillah, plunging into business at once, "at least, until an hour or two ago, to examine the clothes my grandfather was wearing at the time of his death. As a matter of fact he'd been wearing the same clothes for months. I've been through all his pockets. There was nothing of importance—except these letters. I found those in a pocket in the inside of that waistcoat—there! Read them."

The men bent over the unfolded letters, and Ayscough read them aloud.

**"MACPHERSON'S HOTEL, CAPE TOWN,**

"*September 17th*, 1912.

"Dear Sir,—I have sent the little article about which I have already written you and Mr. L. fully, to your address by ordinary registered post. Better put it in your bank till I arrive—shall write you later about date of my arrival. Faithfully yours,

"Stephen Purvis."

"That," remarked Ayscough, glancing at the rest, "clearly refers to whatever it was that Mr. Multenius took from his bank on the morning of his death. It also refers to Mr. Levendale—without doubt."

He drew the other letter to him and read it out.

**"CAPE TOWN,**

"*October 10th*, 1912.

"Dear Sir,—Just a line to say I leave here by s.s. *Golconda* in a day or two—this precedes me by today's mail. I hope to be in England November 15th—due then, anyway—and shall call on you immediately on arrival. Better arrange to have Mr. S. L. to meet you and me at once. Faithfully,

"Stephen Purvis."

"November 15th?" remarked Ayscough. "Mr. Multenius died on November 19th. So—if Purvis did reach here on the 15th he'd probably been about this quarter before the 19th. We know he was at Mrs. Goldmark's restaurant on the 18th, anyway! All right, Miss Wildrose—we'll take these letters with us."

Lauriston stopped behind when the rest of the men went out—to exchange a few words alone with Zillah. When he went into the street, all had gone except Purdie, who was talking with Melky at the entrance to the side-alley.

"That's the sure tip at present, mister," Melky was saying. "Get that done—clear that up. Mr. Lauriston," he went on, "you do what your friend says—we're sorting things out piece by piece."

Purdie took Lauriston's arm and led him away.

"What Melky says is—go and find out what Mr. Killick can prove," he said. "Best thing to do, too, Andie, for us. Now that these detectives are fairly on the hunt, and are in possession of a whole multitude of queer details and facts, we'll just do our bit of business—which is to clear you entirely. There's more reasons than one why we should do that, my man!"

"What're you talking about, John?" demanded Lauriston. "You've some idea in that head of yours!"

"The idea that you and that girl are in love with each other!" said Purdie with a sly look.

"I'll not deny that!" asserted Lauriston, with an ingenuous blush. "We are!"

"Well, you can't ask any girl to marry you, man, while there's the least bit of suspicion hanging over you that you'd a hand in her grandfather's death!" remarked Purdie sapiently. "So we'll just eat a bit of lunch together, and then get a taxi-cab and drive out to find this old gentleman that gave your mother the rings. Come on to the hotel."

"You're spending a fine lot of money over me, John!" exclaimed Lauriston.

"Put it down that I'm a selfish chap that's got interested, and is following his own pleasure!" said Purdie. "Man alive!—I was never mixed up in a detective case before—it beats hunting for animals, this hunting for men!"

By a diligent search in directories and reference books early that morning, Purdie and Lauriston had managed to trace Mr. Edward Killick, who, having been at one time a well-known solicitor in the City, had followed the practice of successful men and retired to enjoy the fruit of his labours in a nice little retreat in the country. Mr. Killick had selected the delightful old-world village of Stanmore as the scene of his retirement, and there, in a picturesque old house, set in the midst of fine trees and carefully trimmed lawns, Purdie and Lauriston found him—a hale and hearty old gentleman, still on the right side of seventy, who rose from his easy chair in a well-stocked library to look in astonishment from the two cards which his servant had carried to him at the persons and faces of their presenters.

"God bless my soul!" he exclaimed. "Are you two young fellows the sons of old friends of mine at Peebles?"

"We are, sir," answered Purdie. "This is Andrew Lauriston, and I am John Purdie. And we're very glad to find that you remember something about our people, Mr. Killick."

Mr. Killick again blessed himself, and after warmly shaking hands with his visitors, bade them sit down. He adjusted his spectacles, and looked both young men carefully over.

"I remember your people very well indeed!" he said. "I used to do a bit of fishing in the Tweed and in Eddleston Water with your father, Mr. Purdie—and I stopped some time with your father and mother, at their house, Mr. Lauriston. In fact, your mother was remarkably kind to me—she nursed me through an illness with which I was seized when I was in

Peebles."

Lauriston and Purdie exchanged glances—by common consent Purdie became spokesman for the two.

"Mr. Killick," he said, "it's precisely about a matter arising out of that illness of yours that we came to see you! Let me explain something first—Andie Lauriston here has been living in London for two years—he's a literary gift, and he hopes to make a name, and perhaps a fortune. I've succeeded to my father's business, and I'm only here in London on a visit. And it's well I came, for Andie wanted a friend. Now, Mr. Killick, before I go further—have you read in the newspapers about what's called the Praed Street Mystery?"

The old gentleman shook his head.

"My dear young sir!" he answered, waving his hand towards his books. "I'm not a great newspaper reader—except for a bit of politics. I never read about mysteries—I've wrapped myself up in antiquarian pursuits since I retired. No!—I haven't read about the Praed Street Mystery—nor even heard of it! I hope neither of you are mixed up in it?"

"Considerably!" answered Purdie. "In more ways than one. And you can be of great help. Mr. Killick—when you left Peebles after your illness, you sent Mrs. Lauriston a present of two valuable rings. Do you remember?"

"Perfectly—of course!" replied the old gentleman. "To be sure!"

"Can you remember, too, from whom you bought those rings?" enquired Purdie eagerly.

"Yes!—as if it were yesterday!" said Mr. Killick. "I bought them from a City jeweller whom I knew very well at that time—a man named Daniel Molteno!"

## CHAPTER TWENTY-THREE
## MR. KILLICK'S OPINION

The old solicitor's trained eye and quick intelligence saw at once that this announcement immediately conveyed some significant meaning to his two young visitors. Purdie and Lauriston, in fact, had immediately been struck by the similarity of the names Molteno and Multenius, and they exchanged another look which their host detected and knew to convey a meaning. He leaned forward in his chair.

"Now, that strikes you—both!" he said. "What's all this about? Better give me your confidence."

"That's precisely what we came here to do, sir," responded Purdie, with alacrity. "And with your permission I'll tell you the whole story. It's a long one, and a complicated one, Mr. Killick!—but I daresay you've heard many intricate stories in the course of your legal experience, and you'll no doubt be able to see points in this that we haven't seen. Well, it's this way—and I'll begin at the beginning."

The old gentleman sat in an attitude of patient and watchful attention while Purdie, occasionally prompted and supplemented by Lauriston, told the whole story of the Praed Street affair, from Lauriston's first visit to the pawnshop up to the events of that morning. Once or twice he asked a question; one or twice he begged the narrator to pause while he considered a point: in the end he drew out his watch—after which he glanced out of his window.

"Do I gather that the taxi-cab which I see outside there is being kept by you two young men?" he asked.

"It is," answered Purdie. "It's important that we should lose no time in getting back to town, Mr. Killick."

"Just so!" agreed Mr. Killick, moving towards his library door. "But I'm going with you—as soon as I've got myself into an overcoat. Now!" he added, a few minutes later, when all three went out to the cab. "Tell the man to drive us straight to that police-station you've been visiting of late—and till we get there, just let me think quietly—I can probably say more about this case than I'm yet aware of. But—if it will give you any relief, I can tell you this at once—I have a good deal to tell. Strange!—strange indeed how things come round, and what a small world this is, after all!"

With this cryptic utterance Mr. Killick sank into a corner of the cab, where he remained, evidently lost in thought, until, nearly an hour later, they pulled up at the door of the police-station. Within five minutes they were closeted with the chief men there—amongst whom were Ayscough and the detective from New Scotland Yard.

"You know me—or of me—some of you?" observed the old solicitor, as he laid a card on the desk by which he had been given a chair. "I was very well known in the City police-courts, you know, until I retired three years ago. Now, these young gentlemen have just told me all the facts of this very strange case, and I think I can throw some light on it—on part of it, anyway. First of all, let me see those two rings about which there has been so much enquiry."

Ayscough produced the rings from a locked drawer; the rest of those present looked on curiously as they were examined and handled by Mr. Killick. It was immediately evident that he had no doubt about his recognition and identification of them—after a moment's inspection of each he pushed them back towards the detective.

"Certainly!" he said with a confidence that carried conviction. "Those are the rings which I gave to Mrs. Lauriston, this young man's mother. I knew them at once. If it's necessary, I can show you the receipt which I got with them from the seller. The particulars are specified in that receipt—and I know that I still have it. Does my testimony satisfy you?"

The chief official present glanced at the man from New Scotland Yard, and receiving a nod from him, smiled at the old solicitor.

"I think we can rely on your evidence, Mr. Killick," he said. "We had to make certain, you know. But these marks—isn't that a curious coincidence, now, when you come to think of it?"

"Not a bit of it!" replied Mr. Killick. "And I'll tell you why—that's precisely what I've come all the way from my own comfortable fireside at Stanmore to do! There's no coincidence at all. I've heard the whole story of this Praed Street affair now from these two lads. And I've no more doubt than I have that I see you, that the old pawnbroker whom you knew hereabouts as Daniel Multenius was the same man Daniel Molteno—from whom I bought those rings, years ago! Not the slightest doubt!"

None of those present made any remark on this surprising announcement, and Mr. Killick went on.

"I was, as some of you may know, in practice in the City—in Moorgate Street, as a matter of fact," he said. "Daniel Molteno was a jeweller in Houndsditch. I occasionally acted for him—professionally. And occasionally when I wanted anything in the way of jewellery, I went to his shop. He was then a man of about fifty, a tall, characteristically Hebraic sort of man, already patriarchal in appearance, though he hadn't a grey hair in his big black beard. He was an interesting man, profoundly learned in the history of precious stones. I remember buying those rings from him very well indeed—I remember, too, what I gave him for them—seventy-five pounds for the two. Those private marks inside them are, of course, his—and so they're just the same as his private marks inside those other rings in the tray. But that's not what I came here to tell you—that's merely preliminary."

"Deeply interesting, anyway, sir," observed Ayscough. "And, maybe, very valuable."

"Not half so valuable as what I'm going to tell you," replied Mr. Killick, with a dry chuckle, "Now, as I understand it, from young Mr. Purdie's account, you're all greatly excited at present over the undoubted connection with this Praed Street mystery of one Mr. Spencer Levendale, who is, I believe, a very rich man, a resident in one of the best parts of this district, and a Member of Parliament. It would appear from all you've discovered, amongst you, up to now, that Spencer Levendale has been privately mixed up with old Daniel Multenius in some business which seems to be connected with South Africa. Now, attend to what I say:—About the time that I knew Daniel Molteno in Houndsditch, Daniel Molteno had a partner—a junior partner, whose name, however, didn't appear over the shop. He was a much younger man than Daniel—in fact, he was quite a young man—I should say he was then about twenty-three or four—not more. He was of medium height, dark, typically Jewish, large dark eyes, olive skin, good-looking, smart, full of go. And his name—the name I knew him by—was Sam Levin." The other men in the room glanced at each other—and one of them softly murmured what all was thinking.

"The same initials!"

"Just so!" agreed Mr. Killick. "That's what struck me—Sam Levin: Spencer Levendale. Very well!—I continue. One day I went to Daniel Molteno's shop to get something repaired, and it struck me that I hadn't seen Sam Levin the last two or three times I had been in. 'Where's your partner?' I asked of Daniel Molteno. 'I haven't seen him lately.' 'Partner no longer, Mr. Killick,' said he. 'We've dissolved. He's gone to South Africa.' 'What to do there?' I asked. 'Oh,' answered Daniel Molteno, 'he's touched with this fever to get at close quarters with the diamond fields! He's gone out there to make a fortune, and come back a millionaire.' 'Well!' I said. 'He's a likely candidate.' 'Oh, yes!' said Daniel. 'He'll do well.' No more was said—and, as far as I can remember, I never saw Daniel Molteno again. It was some time before I had occasion to go that way—when I did, I was surprised to see a new name over the shop. I went in and asked where its former proprietor was. The new shopkeeper told me that Mr. Molteno had sold his business to him. And he didn't know where Mr. Molteno had gone, or whether he'd retired from business altogether; he knew nothing—and evidently didn't care, either, so—that part of my memories comes to an end!"

"Mr. Spencer Levendale is a man of just under fifty," remarked Ayscough, after a thoughtful pause, "and I should say that twenty-five years ago, he'd be just such a man as Mr. Killick has described."

"You can take it from me—considering all that I've been told this afternoon—" said the old solicitor, "that Spencer Levendale is Sam Levin—come back from South Africa, a millionaire. I'm convinced of it! And now then, gentlemen, what does all this mean? There's no doubt that old Multenius and Levendale were secretly mixed up. What in? What's the extraordinary mystery about that book—left in Multenius's back parlour and advertised for immediately by Levendale as if it were simply invaluable? Why has Levendale utterly disappeared? And who is this man Purvis—and what's he to do with it? You've got the hardest nuts to crack—a whole basketful of 'em!—that ever I heard of. And I've had some little experience of crime!"

"I've had some information on Levendale and Purvis this very afternoon," said Ayscough. He turned to the other officials. "I hadn't a chance of telling you of it before," he continued. "I was at Levendale's house at three o'clock, making some further enquiries. I got two pieces of news. To start with—that bottle out of which Levendale filled a small phial, which he put in his waistcoat pocket when he went out for the last time—you remember, Mr. Purdie, that his butler told you of that incident—well, that bottle contains chloroform—I took a chemist there to examine it and some other things. That's item one. The other's a bit of information volunteered by Levendale's chauffeur. The morning after Mr. Multenius's death, and after you, Mr. Lauriston, Mr. Rubinstein, and myself called on Levendale, Levendale went off to the City in his car. He ordered the chauffeur to go through Hyde Park, by the Victoria Gate, and to stop by the Powder Magazine. At the Powder Magazine he got out of the car and walked down towards the bridge on the Serpentine. The chauffeur had him in view all the way, and saw him join a tall man, clean-shaven, much browned, who was evidently waiting for him. They remained in conversation, at the entrance to the bridge, some five minutes or so—then the stranger went across the bridge in the direction of Kensington, and Levendale returned to his car. Now, in my opinion, that strange man was this Purvis we've heard of. And that seems to have been the last time any one we've come across saw him. That night, after his visit to his house, and his taking the phial of chloroform away with him, Levendale utterly disappeared, too—and yet sent a wire to his butler, from close by, next morning, saying he would be away for a few days! Why didn't he call with that message himself!"

Mr. Killick, who had listened to Ayscough with close attention, laughed, and turned to the officials with a sharp look.

"Shall I give you people a bit of my opinion after hearing all this?" he said. "Very well, then—Levendale never did send that wire! It was sent in Levendale's name—to keep things quiet. I believe that Levendale's been trapped—and Purvis with him!"

## CHAPTER TWENTY-FOUR
## THE ORANGE-YELLOW DIAMOND

His various listeners had heard all that the old solicitor had said, with evident interest and attention—now, one of them voiced what all the rest was thinking.

"What makes you think that, Mr. Killick?" asked the man from New

Scotland Yard. "Why should Levendale and Purvis have been trapped?"

Mr. Killick—who was obviously enjoying this return to the arena in which, as some of those present well knew, he had once played a distinguished part, as a solicitor with an extensive police-court practice—twisted round on his questioner with a sly, knowing glance.

"You're a man of experience!" he answered. "Now come!—hasn't it struck you that something went before the death of old Daniel Multenius—whether that death arose from premeditated murder, or from sudden assault? Eh?—hasn't it?"

"What, then?" asked the detective dubiously. "For I can't say that it has—definitely. What do you conjecture did go before that?"

Mr. Killick thumped his stout stick on the floor.

"Robbery!" he exclaimed, triumphantly. "Robbery! The old man was robbed of something! Probably—and there's nothing in these cases like considering possibilities—he caught the thief in the act of robbing him, and lost his life in defending his property. Now, supposing Levendale and Purvis were interested—financially—in that property, and set their wits to work to recover it, and in their efforts got into the hands of— shall we suppose a gang?—and got trapped? Or," concluded Mr. Killick with great emphasis and meaning, "for anything we know—murdered? What about that theory?"

"Possible!" muttered Ayscough. "Quite possible!"

"Consider this," continued the old solicitor. "Levendale is a well-known man—a Member of Parliament—a familiar figure in the City, where he's director of more than one company—the sort of man whom, in ordinary circumstances, you'd be able to trace in a few hours. Now, you tell me that half-a-dozen of your best men have been trying to track Levendale for two days and nights, and can't get a trace of him! What's the inference? A well-known man can't disappear in that way unless for some very grave reason! For anything we know, Levendale—and Purvis with him—may be safely trapped within half-a-mile of Praed Street—or, as I say, they may have been quietly murdered. Of one thing I'm dead certain, anyway—if you want to get at the bottom of this affair, you've got to find those two men!"

"It would make a big difference if we had any idea of what it was that Daniel Multenius had in that packet which he fetched from his bank on the day of the murder," remarked Ayscough. "If there's been robbery, that may have been the thief's object."

"That pre-supposes that the thief knew what was in the packet," said Purdie. "Who is there that could know? We may take it that Levendale and Purvis knew—but who else would?"

"Aye!—and how are we to find that out?" asked the New Scotland Yard man. "If I only knew that much—"

But even at that moment—and not from any coincidence, but from the law of probability to which Mr. Killick had appealed—information on that very point was close at hand. A constable tapped at the door, and entering, whispered a few words to the chief official, who having whispered back, turned to the rest as the man went out of the room.

"Here's something likely!" he said. "There's a Mr. John Purvis, from Devonshire, outside. Says he's the brother of the Stephen Purvis who's name's been in the papers as having mysteriously disappeared, and wants to tell the police something. He's coming in."

The men in the room turned with undisguised interest as the door opened again, and a big, fresh-coloured countryman, well wrapped up in a stout travelling coat, stepped into the room and took a sharp glance at its occupants. He was evidently a well-to-do farmer, this, and quite at his ease—but there was a certain natural anxiety in his manner as he turned to the official, who sat at the desk in the centre of the group.

"You're aware of my business, sir?" he asked quietly.

"I understand you're the brother of the Stephen Purvis we're wanting to find in connection with this Praed Street mystery," answered the official. "You've read of that in the newspaper, no doubt, Mr. Purvis? Take a seat—you want to tell us something? As a matter of fact, we're all discussing the affair!"

The caller took the chair which Ayscough drew forward and sat down, throwing open his heavy overcoat, and revealing a whipcord riding-suit of light fawn beneath it.

"You'll see I came here in a hurry, gentlemen," he said, with a smile. "I'd no thoughts of coming to London when I left my farm this morning, or I'd have put London clothes on! The fact is—I farm at a very out-of-the-way place between Moretonhampstead and Exeter, and I never see the daily papers except when I drive into Exeter twice a week. Now when I got in there this morning, I saw one or two London papers—last night's they were—and read about this affair. And I read enough to know that I'd best get here as quick as possible!—so I left all my business there and then, and caught the very next express to Paddington. And here I am! And now—have you heard anything of my brother Stephen more than what's in the papers? I've seen today's, on the way up."

"Nothing!" answered the chief official. "Nothing at all! We've purposely kept the newspapers informed, and what there is in the morning's papers is the very latest. So—can you tell us anything?"

"I can tell you all I know myself," replied John Purvis, with a solemn shake of his head. "And I should say it's a good deal to do with Stephen's disappearance—in which, of course, there's some foul play! My opinion, gentlemen, is that my brother's been murdered! That's about it!"

No one made any remark—but Mr. Killick uttered a little murmur of comprehension, and nodded his head two or three times.

"Murdered, poor fellow, in my opinion," continued John Purvis. "And I'll tell you why I think so. About November 8th or 9th—I can't be sure to a day—I got a telegram from Stephen, sent off from Las Palmas, in the Canary Islands, saying he'd be at Plymouth on the 15th, and asking me to meet him there. So I went to Plymouth on the morning of the 15th. His boat, the *Golconda*, came in at night, and we went to an hotel together and stopped the night there. We hadn't met for some years, and of course he'd a great deal to tell—but he'd one thing in particular—he'd struck such a piece of luck as he'd never had in his life before!—and he hadn't been one of the unlucky ones, either!"

"What was this particular piece of luck?" asked Mr. Killick.

John Purvis looked round as if to make sure of general attention.

"He'd come into possession, through a fortunate bit of trading, up country in South Africa, of one of the finest diamonds ever discovered!" he answered. "I know nothing about such things, but he said it was an orange-yellow diamond that would weigh at least a hundred and twenty carats when cut, and was worth, as far as he could reckon, some eighty to ninety thousand pounds. Anyway, that was what he'd calculated he was going to get for it here in London—and what he wanted to see me about, in addition to telling me of his luck, was that he wanted to buy a real nice bit of property in Devonshire, and settle down in the old country. But—I'm afraid his luck's turned to a poor end! Gentlemen!—I'm certain my brother's been murdered for that diamond!"

The police officials, as with one consent, glanced at Mr. Killick, and by their looks seemed to invite his assistance. The old gentleman nodded and turned to the caller.

"Now, Mr. Purvis," he said, "just let me ask you a few questions. Did your brother tell you that this diamond was his own, sole property?"

"He did, sir!" answered the farmer. "He said it was all his own."

"Did he tell you where it was—what he had done with it?"

"Yes! He said that for some years he'd traded in small parcels of such things with two men here in London—Multenius and Levendale—he knew both of them. He'd sent the diamond on in advance to Multenius, by ordinary registered post, rather than run the risk of carrying it himself."

"I gather from that last remark that your brother had let some other person or persons know that he possessed this stone?" said Mr. Killick. "Did he mention that? It's of importance."

"He mentioned no names—but he did say that one or two knew of his luck, and he'd an idea that he'd been watched in Cape Town, and followed on the *Golconda*," replied John Purvis. "He laughed about that, and said he wasn't such a fool as to carry a thing like that on him."

"Did he say if he knew for a fact that the diamond was delivered to Multenius?" asked Mr. Killick.

"Yes, he did. He found a telegram from Multenius at Las Palmas, acknowledging the receipt. He mentioned to me that Multenius would put the diamond in his bank, till he got to London himself."

Mr. Killick glanced at the detective—the detectives nodded.

"Very good," continued Mr. Killick. "Now then—: you'd doubtless talk a good deal about this matter—did your brother tell you what was to be done with the diamond? Had he a purchaser in view?"

"Yes, he said something about that," replied John Purvis. "He said that Multenius and Levendale would make—or were making—what he called a syndicate to buy it from him. They'd have it cut—over in Amsterdam, I think it was. He reckoned he'd get quite eighty thousand from the syndicate."

"He didn't mention any other names than those of Multenius and Levendale?"

"No—none!"

"Now, one more question. Where did your brother leave you—at Plymouth?"

"First thing next morning," said John Purvis. "We travelled together as far as Exeter. He came on to Paddington—I went home to my farm. And I've never heard of him since—till I read all this in the papers."

Mr. Killick got up and began to button his overcoat. He turned to the police.

"Now you know what we wanted to know!" he said. "That diamond is at the bottom of everything! Daniel Multenius was throttled for that diamond—Parslett's death arose out of that diamond—everything's arisen from that diamond! And, now that you police folks know all this—you know what to do. You want the man, or men, who were in Daniel Multenius's shop about five o'clock on that particular day, and who carried off that diamond. Mr. Purvis!—are you staying in town?"

The farmer shook his head—but not in the negative.

"I'm not going out of London, till I know what's become of my brother!"

he said.

"Then come with me," said Mr. Killick. He said a word or two to the police, and then, beckoning Lauriston and Purdie to follow with Purvis, led the way out into the street. There he drew Purdie towards him. "Get a taxi-cab," he whispered, "and we'll all go to see that American man you've told me of—Guyler. And when we've seen him, you can take me to see Daniel Multenius's granddaughter."

## CHAPTER TWENTY-FIVE
## THE DEAD MAN'S PROPERTY

Old Daniel Multenius had been quietly laid to rest that afternoon, and at the very moment in which Mr. Killick and his companions were driving away from the police station to seek Stuyvesant Guyler at his hotel, Mr. Penniket was closeted with Zillah and her cousin Melky Rubinstein in the back-parlour of the shop in Praed Street—behind closed and locked doors which they had no intention of opening to anybody. Now that the old man was dead and buried, it was necessary to know how things stood with respect to his will and his property, and, as Mr. Penniket had remarked as they drove back from the cemetery, there was no reason why they should not go into matters there and then. Zillah and Melky were the only relations—and the only people concerned, said Mr. Penniket. Five minutes would put them in possession of the really pertinent facts as regards the provisions of the will—but there would be details to go into. And now they were all three sitting round the table, and Mr. Penniket had drawn two papers from his inner pocket—and Zillah regarding him almost listlessly, and Melky with one of his quietly solemn expression. Each had a pretty good idea of what was coming and each regarded the present occasion as no more than a formality.

"This is the will," said Mr. Penniket, selecting and unfolding one of the documents. "It was made about a year ago—by me. That is, I drafted it. It's a short, a very short and practical will, drafted from precise instructions given to me by my late client, your grandfather. I may as well tell you in a few words what it amounts to. Everything that he left is to be sold—this business as a going concern; all his shares; all his house property. The whole estate is to be realized by the executors—your two selves. And when that's done, you're to divide the lot—equally. One half is yours, Miss Wildrose; Mr. Rubinstein, the other half is yours. And," concluded Mr. Penniket, rubbing his hands, "you'll find you're very fortunate—not to say wealthy—young people, and I congratulate you on your good fortune! Now, perhaps, you'd like to read the will?"

Mr. Penniket laid the will on the table before the two cousins, and they bent forward and read its legal phraseology. Zillah was the first to look up and to speak.

"I never knew my grandfather had any house property," she said. "Did you, Melky?"

"S'elp me, Zillah, if I ever knew what he had in that way!" answered Melky. "He had his secrets and he could be close. No—I never knew of his having anything but his business. But then, I might have known that he'd invest his profits in some way or other."

The solicitor unfolded the other document.

"Here's a schedule, prepared by Mr. Multenius himself, and handed by him to me not many weeks ago, of his property outside this business," he remarked. "I'll go through the items. Shares in the Great Western Railway. Shares in the London, Brighton, and South Coast Railway. Government Stock. Certain American Railway Stock. It's all particularized—and all gilt-edged security. Now then, about his house property. There's a block of flats at Hampstead. There are six houses at Highgate. There are three villas in the Finchley Road. The rents of all these have been collected by Messrs. Holder and Keeper, estate agents, and evidently paid by them direct to your esteemed relative's account at his bank. And then—to wind up—there is a small villa in Maida Vale, which he let furnished—you never heard of that?"

"Never!" exclaimed Zillah, while Melky shook his head.

"There's a special note about that at the end of this schedule," said Mr. Penniket. "In his own hand—like all the rest. This is what he says. 'N. B. Molteno Lodge, Maida Vale—all the furniture, pictures, belongings in this are mine—I have let it as a furnished residence at £12 a month, all clear, for some years past. Let at present, on same terms, rent paid quarterly, in advance, to two Chinese gentlemen, Mr. Chang Li and Mr. Chen Li—good tenants."

Zillah uttered another sharp exclamation and sprang to her feet. She walked across to an old-fashioned standup desk which stood in a corner of the parlour, drew a bunch of keys from her pocket, and raised the lid.

"That explains something!" she said. "I looked into this desk the other day—grandfather used to throw letters and papers in there sometimes, during the day, and then put them away at night. Here's a cheque here that puzzled me—I don't know anything about it. But—it'll be a quarter's rent for that house. Look at the signatures!"

She laid a cheque before Melky and Mr. Penniket and stood by while they looked at it. There was nothing remarkable about the cheque—made out to Mr. Daniel Multenius on order for £36—except the two odd looking names at its foot—*Chang Li: Chen Li*. Otherwise, it was just like all other cheques—and it was on a local bank, in Edgware Road, and duly crossed. But Melky instantly observed the date, and put one of his long fingers to it.

"November 18th," he remarked. "The day he died. Did you notice that, Zillah?"

"Yes," answered Zillah. "It must have come in by post and he's thrown it, as he often did throw things, into that desk. Well—that's explained! That'll be the quarter's rent, then, for this furnished house, Mr. Penniket?"

"Evidently!" agreed the solicitor. "Of course, there's no need to give notice to these two foreigners—yet. It'll take a little time to settle the estate, and you can let them stay on awhile. I know who they are—your grandfather mentioned them—two medical students, of University College. They're all right. Well, now, that completes the schedule. As regards administering the estate—"

A sudden gentle but firm knock at the side-door brought Zillah to her feet again.

"I know that knock," she remarked. "It's Ayscough, the detective. I suppose he may come in, now?"

A moment later Ayscough, looking very grave and full of news, had joined the circle round the table. He shook his head as he glanced at Mr. Penniket.

"I came on here to give you a bit of information," he said. "There's been an important development this afternoon. You know the name of this Stephen Purvis that's been mentioned as having been about here? Well, this afternoon his brother turned up from Devonshire. He wanted to see us—to tell us something. He thinks Stephen's been murdered!"

"On what grounds?" asked the solicitor.

"It turns out Stephen had sent Mr. Multenius a rare fine diamond—uncut—from South Africa," answered Ayscough. "Worth every penny of eighty thousand pounds!"

He was closely watching Zillah and Melky as he gave this piece of news, and he was quick to see their utter astonishment. Zillah turned to the solicitor; Melky slapped the table.

"That's been what the old man fetched from his bank that day!" he exclaimed. "S'elp me if I ain't beginning to see light! Robbery—before murder!"

"That's about it," agreed Ayscough. "But I'll tell you all that's come out."

He went on to narrate the events of the afternoon, from the arrival of Mr. Killick and his companions at the police station to the coming of John Purvis, and his three listeners drank in every word with rising interest. Mr. Penniket became graver and graver.

"Where's Mr. Killick now—and the rest of them?" he asked in the end.

"Gone to find that American chap—Guyler," answered Ayscough. "They did think he might be likely—having experience of these South African matters—to know something how Stephen Purvis may have been followed. You see—you're bound to have some theory! It looks as if Stephen Purvis had been tracked—for the sake of that diamond. The thieves probably tracked it to this shop—most likely attacked Mr. Multenius for it. They'd most likely been in here just before young Lauriston came in."

"But where does Stephen Purvis come in—then?" asked Mr. Penniket.

"Can't say yet—," replied Ayscough, doubtfully. "But—it may be that he—and Levendale—got an idea who the thieves were, and went off after them, and have got—well, trapped, or, as John Purvis suggests, murdered. It's getting a nicer tangle than ever!"

"What's going to be done?" enquired the solicitor.

"Why!" said Ayscough. "At present, there's little more to be done than what is being done! There's no end of publicity in the newspapers about both Levendale and Purvis. Every newspaper reporter in London's on the stretch for a thread of news of 'em! And we're getting posters and bills out, all over, advertising for them—those bills'll be outside every police-station in London—and over a good part of England—by tomorrow noon. And, of course, we're all at work. But you see, we haven't so far, the slightest clue as to the thieves! For there's no doubt, now, that it was theft first, and the rest afterwards."

Mr. Penniket rose and gathered his papers together.

"I suppose," he remarked, "that neither of you ever heard of this diamond, nor of Mr. Multenius having charge of it? No—just so. An atmosphere of secrecy all over the transaction. Well—all I can say, Ayscough, is this—you find Levendale. He's the man who knows."

When the solicitor had gone, Ayscough turned to Zillah.

"You never saw anything of any small box, packet, or anything of that sort, lying about after your grandfather's death?" he asked. "I'm thinking of what that diamond had been enclosed in, when he brought it from the bank. My notion is that he was examining that diamond when he was attacked, and in that case the box he'd taken it from would be lying about, or thrown aside."

"You were in here yourself, before me," said Zillah.

"Quite so—but I never noticed anything," remarked Ayscough.

"Neither have I," replied Zillah. "And don't you think that whoever seized that diamond would have the sense to snatch up anything connected with it! I believe in what Mr. Penniket said just now—you find Levendale. If there's a man living who knows who killed my grandfather, Levendale's that man. You get him."

Mrs. Goldmark came in just then, to resume her task of keeping Zillah company, and the detective left. Melky snatched up his overcoat and followed him out, and in the side-passage laid a hand on his arm.

"Look here, Mr. Ayscough!" he whispered confidentially. "I want you! There's something turned up in there, just now, that I ain't said a word about to either Penniket or my cousin—but I will to you. Do you know what, Mr. Ayscough—listen here;"—and he went on to tell the detective the story of the furnished house in Maida Vale, its Chinese occupants, and their cheque. "Dated that very day the old man was scragged!" exclaimed Melky. "Now, Mr. Ayscough, supposing that one o' those Chinks called here with that cheque that afternoon when Zillah was out, and found the old man alone, and that diamond in his hand—eh?"

Ayscough started and gave a low, sharp whistle.

"Whew!" he said. "By George, that's an idea! Where's this house, do you say? Molteno Lodge, Maida Vale? I know it—small detached house in a garden. I say!—let's go and take a look round there!"

"It's what I was going to propose—and at once," responded Melky. "Come on—but on the way, we'll pay a bit of a call. I want to ask a question of Dr. Mirandolet."

## CHAPTER TWENTY-SIX
## THE RAT

Ayscough and Melky kept silence, until they had exchanged the busy streets for the quieter by-roads which lie behind the Paddington Canal—then, as they turned up Portsdown Road, the detective tapped his companion's arm.

"What do you know about these two Chinese chaps that have this furnished house of yours?" he asked. "Much?—or little?"

"We don't know nothing at all, Mr. Ayscough—me and my cousin Zillah," replied Melky. "Never heard of 'em! Never knew they were there! Never knew the old man had furnished house to let in Maida Vale! He was close, the old man was, about some things. That was one of 'em. However, Mr. Penniket, he knew of this—but only recently. He says they're all right—medical students at one of the hospitals—yes, University College. That's in Gower Street, ain't it? The old man—he put in a note about there here Molteno Lodge that these Chinks were good tenants. I know what he'd mean by that!—paid their rent regular, in advance."

"Oh, I know they've always plenty of money, these chaps!" observed Ayscough. "I've been wondering if I'd ever seen these two. But Lor' bless you!—there's such a lot o' foreigners in this quarter, especially Japanese and Siamese—law students and medical students and such like—that you'd never notice a couple of Easterns particularly—and I've no doubt they wear English clothes. Now, what do you want to see this doctor for?" he asked as they halted by Dr. Mirandolet's door. "Anything to do with the matter in hand?"

"You'll see in a minute," replied Melky as he rang the bell. "Just a notion that occurred to me. And it has got to do with it."

Dr. Mirandolet was in, and received his visitors in a room which was half-surgery and half-laboratory, and filled to the last corner with the evidences and implements of his profession. He was wearing a white linen operating jacket, and his dark face and black hair looked all the darker and blacker because of it. Melky gazed at him with some awe as he dropped into the chair which Mirandolet indicated and found the doctor's piercing eyes on him.

"Just a question or two, mister!" he said, apologetically. "Me and Mr. Ayscough there is doing a bit of looking into this mystery about Mr. Multenius, and knowing as you was a big man in your way, it struck me you'd tell me something. I was at that inquest on Parslett, you know, mister."

Mirandolet nodded and waited, and Melky gained courage.

"Mister!" he said, suddenly bending forward and tapping the doctor's knee in a confidential fashion. "I hear you say at that inquest as how you'd lived in the East?"

"Yes!" replied Mirandolet. "Many years. India—Burmah—China!"

"You know these Easterns, mister, and their little way?" suggested Melky. "Now, would it be too much—I don't want to get no professional information, you know, if it ain't etiquette!—but would it be too much to ask you if them folks is pretty good hands at poisoning?"

Mirandolet laughed, showing a set of very white teeth, and glared at Ayscough with a suggestion of invitation to join in his amusement. He clapped Melky on the shoulder as if he had said something diverting.

"Good hands, my young friend?" he exclaimed. "The very best in the world! Past masters! Adepts. Poison you while they look at you!"

"Bit cunning and artful about it, mister?" suggested Melky.

"Beyond your conception, my friend," replied Mirandolet. "Unless I very much mistake your physiognomy, you yourself come of an ancient race which is not without cunning and artifice—but in such matters as you refer to, you are children, compared to your Far East folk."

"Just so, mister—I believe you!" said Melky, solemnly. "And—which of 'em, now, do you consider the cleverest of the lot—them as you say you've lived amongst, now? You mentioned three lots of 'em, you know—Indians, Burmese, Chinese. Which would you consider the artfullest of them three—if it came to a bit of real underhand work, now?"

"For the sort of thing you're thinking of, my friend," answered Mirandolet, "you can't beat a Chinaman. Does that satisfy you?"

Melky rose and glanced at the detective before turning to the doctor.

"Mister," he said, "that's precisely what I should ha' said myself. Only—I wanted to know what a big man like you thought. Now, I know! Much obliged to you, mister. If there's ever anything I can do for you, doctor—if you want a bit of real good stuff—jewellery, you know—at dead cost price—"

Mirandolet laughed and clapping Melky's shoulder again, looked at Ayscough.

"What's our young friend after?" he asked, good-humouredly. "What's his game?"

"Hanged if I know, doctor!" said Ayscough, shaking his head. "He's got some notion in his head. Are you satisfied, Mr. Rubinstein?"

Melky was making for the door.

"Ain't I just said so?" he answered. "You come along of me, Mr. Ayscough, and let's be getting about our business. Now, look here!" he said, taking the detective's arm when they had left the house. "We're going to take a look at them Chinks. I've got it into my head that they've something to do with this affair—and I'm going to see 'em, and to ask 'em a question or two. And—you're coming with me!"

"I say, you know!" remarked Ayscough. "They're respectable gentlemen—even if they are foreigners. Better be careful—we don't know anything against 'em."

"Never you fear!" said Melky. "I'll beat 'em all right. Ain't I got a good excuse, Mr. Ayscough? Just to ask a civil question. Begging their pardons for intrusion, but since the lamented death of Mr. Daniel Multenius, me and Miss Zillah Wildrose has come into his bit of property, and does the two gentlemen desire to continue their tenancy, and is there anything we can do to make 'em comfortable—see? Oh, I'll talk to 'em all right!"

"What're you getting at, all the same?" asked the detective. "Give it a title!"

Melky squeezed his companion's arm.

"I want to see 'em," he whispered. "That's one thing. And I want to find out how that last cheque of theirs got into our back-parlour! Was it sent by post—or was it delivered by hand? And if by hand—who delivered it?"

"You're a cute 'un, you are!" observed Ayscough. "You'd better join us."

"Thank you, Mr. Ayscough, but events has happened which'll keep me busy at something else," said Melky, cheerfully. "Do you know that my good old relative has divided everything between me and my cousin?—I'm a rich man, now, Mr. Ayscough. S'elp me!—I don't know how rich I am. It'll take a bit o' reckoning."

"Good luck to you!" exclaimed the detective heartily. "Glad to hear it! Then I reckon you and your cousin'll be making a match of it—keeping the money in the family, what?"

Melky laid his finger on the side of his nose.

"Then you think wrong!" he said. "There'll be marriages before long—for both of us—but it'll not be as you suggest! There's Molteno Lodge, across the road there—s'elp me, I've often seen that bit of a retreat from the top of a 'bus, but I never knew it belonged to the poor old man!"

They had now come to the lower part of Maida Vale, where many detached houses stand in walled-in gardens, isolated and detached from each other—Melky pointed to one of the smaller ones—a stucco villa, whose white walls shone in the November moonlight. Its garden, surrounded by high walls, was somewhat larger than those of the neighbouring houses, and was filled with elms rising to a considerable height and with tall bushes growing beneath them.

"Nice, truly rural sort of spot," said Melky, as they crossed the road and approached the gate in the wall. "And—once inside—uncommon private, no doubt! What do you say, Mr. Ayscough?"

The detective was examining the gate. It was a curious sort of gate, set between two stout pillars, and fashioned of wrought ironwork, the meshes of which were closely intertwined. Ayscough peered through the upper part and saw a trim lawn, a bit of statuary, a garden seat, and all the rest of the appurtenances common to a London garden whose owners wish to remind themselves of rusticity—also, he saw no signs of life in the house at the end of the garden.

"There's no light in this house," he remarked, trying the gate. "Looks to me as if everybody was out. Are you going to ring?"

Melky pointed along the front of the wall.

"There's a sort of alley going up there, between this house and the next," he said. "Come round—sure to be a tradesman's entrance—a side-door—up there."

"Plenty of spikes and glass-bottle stuff on those walls, anyhow!" remarked Ayscough, as they went round a narrow alley to the rear of the villa. "Your grandfather evidently didn't intend anybody to get into these premises very easily, Mr. Rubinstein. Six-foot walls and what you might call regular fortifications on top of 'em! What are you going to do, now?"

Melky had entered a recess in the side-wall and was examining a stout door on which, plainly seen in the moonlight, were the words *Tradesman's Entrance*. He turned the handle—and uttered an exclamation.

"Open!" he said. "Come on, Mr. Ayscough—we're a-going in! If there is anybody at home, all right—if there ain't, well, still all right. I'm going to have a look round."

The detective followed Melky into a paved yard at the back of the villa. All was very still there—and the windows were dark.

"No lights, back or front," remarked Ayscough. "Can't be anybody in. And I say—if either of those Chinese gents was to let himself in with his key at the front gate and find us prowling about, it wouldn't look very well, would it, now? Why not call again—in broad daylight?"

"Shucks!" said Melky. "Ain't I one o' the landlords of this desirable bit o' property? And didn't we find that door open? Come round to the front."

He set off along a gravelled path which ran round the side of the house, and ascended the steps to the porticoed front door. And there he rang the bell—and he and his companion heard its loud ringing inside the house. But no answer came—and the whole place seemed darker and stiller than before.

"Of course there's nobody in!" muttered Ayscough. "Come on—let's get out of it."

Melky made no answer. He walked down the steps, and across the lawn beneath the iron-work gate in the street wall. A thick shrubbery of holly and laurel bushes stood on his right—and as he passed it something darted out—something alive and alert and sinuous—and went scudding away across the lawn.

"Good Lord!" said Ayscough. "A rat! And as big as a rabbit!"

Melky paused, looked after the rat, and then at the place from which it had emerged. And suddenly he stepped towards the shrubbery and drew aside the thick cluster of laurel branches. Just as suddenly he started back on the detective, and his face went white in the moonbeams.

"Mr. Ayscough!" he gasped. "S'elp me!—there's a dead man here! Look for yourself!"

## CHAPTER TWENTY-SEVEN
## THE EMPTY HOUSE

Ayscough had manifested a certain restiveness and dislike to the proceedings ever since his companion had induced him to enter the back door of Molteno Lodge—these doings appeared to him informal and irregular. But at Melky's sudden exclamation his professional instincts were aroused, and he started forward, staring through the opening in the bushes made by Melky's fingers.

"Good Lord!" he said. "You're right. One of the Chinamen!"

The full moon was high in a cloudless sky by that time, and its rays fell full on a yellow face—and on a dark gash that showed itself in the yellow neck below. Whoever this man was, he had been killed by a savage knifethrust that had gone straight and unerringly through the jugular vein. Ayscough pointed to a dark wide stain which showed on the earth at the foot of the bushes.

"Stabbed!" he muttered. "Stabbed to death! And dragged in here—look at that—and that!"

He turned, pointing to more stains on the gravelled path behind them—stains which extended, at intervals, almost to the entrance door in the outer wall. And then he drew a box of matches from his pocket, and striking one, went closer and held the light down to the dead man's face. Melky, edging closer to his elbow, looked, too.

"One of those Chinamen, without a doubt!" said Ayscough, as the match flickered and died out. "Or, at any rate, a Chinaman. And—he's been dead some days! Well!—this is a go!"

"What's to be done?" asked Melky. "It's murder!"

Ayscough looked around him. He was wondering how it was that a dead man could lie in that garden, close to a busy thoroughfare, along which a regular stream of traffic of all descriptions was constantly passing, for several days, undetected. But a quick inspection of the surroundings explained matters. The house itself filled up one end of the garden; the other three sides were obscured from the adjacent houses and from the street by high walls, high trees, thick bushes. The front gate was locked or latched—no one had entered—no one, save the owner of the knife that had dealt that blow, had known a murdered man lay there behind the laurels. Only the rat, started by Melky's footsteps, had known.

"Stay here!" said Ayscough. "Well—inside the gate, then—don't come out—I don't want to attract attention. There'll be a constable somewhere about."

He walked down to the iron-work gate, Melky following close at his heels, found and unfastened the patent latch, and slipped out into the road. In two minutes he was back again with a policeman. He motioned the man inside and once more fastened the door.

"As you know this beat," he said quietly, as if continuing a conversation already begun, "you'll know the two Chinese gentlemen who have this house?"

"Seen 'em—yes," replied the policeman. "Two quiet little fellows—seen 'em often—generally of an evening."

"Have you seen anything of them lately?" asked Ayscough.

"Well, now I come to think of it, no, I haven't," answered the policeman. "Not for some days."

"Have you noticed that the house was shut up—that there were no lights in the front windows?" enquired the detective.

"Why, as a matter of fact, Mr. Ayscough," said the policeman, "you never do see any lights here—the windows are shuttered. I know that, because I used to give a look round when the house was empty."

"Do you know what servants they kept—these two?" asked Ayscough.

"They kept none!" answered the policeman. "Seems to me—from what bit I saw, you know—they used the house for little more than sleeping in. I've seen 'em go out of a morning, with books and papers under their arms, and come home at night—similar. But there's no servants there. Anything wrong, Mr. Ayscough?"

Ayscough moved toward the bushes.

"There's this much wrong," he answered. "There's one of 'em lying dead behind those laurels with a knife-thrust through his throat! And I should say, from the look of things, that he's been lying there several days. Look here!"

The policeman looked—and beyond a sharp exclamation, remained stolid. He glanced at his companions, glanced round the garden—and suddenly pointed to a dark patch on the ground.

"There's blood there!" he said. "Blood!"

"Blood!" exclaimed Ayscough. "There's blood all the way down this path! The man's been stabbed as he came in at that door, and his body was then dragged up the path and thrust in here. Now then!—off you go to the station, and tell 'em what we've found. Get help—he'll have to be taken to the mortuary. And you'll want men to keep a watch on this house—tell the inspector all about it and say I'm here. And here—leave me that lamp of yours."

The policeman took off his bull's eye lantern and handed it over. Ayscough let him out of the door, and going back to Melky, beckoned him towards the house.

"Let's see if there's any way of getting in here," he said. "My conscience, Mr. Rubinstein!—you must have had some instinct about coming here

115

tonight! We've hit on something—but Lord bless me if I know what it is!"

"Mr. Ayscough!" said Melky. "I hadn't a notion of aught like that—it's give me a turn! But don't I know what it means, Mr. Ayscough—not half! It's all of a piece with the rest of it! Murder, Mr. Ayscough—bloody murder! All on account of that orange-yellow diamond we've heard of—at last. Ah!—if I'd known there was that at the bottom of this affair, I'd ha' been a bit sharper in coming to conclusions, I would so! Diamond worth eighty thousand pounds—."

Ayscough, who had been busy at the front door of the house, suddenly interrupted his companion's reflections.

"The door's open!" he exclaimed. "Open! Not even on the latch. Come on!"

Melky shrank back at the prospect of the unlighted hall. There was a horror in the garden, in that bright moonlight—what might there not be in that black, silent house?

"Well, turn that there bull's eye on!" he said. "I don't half fancy this sort of exploration. We'd ought to have had revolvers, you know."

Ayscough turned on the light and advanced into the hall. There was nothing there beyond what one would expect to see in the hall of a well-furnished house, nor was there anything but good furniture, soft carpets, and old pictures to look at in the first room into which he and Melky glanced. But in the room behind there were evidences of recent occupation—a supper-table was laid: there was food on it, a cold fowl, a tongue—one plate had portions of both these viands laid on it, with a knife and fork crossed above them; on another plate close by, a slice of bread lay, broken and crumbled—all the evidences showed that supper had been laid for two, that only one had sat down to it: that he had been interrupted at the very beginning of his meal—a glass half-full of a light French wine stood near the pushed-aside plate.

"Looks as if one of 'em had been having a meal, had had to leave it, and had never come back to it," remarked Ayscough. "Him outside, no doubt. Let's see the other rooms."

There was nothing to see beyond what they would have expected to see—except that in one of the bedrooms, in a drawer pulled out from a dressing-table and left open, lay a quantity of silver and copper, with here and there a gold coin shining amongst it. Ayscough made a significant motion of his head at the sight.

"Another proof of—hurry!" he said. "Somebody's cleared out of this place about as quick as he could! Money left lying about—unfinished meal—door open—all sure indications. Well, we've seen enough for the present. Our people'll make a thorough search later. Come downstairs again."

Neither Ayscough nor Melky were greatly inclined for conversation or speculation, and they waited in silence near the gate, both thinking of the still figure lying behind the laurel bushes until the police came. Then followed whispered consultations between Ayscough and the inspector, and arrangements for the removal of the dead man to the mortuary and the guardianship and thorough search of the house—and that done, Ayscough beckoned Melky out into the road.

"Glad to be out of that—for this time, anyway!" he said, with an air of relief. "There's too much atmosphere of murder and mystery—what they call Oriental mystery—for me in there, Mr. Rubinstein! Now then, there's something we can do, at once. Did I understand you to say these two were medical students at University College?"

"So Mr. Penniket said," replied Melky. "S'elp me! I never heard of 'em till this afternoon!"

"You're going to hear a fine lot about 'em before long, anyway!" remarked Ayscough.

"Well—we'll just drive on to Gower Street—somebody'll know something about 'em there, I reckon."

He walked forward until he came to the cab-rank at the foot of St. John's Wood Road, where he bundled Melky into a taxi-cab, and bade the driver get away to University College Hospital at his best pace. There was little delay in carrying out that order, but it was not such an easy task on arrival at their destination to find any one who could give Ayscough the information he wanted. At last, after they had waited some time in a reception room a young member of the house-staff came in and looked an enquiry.

"What is it you want to know about these two Chinese students?" he asked a little impatiently, with a glance at Ayscough's card. "Is anything wrong?"

"I want to know a good deal!" answered Ayscough. "If not just now, later. You know the two men I mean—Chang Li and Chen Li—brothers, I take it?"

"I know them—they've been students here since about last Christmas," answered the young surgeon. "As a matter of fact they're not brothers—though they're very much alike, and both have the same surname—if Li is a surname. They're friends—not brothers, so they told us."

"When did you see them last?" asked Ayscough.

"Not for some days, now you mention it," replied the surgeon. "Several days. I was remarking on that today—I missed them from a class."

"You say they're very much alike," remarked the detective. "I suppose you can tell one from the other?"

"Of course! But—what is this? I see you're a detective sergeant. Are they in any bother—trouble?"

"The fact of the case," answered Ayscough, "is just this—one of them's lying dead at our mortuary, and I shall be much obliged if you'll step into my cab outside and come and identify him. Listen—it's a case of murder!"

Twenty minutes later, Ayscough, leading the young house-surgeon into a grim and silent room, turned aside the sheet from a yellow face.

"Which one of 'em is it?" he asked.

The house-surgeon started as he saw the wound in the dead man's throat.

"This is Chen!" he answered.

## CHAPTER TWENTY-EIGHT
## THE £500 BANK NOTE

Ayscough drew the sheet over the dead man's face and signed to his companion to follow him outside, to a room where Melky Rubinstein, still gravely meditating over the events of the evening, was awaiting their reappearance.

"So that," said Ayscough, jerking his thumb in the direction of the mortuary, "that's Chen Li! You're certain?"

"Chen Li! without a doubt!" answered the house-surgeon. "I know him well!"

"The younger of the two?" suggested Ayscough.

The house-surgeon shook his head.

"I can't say as to that," he answered. "It would be difficult to tell which of two Chinese, of about the same age, was the older. But that's Chen. He and the other, Chang Li, are very much alike, but Chen was a somewhat smaller and shorter man."

"What do you know of them?" inquired Ayscough. "Can you say what's known at your hospital?"

"Very little," replied the house-surgeon. "They entered, as students there—we have several foreigners—about last Christmas—perhaps at the New Year. All that I know of them is that they were like most Easterns—very quiet, unassuming, inoffensive fellows, very assiduous in their studies and duties, never giving any trouble, and very punctual in their attendance."

"And, you say, they haven't been seen at the hospital for some days?" continued Ayscough. "Now, can you tell me—it's important—since what precise date they've been absent?"

The house-surgeon reflected for a moment—then he suddenly drew out a small memorandum book from an inner pocket.

"Perhaps I can," he answered, turning the pages over. "Yes—both these men should have been in attendance on me—a class of my own, you know—on the 20th, at 10.35. They didn't turn up. I've never seen them since—in fact, I'm sure they've never been at the hospital since."

"The 20th?" observed Ayscough. He looked at Melky, who was paying great attention to the conversation. "Now let's see—old Mr. Multenius met his death on the afternoon of the 18th. Parslett was poisoned on the night of the 19th. Um!"

"And Parslett was picked up about half-way between the Chink's house and his own place, Mr. Ayscough—don't you forget that!" muttered Melky. "I'm not forgetting—don't you make no error!"

"You don't know anything more that you could tell us about these two?" asked the detective, nodding reassuringly at Melky and then turning to the house-surgeon. "Any little thing?—you never know what helps."

"I can't!" said the house-surgeon, who was obviously greatly surprised by what he had seen and heard. "These Easterns keep very much to themselves, you know. I can't think of anything."

"Don't know anything of their associates—friends—acquaintances?" suggested Ayscough. "I suppose they had some—amongst your students?"

"I never saw them in company with anybody—particularly—except a young Japanese who was in some of their classes," replied the house-surgeon. "I have seen them talking with him—in Gower Street."

"What's his name?" asked Ayscough, pulling out a note-book.

"Mr. Mori Yada," answered the house-surgeon promptly. "He lives in Gower Street—I don't know the precise number of the house. Yes, that's the way to spell his name. He's the only man I know who seemed to know these two."

"Have you seen him lately?" asked Ayscough.

"Oh, yes—regularly—today, in fact," said the house-surgeon.

He waited a moment in evident expectation of other questions; as the detective asked none—"I gather," he remarked, "that Chang Li has disappeared?"

"The house these two occupied is empty," replied Ayscough.

"I am going to suggest something," said the house-surgeon. "I know—from personal observation—that there is a tea-shop in Tottenham Court Road—a sort of quiet, privately-owned place—Pilmansey's—which these two used to frequent. I don't know if that's of any use to you?"

"Any detail is of use, sir," answered Ayscough, making another note. "Now, I'll tell this taxi-man to drive you back to the hospital. I shall call there tomorrow morning, and I shall want to see this young Japanese gentleman, too. I daresay you see that this is a case of murder—and there's more behind it!"

"You suspect Chang Li?" suggested the house-surgeon as they went out to the cab.

"Couldn't say that—yet," replied Ayscough, grimly. "For anything I know, Chang Li may have been murdered, too. But I've a pretty good notion what Chen Li was knifed for!"

When the house-surgeon had gone away, Ayscough turned to Melky.

"Come back to Molteno Lodge," he said. "They're searching it. Let's see if they've found anything of importance."

The house which had been as lifeless and deserted when Melky and the detective visited it earlier in the evening was full enough of energy and animation when they went back. One policeman kept guard at the front gate; another at the door of the yard; within the house itself, behind closed doors and drawn shutters and curtains, every room was lighted and the lynx-eyed men were turning the place upside down. One feature of the search struck the newcomers immediately—the patch of ground whereon Melky had found the dead man had been carefully roped off. Ayscough made a significant motion of his hand towards it.

"Good!" he said, "that shows they've found footprints. That may be useful. Let's hear what else they've found."

The man in charge of these operations was standing within the dining-room when Ayscough and Melky walked in, and he at once beckoned them into the room and closed the door.

"We've made two or three discoveries," he said, glancing at Ayscough. "To start with, there were footprints of a rather unusual sort round these bushes where the man was lying—so I've had it carefully fenced in around there—we'll have a better look at 'em, in daylight. Very small prints, you understand—more like a woman's than a man's."

Ayscough's sharp eyes turned to the hearth—there were two or three pairs of slippers lying near the fender and he pointed to them.

"These Chinamen have very small feet, I believe," he said. "The footprints are probably theirs. Well—what else?"

"This," answered the man in charge, producing a small parcel from the side-pocket of his coat, and proceeding to divest it of a temporary wrapping. "Perhaps Mr. Rubinstein will recognize it. We found it thrown away in a fire-grate in one of the bedrooms upstairs—you see, it's half burnt."

He produced a small, stoutly-made cardboard box, some three inches square, the outer surface of which was covered with a thick, glossy-surfaced dark-green paper, on which certain words were deeply impressed in gilt letters. The box was considerably charred and only fragments of the lettering on the lid remained intact—but it was not difficult to make out what the full wording had been.

.... *enius,*

.. *.nd jeweller,*

.. *ed Street.*

"That's one of the late Mr. Multenius's boxes," affirmed Melky at once. "Daniel Multenius, Pawnbroker and Jeweller, Praed Street—that's the full wording. Found in a fireplace, d'ye say, mister? Ah—and what had he taken out of it before he threw the box away, now, Mr. Ayscough—whoever it was that did throw it away?"

"That blessed orange and yellow diamond, I should think!" said Ayscough. "Of course! Well, anything else?"

The man in charge carefully wrapped up and put away the jeweller's box; then, with a significant glance at his fellow-detective, he slipped a couple of fingers into his waistcoat pocket and drew out what looked like a bit of crumpled paper.

"Aye!" he answered. "This! Found it—just there! Lying on the floor, at the end of this table."

He opened out the bit of crumpled paper as he spoke and held it towards the other two. Ayscough stared, almost incredulously, and Melky let out a sharp exclamation.

"S'elp us!" he said. "A five-hundred-pound bank-note!"

"That's about it," remarked the exhibitor. "Bank of England note for five hundred of the best! And—a good 'un, too. Lying on the floor."

"Take care of it," said Ayscough laconically. "Well—you haven't found any papers, documents, or anything of that sort, that give any clue?"

"There's a lot of stuff there," answered the man in charge, pointing to a pile of books and papers on the table, "but it seems to be chiefly exercises and that sort of thing. I'll look through it myself, later."

"See if you can find any letters, addresses, and so on," counselled Ayscough. He turned over some of the books, all of them medical works and text-books, opening some of them at random. And suddenly he caught sight of the name which the house-surgeon had given him half-an-hour before, written on a fly-leaf: Mori Yada, 491, Gower Street—and an idea came into his mind. He bade the man in charge keep his eyes open and leave nothing unexamined, and tapping Melky's arm, led him outside. "Look here!" he said, drawing out his watch, as they crossed the hall, "it's scarcely ten o'clock, and I've got the address of that young Jap. Come on—we'll go and ask him a question or two."

So for the second time that evening, Melky, who was beginning to feel as if he were on a chase which pursued anything but a straight course, found himself in Gower Street again, and followed Ayscough along, wondering what was going to happen next, until the detective paused at the door of a tall house in the middle of the long thoroughfare and rang the bell. A smart maid answered that ring and looked dubiously at Ayscough as he proffered a request to see Mr. Mori Yada. Yes—Mr. Yada was at home, but he didn't like to see any one, of an evening when he was at his studies, and—in fact he'd given orders not to be disturbed at that time.

"I think he'll see me, all the same," said Ayscough, drawing out one of his professional cards. "Just give him that, will you, and tell him my business is very important."

He turned to Melky when the girl, still looking unwilling, had gone away upstairs, and gave him a nudge of the elbow.

"When we get up there—as we shall," whispered Ayscough, "you watch this Jap chap while I talk to him. Study his face—and see if anything surprises him."

"Biggest order, mister—with a Jap!" muttered Melky. "Might as well tell me to watch a stone image—their faces is like wood!"

"Try it!" said Ayscough. "Flicker of an eyelid—twist of the lip—anything! Here's the girl back again."

A moment later Melky, treading close on the detective's heels, found himself ushered into a brilliantly-lighted, rather over-heated room, somewhat luxuriously furnished, wherein, in the easiest of chairs, a cigar in his lips, a yellow-backed novel in his hand, sat a slimly-built, elegant young gentleman whose face was melting to a smile.

## CHAPTER TWENTY-NINE
## MR. MORI YADA

Ayscough was on his guard as soon as he saw that smile. He had had some experience of various national characteristics in his time, and he knew that when an Eastern meets you with a frank and smiling countenance you had better keep all your wits about you. He began the exercise of his own with a polite bow—while executing it, he took a rapid inventory of Mr. Mori Yada. About—as near as he could judge—two or three and twenty; a black-haired, black-eyed young gentleman; evidently fastidious about his English clothes, his English linen, his English ties, smart socks, and shoes—a good deal of a dandy, in short—

and, judging from his surroundings, very fond of English comfort—and not averse to the English custom of taking a little spirituous refreshment with his tobacco. A decanter stood on the table at his elbow; a syphon of mineral water reared itself close by; a tumbler was within reach of Mr. Yada's slender yellowish fingers.

"Servant, sir!" said Ayscough. "Detective Sergeant Ayscough of the Criminal Investigation Department—friend of mine, this, sir, Mr. Yada, I believe—Mr. Mori Yada?"

Mr. Yada smiled again, and without rising, indicated two chairs.

"Oh, yes!" he said in excellent English accents. "Pleased to see you—will you take a chair—and your friend! You want to talk to me?"

Ayscough sat down and unbuttoned his overcoat.

"Much obliged, sir," he said. "Yes—the fact is, Mr. Yada, I called to see you on a highly important matter that's arisen. Your name, sir, was given to me tonight by one of the junior house-surgeons at the hospital up the street—Dr. Pittery."

"Oh, yes, Dr. Pittery—I know," agreed Yada. "Yes?"

"Dr. Pittery tells me, sir," continued Ayscough, "that you know two Chinese gentlemen who are fellow-students of yours at the hospital, Mr. Yada?"

The Japanese bowed his dark head and blew out a mouthful of smoke from his cigar.

"Yes!" he answered readily, "Mr. Chang Li—Mr. Chen Li. Oh, yes!"

"I want to ask you a question, Mr. Yada," said Ayscough, bending forward and assuming an air of confidence. "When did you see those two gentlemen last—either of them?"

Yada leaned back in his comfortably padded chair and cast his quick eyes towards the ceiling. Suddenly he jumped to his feet.

"You take a little drop of whisky-and-soda?" he said hospitably, pushing a clean glass towards Ayscough. "Yes—I will get another glass for your friend, too. Help yourselves, please, then—I will look in my diary for an answer to your question. You excuse me, one moment."

He walked across the room to a writing cabinet which stood in one corner, and took up a small book that lay on the blotting-pad; while he turned over its pages, Ayscough, helping himself and Melky to a drink, winked at his companion with a meaning expression.

"I have not seen either Mr. Chang Li or Mr. Chen Li since the morning of the 18th November," suddenly said Yada. He threw the book back on the desk, and coming to the hearthrug, took up a position with his back to the fire and his hands in the pockets of his trousers. He nodded politely as his visitors raised their glasses to him. "Is anything the matter,

Mr. Detective-Sergeant?" he asked.

Ayscough contrived to press his foot against Melky's as he gave a direct answer to this question.

"The fact of the case is, Mr. Yada," he said, "one of these two young men has been murdered! murdered, sir!"

Yada's well-defined eyebrows elevated themselves—but the rest of his face was immobile. He looked fixedly at Ayscough for a second or two—then he let out one word.

"Which?"

"According to Dr. Pittery—Chen Li," answered Ayscough. "Dr. Pittery identified him. Murdered, Mr. Yada, murdered! Knifed!—in the throat."

The reiteration of the word murdered appeared to yield the detective some sort of satisfaction—but it apparently made no particular impression on the Japanese. Again he rapped out one word.

"Where?"

"His body was found in the garden of the house they rented in Maida Vale," replied Ayscough. "Molteno Lodge. No doubt you've visited them there, Mr. Yada?"

"I have been there—yes, a few times," assented Yada. "Not very lately. But—where is Chang Li?"

"That's what we don't know—and what we want to know," said Ayscough. "He's not been seen at the hospital since the 20th. He didn't turn up there—nor Chen, either, at a class, that day. And you say you haven't seen them either since the 18th?"

"I was not at the hospital on the 19th," replied Yada. He threw away the end of his cigar, picked up a fresh one from a box which stood on the table, pushed the box towards his visitors, and drew out a silver matchbox. "What are the facts of this murder, Mr. Detective-Sergeant?" he asked quietly. "Murder is not done without some object—as a rule."

Ayscough accepted the offered cigar, passed the box to Melky and while he lighted his selection, thought quietly. He was playing a game with the Japanese, and it was necessary to think accurately and quickly. And suddenly he made up his mind and assumed an air of candour.

"It's like this, Mr. Yada," he said. "I may as well tell you all about it. You've doubtless read all about this Praed Street mystery in the newspapers? Well, now, some very extraordinary developments have arisen out of the beginnings of that, it turns out."

Melky sat by, disturbed and uncomfortable, while Ayscough reeled off a complete narrative of the recent discoveries to the suave-mannered, phlegmatic, calmly-listening figure on the hearthrug. He did not understand the detective's doings—it seemed to him the height of folly to

124

tell a stranger, and an Eastern stranger at that, all about the fact that there was a diamond worth eighty thousand pounds at the bottom of these mysteries and murders. But he discharged his own duties, and watched Yada intently—and failed to see one single sign of anything beyond ordinary interest in his impassive face.

"So there it is, sir," concluded Ayscough. "I've no doubt whatever that Chen Li called at Multenius's shop to pay the rent; that he saw the diamond in the old man's possession and swagged him for it; that Parslett saw Chen Li slip away from that side-door and, hearing of Multenius's death, suspected Chen Li of it and tried to blackmail him; that Chen Li poisoned Parslett—and that Chen Li himself was knifed for that diamond. Now—by whom? Chang Li has—disappeared!"

"You suspect Chang Li?" asked Yada.

"I do," exclaimed Ayscough. "A Chinaman—a diamond worth every penny of eighty thousand pounds—Ah!" He suddenly lifted his eyes to Yada with a quick enquiry. "How much do you know of these two?" he asked.

"Little—beyond the fact that they were fellow-students of mine," answered Yada. "I occasionally visited them—occasionally they visited me—that is all."

"Dr. Pittery says they weren't brothers?" suggested Ayscough.

"So I understood," assented Yada. "Friends."

"You can't tell us anything of their habits?—haunts?—what they usually did with themselves when they weren't at the hospital?" asked the detective.

"I should say that when they weren't at the hospital, they were at their house—reading," answered Yada, drily. "They were hard workers."

Ayscough rose from his chair.

"Well, much obliged to you, sir," he said. "As your name was mentioned as some sort of a friend of theirs, I came to you. Of course, most of what I've told you will be in all the papers tomorrow. If you should hear anything of this Chang Li, you'll communicate with us, Mr. Yada?"

The Japanese smiled—openly.

"Most improbable, Mr. Detective-Sergeant!" he answered. "I know no more than what I have said. For more information, you should go to the Chinese Legation."

"Good idea, sir—thank you," said Ayscough.

He bowed himself and Melky out; once outside the street-door he drew his companion away towards a part which lay in deep shadow. Some repairing operations to the exterior of a block of houses were going on there; underneath a scaffolding which extended over the sidewalk

Ayscough drew Melky to a halt.

"You no doubt wondered why I told that chap so much?" he whispered. "Especially about that diamond! But I had my reasons—and particularly for telling him about its value."

"It isn't what I should ha' done, Mr. Ayscough," said Melky, "and it didn't ought to come out in the newspapers, neither—so I think! 'Tain't a healthy thing to let the public know there's an eighty-thousand pound diamond loose somewhere in London—and as to telling that slant-eyed fellow in there—"

"You wait a bit, my lad!" interrupted Ayscough. "I had my reasons—good 'uns. Now, look here, we're going to watch that door awhile. If the Jap comes out—as I've an idea he will—we're going to follow. And as you're younger, and slimmer, and less conspicuous than I am, if he should emerge, keep on the shadowy side of the street, at a safe distance, and follow him as cleverly as you can. I'll follow you."

"What new game's this?" asked Melky.

"Never mind!" replied Ayscough. "And, if it does come to following, and he should take a cab, contrive to be near—there's a good many people about, and if you're careful he'll never see you. And—there, now, what did I tell you? He's coming out, now! Be handy—more depends on it than you're aware of."

Yada, seen clearly in the moonlight which flooded that side of the street, came out of the door which they had left a few minutes earlier. His smart suit of grey tweed had disappeared under a heavy fur-collared overcoat; a black bowler hat surmounted his somewhat pallid face. He looked neither to right nor left, but walked swiftly up the street in the direction of the Euston Road. And when he had gone some thirty yards, Ayscough pushed Melky before him out of their retreat.

"You go first," he whispered, "I'll come after you. Keep an eye on him as far as you can—didn't I tell you he'd come out when we'd left? Be wary!"

Melky slipped away up the street on the dark side and continued to track the slim figure quickly advancing in the moonlight. He followed until they had passed the front of the hospital—a few yards further, and Yada suddenly crossed the road in the direction of the Underground Railway. He darted in at the entrance to the City-bound train, and disappeared, and Melky, uncertain what to do, almost danced with excitement until Ayscough came leisurely towards him. "Quick! quick!" exclaimed Melky. "He's gone down there—City trains. He'll be off unless you're on to him!"

But Ayscough remained quiescent and calmly relighted his cigar.

"All right, my lad," he said. "Let him go—just now. I've seen—what I expected to see!"
## CHAPTER THIRTY
## THE MORTUARY

Melky, who had grown breathless in his efforts to carry out his companion's wishes, turned and looked at him with no attempt to conceal his wonder.

"Well, s'elp me if you ain't a cool 'un, Mr. Ayscough!" he exclaimed. "Here you troubles to track a chap to this here Underground Railway, seen him pop into it like a rabbit into a hole—and let's him go! What did we follow him up Gower Street for? Just to see him set off for a ride?"

"All right, my lad!" repeated Ayscough. "You don't quite understand our little ways. Wait here a minute."

He drew one of his cards from his pocket and carrying it into the booking office exchanged a few words with the clerk at the window. Presently he rejoined Melky. "He took a ticket for Whitechapel," remarked Ayscough as he strolled quietly up. "Ah! now what does a young Japanese medical student want going down that way at eleven o'clock at night? Something special, no doubt, Mr. Rubinstein. However, I'm going westward just now. Just going to have a look in at the Great Western Hotel, to see if Mr. Purdie heard anything from that American chap—and then I'm for home and bed. Like to come to the hotel with me?"

"Strikes me we might as well make a night of it!" remarked Melky as they recrossed the road and sought a west-bound train. "We've had such an evening as I never expected! Mr. Ayscough! when on earth is this going to come to something like a clearing-up?"

Ayscough settled himself in a corner of a smoking-carriage and leaned back.

"My own opinion," he said, "is that it's coming to an end. Tomorrow, the news of the Chinaman's murder'll be the talk of the town. And if that doesn't fetch Levendale out of whatever cranny he's crept into, hanged if I know what will!"

"Ah! you think that, do you?" said Melky. "But—why should that news fetch him out?"

"Don't know!" replied Ayscough, almost unconcernedly. "But I'm almost certain that it will. You see—I think Levendale's looking for Chen Li. Now, if Levendale hears that Chen Li's lying dead in our mortuary—what? See?"

Melky murmured that Mr. Ayscough was a cute 'un, and relapsed into thought until the train pulled up at Praed Street. He followed the detective up the streets and across the road to the hotel, dumbly wondering how many times that day he had been in and about that quarter on this apparently interminable chase. He was getting dazed—but Ayscough who was still smoking the cigar which Yada had given him, strode along into the hotel entrance apparently as fresh as paint.

Purdie had a private sitting-room in connection with his bedroom, and there they found him and Lauriston, both smoking pipes and each evidently full of thought and speculation. They jumped to their feet as the detective entered.

"I say!" exclaimed Lauriston. "Is this true?—this about the Chinese chap? Is it what they think at your police-station?—connected with the other affairs? We've been waiting, hoping you'd come in!"

"Ah!" said Ayscough, dropping into a chair. "We've been pretty busy, me and Mr. Rubinstein there—we've had what you might call a pretty full evening's work of it. Yes—it's true enough, gentlemen—another step in the ladder—another brick in the building! We're getting on, Mr. Purdie, we're getting on! So you've been round to our place?—they told you, there!"

"They gave us a mere outline," answered Purdie. "Just the bare facts. I suppose you've heard nothing of the other Chinaman?"

"Not a circumstance—as yet," said Ayscough. "But I'm in hopes—I've done a bit, I think, towards it—with Mr. Rubinstein's help, though he doesn't quite understand my methods. But you, gentlemen—I came in to hear if you'd anything to tell about Guyler. What did he think about what John Purvis had to tell us this afternoon?"

"He wasn't surprised," answered Purdie. "Don't you remember that he assured us from the very start that diamonds would be found to be at the bottom of this. But he surprised us!"

"Aye? How?" asked Ayscough. "Some news?"

"Guyler swears that he saw Stephen Purvis this very morning," replied Purdie. "He's confident of it!"

"Saw Stephen Purvis—this very morning!" exclaimed Ayscough. "Where, now?"

"Guyler had business down in the City—in the far end of it," said Purdie. "He was crossing Bishopsgate when he saw Stephen Purvis—he swears it was Stephen Purvis!—nothing can shake him! He, Purvis, was just turning the corner into a narrow alley running out of the street. Guyler rushed after him—he'd disappeared. Guyler waited, watching that alley, he says, like a cat watches a mouse-hole—and all in vain. He watched for an hour—it was no good."

"Pooh!" said Ayscough. "If it was Purvis, he'd walked straight through the alley and gone out at the other end."

"No!" remarked Lauriston. "At least, not according to Guyler. Guyler says it was a long, narrow alley—Purvis could have reached one end by the time he'd reached the other. He says—Guyler—that on each side of that alley there are suites of offices—he reckoned there were a few hundred separate offices in the lot, and that it would take him a week to make enquiry at the doors of each. But he's certain that Purvis disappeared into one block of them and dead certain that it was Stephen Purvis that he saw. So—Purvis is alive!"

"Where's the other Purvis—the farmer?" asked Ayscough.

"Stopping with Guyler at the Great Northern," answered Lauriston. "We've all four been down in the City, looking round, this evening. Guyler and John Purvis are going down again first thing in the morning. John Purvis, of course, is immensely relieved to know that Guyler's certain about his brother. I say!—do you know what Guyler's theory is about that diamond of Stephen's?"

"No—and what might Mr. Guyler's theory be, now Mr. Lauriston?" enquired the detective. "There's such a lot of ingenious theories about that one may as well try to take in another. Mr. Rubinstein there is about weary of theories."

But Melky was pricking his ears at the mere mention of anything relating to the diamond.

"That's his chaff, Mr. Lauriston," he said. "Never mind him! What does Guyler think?"

"Well, of course, Guyler doesn't know yet about the Chinese development," said Lauriston. "Guyler thinks the robbery has been the work of a gang—a clever lot of diamond thieves who knew about Stephen Purvis's find of the orange-yellow thing and put in a lot of big work about getting it when it reached England. And he believes that that gang has kidnapped Levendale, and that Stephen Purvis is working in secret to get at them. That's Guyler's notion, anyhow."

"Well!" said Ayscough. "And there may be something in it! For this search—how do we know that at any rate one of these Chinamen mayn't have had some connection with this gang? You never know—and to get a dead straight line at a thing's almost impossible. However, we've taken steps to have the news about the diamond and about this Chen Li appear in tomorrow morning's papers, and if that doesn't rouse the whole town—"

A tap at the door prefaced the entrance of a waiter, who looked apologetically at its inmates.

"Beg pardon, gentlemen," he said, "Mr. Ayscough? Gentleman outside would like a word with you, if you please, sir."

Ayscough picked up his hat and walked out—there, waiting a little way down the corridor, an impressive figure in his big black cloak and wide-brimmed hat, stood Dr. Mirandolet. He strode forward as the detective advanced.

"I heard you were here, so I came up," he said, leading Ayscough away.

"Look here, my friend—one of your people has told me of this affair at Molteno Lodge—the discovery of the Chinaman's dead body."

"That young fellow, Rubinstein, who called on you early this evening, and got me to accompany him discovered it," said Ayscough, who was wondering what the doctor was after. "I was with him."

"I have heard, too," continued Mirandolet, "also from one of your people, about the strange story of the diamond which came out this afternoon, from the owner's brother. Now—I'll tell you why after—I want to see that dead Chinaman! I've a particular reason. Will you come with me to the mortuary?"

Ayscough's curiosity was aroused by Mirandolet's manner, and without going back to Purdie's room, he set out with him. Mirandolet remained strangely silent until they came to the street in which the mortuary stood.

"A strange and mysterious matter this, my friend!" he said. "That little Rubinstein man might have had some curious premonition when he came to me tonight with his odd question about Chinese!"

"Just what I said myself, doctor!" agreed Ayscough.

"It did look as if he'd a sort of foreboding, eh? But—Hullo!"

He stopped short as a taxi-cab driven at a considerable speed, came rushing down the street and passing them swiftly turned into the wider road beyond. And the sudden exclamation was forced from his lips because it seemed to him that as the cab sped by he saw a yellow-hued face within it—for the fraction of a second. Quick as that glimpse was, Ayscough was still quicker as he glanced at the number on the back of the car—and memorized it.

"Odd!" he muttered, "odd! Now, I could have sworn—" He broke off, and hurried after Mirandolet who had stridden ahead. "Here we are, doctor," he said, as they came to the door of the mortuary. "There's a man on night duty here, so there's no difficulty about getting in."

There was a drawing of bolts, a turning of keys; the door opened, and a man looked out and seeing Ayscough and Dr. Mirandolet, admitted them into an ante-room and turned up the gas.

"We want to see that Chinaman, George," said the detective. "Shan't keep you long."

"There's a young foreign doctor just been to see him, Mr. Ayscough," said the man. "You'd pass his car down the street—he hasn't been gone three minutes. Young Japanese—brought your card with him."

Ayscough turned on the man as if he had given him the most startling news in the world.

"What?" he exclaimed, "Japanese? Brought my card?"

"Showed me it as soon as he got here," answered the attendant, surprised at Ayscough's amazement. "Said you'd given it to him, so that he could call here and identify the body. So, of course, I let him go in."

Ayscough opened his mouth in sheer amazement. But before he could get out a word, Mirandolet spoke, seizing the mortuary-keeper by the arm in his eagerness.

"You let that man—a Japanese—see the dead Chinaman—*alone*?" he demanded.

"Why, of course!" the attendant answered surlily. "He'd Mr. Ayscough's card, and—"

Mirandolet dropped the man's arm and threw up his own long white hands.

"Merciful Powers!" he vociferated. "He has stolen the diamond!"

## CHAPTER THIRTY-ONE
## THE MIRANDOLET THEORY

The silence that followed on this extraordinary exclamation was suddenly broken: the mortuary keeper, who had been advancing towards a door at the side of the room, dropped a bunch of keys. The strange metallic sound of their falling roused Ayscough, who had started aside, and was staring, open-mouthed, at Mirandolet's waving hands. He caught the doctor by the arm.

"What on earth do you mean?" he growled. "Speak man—what is it?"

Mirandolet suddenly laughed.

"What is it?" he exclaimed. "Precisely what I said, in plain language! That fellow has, of course, gone off with the diamond—worth eighty thousand pounds! Your card!—Oh, man, man, whatever have you been doing? Be quick!—who is this Japanese?—how came he by your card? Quick, I say!—if you want to be after him!"

"Hanged if I know what this means!" muttered Ayscough. "As to who he is—if he's the fellow I gave a card to, he's a young Japanese medical student, one Yada, that was a friend of those Chinese—I called on him tonight, with Rubinstein, to see if we could pick up a bit of information. Of course, I sent in my professional card to him. But—we saw him set off to the East End!"

"Bah!" laughed Mirandolet. "He has—what you call done you brown, my friend! He came—here! And he has got away—got a good start—with that diamond in his pocket!"

"What the devil do you mean by that?" said Ayscough, hotly. "Diamond! Diamond! Where should he find the diamond—here? In a deadhouse? What are you talking about?"

Mirandolet laughed again, and giving the detective a look that was very like one of pitying contempt, turned to the amazed mortuary keeper.

"Show us that dead man!" he said.

The mortuary keeper, who had allowed his keys to lie on the floor during this strange scene, picked them up, and selecting one, opened, and threw back the door by which he was standing. He turned on the light in the mortuary chamber, and Mirandolet strode in, with Ayscough, sullen and wondering, at his heels.

Chen Li lay where the detective had last seen him, still and rigid, the sheet drawn carefully over his yellow face. Without a word Mirandolet drew that sheet aside, and motioning his companion to draw nearer, pointed to a skull-cap of thin blue silk which fitted over the Chinaman's head.

"You see that!" he whispered. "You know what's beneath it!—something that no true Chinaman ever parts with, even if he does come to Europe, and does wear English dress and English headgear—his pigtail! Look here!"

He quietly moved the skull-cap, and showed the two astonished men a carefully-coiled mass of black hair, wound round and round the back of the head. And into it he slipped his own long, thin fingers—to draw them out again with an exclamation which indicated satisfaction with his own convictions.

"Just as I said," he remarked. "Gone! Mr. Detective—that's where Chen Li hid the diamond—and that Japanese man has got it. And now—you'd better be after him—half-an-hour's start to him is as good as a week's would be to you."

He drew the sheet over the dead face and strode out, and Ayscough followed, angry, mystified, and by no means convinced.

"Look here!" he said, as they reached the ante-room; "that's all very well, Dr. Mirandolet, but it's only supposition on your part!"

"Supposition that you'll find to be absolute truth, my good friend!" retorted Mirandolet, calmly. "I know the Chinese—better than you think. As soon as I heard of this affair tonight, I came to you to put you up to the Chinese trick of secreting things of value in their pigtails—it did not occur to me that the diamond might be there in this case, but I thought you would probably find something. But when we reached this mortuary, and I heard that a Japanese had been here, presenting your card when he had no business to present it, I guessed immediately what had happened—and now that you tell me that you told him all about this affair, well—I am certain of my assertion. Mr. Detective—go after the diamond!"

He turned as if to leave the place, and Ayscough followed.

"He mayn't been after the diamond at all!" he said, still resentful and incredulous. "Is it very likely he'd think it to be in that dead chap's pigtail when the other man's missing? It's Chang that's got that diamond—not Chen."

"All right, my friend!" replied Mirandolet. "Your wisdom is superior to mine, no doubt. So—I wish you good-night!"

He strode out of the place and turned sharply up the street, and Ayscough, after a growl or two, went back to the mortuary keeper.

"How long was that Jap in there?" he asked, nodding at the death chamber.

"Not a minute, Mr. Ayscough!" replied the man. "In and out again, as you might say."

"Did he say anything when he came out?" enquired the detective.

"He did—two words," answered the keeper. "He said, 'That's he!' and walked straight out, and into his car."

"And when he came he told you I'd sent him?" demanded Ayscough.

"Just that—and showed me your card," assented the man. "Of course, I'd no reason to doubt his word."

"Look here, George!" said Ayscough, "you keep this to yourself! Don't say anything to any of our folks if they come in. I don't half believe what that doctor said just now—but I'll make an enquiry or two. Mum's the word, meanwhile. You understand, George?"

George answered that he understood very well, and Ayscough presently left him. Outside, in the light of the lamp set over the entrance to the mortuary, he pulled out his watch. Twelve o'clock—midnight. And somewhere, that cursed young Jap was fleeing away through the London streets—having cheated him, Ayscough, at his own game!

He had already reckoned things up in connection with Yada. Yada had been having him—even as Melky Rubinstein had suspected and suggested—all through that conversation at Gower Street. Probably, Yada, from his window in the drawing-room floor of his lodging-house, had watched him and Melky slip across the street and hide behind the hoarding opposite. And then Yada had gone out, knowing he was to be followed, and had tricked them beautifully, getting into an underground train going east, and, in all certainty, getting out again at the next station, chartering a cab, and returning west—with Ayscough's card in his pocket. But Ayscough knew one useful thing—he had memorized the letters and numbers of the taxi-cab in which Yada had sped by him and Mirandolet, L.C. 2571—he had kept repeating that over and over. Now he took out his note-book and jotted it down—and that done he set off to the police-station, intent first of all on getting in touch with New Scotland Yard by means of the telephone.

Ayscough, like most men of his calling in London, had a considerable amount of general knowledge of things and affairs, and he summoned it to his aid in this instance. He knew that if the Japanese really had become possessed of the orange and yellow diamond (of which supposition, in spite of Mirandolet's positive convictions, he was very sceptical) he would most certainly make for escape. He would be off to the Continent, hot foot. Now, Ayscough had a good acquaintance with the Continental train services—some hours must elapse before Yada could possibly get a train for Dover, or Folkstone, or Newhaven, or the shortest way across, or to any other ports such as Harwich or Southampton, by a longer route. Obviously, the first thing to do was to have the stations at Victoria, and Charing Cross, and Holborn Viaduct, and London Bridge carefully watched for Yada. And for two weary hours in the middle of the night he was continuously at work on the telephone, giving instructions and descriptions, and making arrangements to spread a net out of which the supposed fugitive could not escape.

And when all that was at last satisfactorily arranged, Ayscough was conscious that it might be for nothing. He might be on a wrong track altogether—due to the suspicions and assertions of that queer man, Mirandolet. There might be some mystery—in Ayscough's opinion there always was mystery wherever Chinese or Japanese or Hindus were concerned. Yada might have some good reason for wishing to see Chen Li's dead body, and have taken advantage of the detective's card to visit it. This extraordinary conduct might be explained. But meanwhile Ayscough could not afford to neglect a chance, and tired as he was, he set out to find the driver of the taxicab whose number he had carefully set down in his notebook.

There was little difficulty in this stage of the proceedings; it was merely a question of time, of visiting a central office and finding the man's name and address. By six o'clock in the morning Ayscough was at a small house in a shabby street in Kentish Town, interviewing a woman who had just risen to light her fire, and was surlily averse to calling up a husband, who, she said, had not been in bed until nearly four. She was not any more pleased when Ayscough informed her of his professional status—but the man was fetched down.

"You drove a foreigner—a Japanese—to the mortuary in Paddington last night?" said Ayscough, plunging straight into business, after telling the man who he was. "I saw him—just a glimpse of him—in your cab, and I took your number. Now, where did you first pick him up?"

"Outside the Underground, at King's Cross," replied the driver promptly.

This was precisely what Ayscough had expected; so far, so good; his own prescience was proving sure.

"Anything wrong, mister?" asked the driver.

"There may be," said Ayscough. "Well—you picked him up there, and drove him straight to the mortuary?"

"No—I didn't," said the man. "We made a call first. Euston. He went in there, and, I should say, went to the left luggage office, 'cause he came back again with a small suit-case—just a little 'un. Then we went on to that mortuary."

Euston! A small suit-case! More facts—Ayscough made notes of them.

"Well," he said, "and when you drove away from the mortuary, where did you go then?"

"Oxford Circus," answered the driver, "set him down—his orders—right opposite the Tube Station—t'other side of the street."

"Did you see which way he went—then?" enquired Ayscough.

"I did. Straight along Oxford Street—Tottenham Court Road way," said the driver, "carrying his suitcase—which it was, as I say, on'y a little 'un—and walking very fast. Last I see of him was that, guv'nor."

Ayscough went away and got back to more pretentious regions. He was dead tired and weary with his night's work, and glad to drop in at an early-opened coffee-shop and get some breakfast. While he ate and drank a boy came in with the first editions of the newspapers. Ayscough picked one up—and immediately saw staring headlines:—

**THE PADDINGTON MYSTERIES. NEW AND STARTLING FEATURES. DIAMOND WORTH £80,000 BEING LOOKED FOR MURDER IN MAIDA VALE**

Ayscough laid down the paper and smiled. Levendale—if not dead—could scarcely fail to see that!

**CHAPTER THIRTY-TWO**
**ONE O'CLOCK MIDNIGHT**

Five minutes after Ayscough had gone away with Dr. Mirandolet the hotel servant who had summoned him from Purdie's sitting-room knocked at the door for the second time and put a somewhat mystified face inside.

"Beg pardon, sir," he said, glancing at Purdie, who was questioning Melky Rubinstein as to the events of the evening in their relation to the house in Maida Vale. "Two ladies outside, sir—waiting to see you. But they don't want to come in, sir, unless they know who's here—don't want to meet no strangers, sir."

Purdie jumped to his feet, and putting the man aside looked into the dimly-lighted corridor. There, a few paces away, stood Zillah—and, half hidden by her, Mrs. Goldmark.

"Come in—come in!" he exclaimed. "Nobody here but Andie Lauriston and

Melky Rubinstein. You've something to tell—something's happened?"

He ushered them into the room, sent the hotel servant, obviously in a state of high curiosity about these happenings, away, and closed the door.

"S'elp me!" exclaimed Melky, "there ain't no other surprises, Zillah? You ain't come round at this time o' night for nothing! What you got to tell, Zillah?—another development?"

"Mrs. Goldmark has something to tell," answered Zillah. "We didn't know what to do, and you didn't come, Melky—nobody come—and so we locked the house and thought of Mr. Purdie. Mrs. Goldmark has seen somebody!"

"Who?" demanded Melky. "Somebody, now? What somebody?"

"The man that came to her restaurant," replied Zillah. "The man who lost the platinum solitaire!"

Mrs. Goldmark who had dropped into the chair which Purdie had drawn to the side of the table for her, wagged her head thoughtfully.

"This way it was, then," she said, with a dramatic suggestion of personal enjoyment in revealing a new feature of the mystery, "I have a friend who lives in Stanhope Street—Mrs. Isenberg. She sends to me at half-past-ten to tell me she is sick. I go to see her—immediate. I find her very poorly—so! I stop with her till past eleven, doing what I can. Then her sister, she comes—I can do no more—I come away. And I walk through Sussex Square, as my road back to Praed Street and Zillah. But before I am much across Sussex Square, I stop—sudden, like that! For what? Because—I see a man! That man! Him what drops his cuff-link on my table. Oh, yes!"

"You're sure it was that man, Mrs. Goldmark?" enquired Melky, anxiously. "You don't make no mistakes, so?"

"Do I mistake myself if I say I see you, Mr. Rubinstein?" exclaimed Mrs. Goldmark, solemnly and with emphasis. "No, I don't make no mistakes at all. Is there not gas lamps?—am I not blessed with good eyes? I see him—like as I see you there young gentleman and Zillah. Plain!"

"Well—and what was he doing?" asked Purdie, desirous of getting at facts. "Did he come out of a house, or go into one, or—what?"

"I tell you," replied Mrs. Goldmark, "everything I tell you—all in good time. It is like this. A taxicab comes up—approaching me. It stops—by the pavement. Two men—they get out. Him first. Then another. They pay the driver—then they walk on a little—just a few steps. They go into a house. The other man—he lets them into that house. With a latch-key. The door opens—shuts. They are inside. Then I go to Zillah and tell her what I see. So!"

The three young men exchanged glances, and Purdie turned to the informant.

"Mrs. Goldmark," he said, "did you know the man who opened the door?"

"Not from another!" replied Mrs. Goldmark. "A stranger to me!"

"Do you know Mr. Levendale—by sight?" asked Purdie.

"Often, since all this begins, I ask myself that question," said Mrs. Goldmark, "him being, so to speak, a neighbour. No, that I do not, not being able to say he was ever pointed out to me."

"Well, you can describe the man who pulled out his latch-key and opened the door, anyhow," remarked Purdie. "You took a good look at him, I suppose!"

"And a good one," answered Mrs. Goldmark. "He was one of our people—I saw his nose and his eyes. And I was astonished to see so poor-looking a man have a latch-key to so grand a mansion as that!—he was dressed in poor clothes, and looked dirty and mean."

"A bearded dark man?" suggested Purdie.

"Not at all," said Mrs. Goldmark. "A clean-shaved man—though dark he might be."

Purdie looked at Melky and shook his head.

"That's not Levendale!" he said, "Clean-shaven! Levendale's bearded and mustached—and I should say a bit vain of his beard. Um! you're dead certain, Mrs. Goldmark, about the other man?"

"As that I tell you this," insisted Mrs. Goldmark. "I see him as plain as what I see him when he calls at my establishment and leaves his jewellery on my table. Oh, yes—I don't make no mistake, Mr. Purdie."

Purdie looked again at Melky—this time with an enquiry in his glance.

"Don't ask me, Mr. Purdie!" said Melky. "I don't know what to say. Sounds like as if these two went into Levendale's house. But what man would have a latch-key to that but Levendale himself? More mystery!—ain't I full of it already? Now if Mr. Ayscough hadn't gone away—"

"Look here!" said Purdie, coming to a sudden decision, "I'm going round there. I want to know what this means—I'm going to know. You ladies had better go home. If you others like to come as far as the corner of Sussex Square, come. But I'm going to Levendale's house alone. I'll find something out."

He said no more until, Zillah and Mrs. Goldmark having gone homeward, and he and his two companions having reached a side street leading into Sussex Square, he suddenly paused and demanded their attention!

"I've particular reasons for wanting to go into that house alone," he said. "There's no danger—trust me. But—if I'm not out again in a quarter of an hour or so, you can come there and ask for me. My own impression is that I shall find Levendale there. And—as you're aware, Andie—I know Levendale." He left them standing in the shadow of a projecting portico and going up to Levendale's front door, rang the bell. There was no light in any of the windows; all appeared to be in dead stillness in the house; somewhere, far off in the interior, he heard the bell tinkle. And suddenly, as he stood waiting and listening, he heard a voice that sounded close by him and became aware that there was a small trap or grille in the door, behind which he made out a face.

"Who is that?" whispered the voice.

"John Purdie—wanting to see Mr. Levendale," he answered promptly.

The door was just as promptly opened, and as Purdie stepped within was as quickly closed behind him. At the same instant the click of a switch heralded a flood of electric light, and he started to see a man standing at his side—a man who gave him a queer, deprecating smile, a man who was not and yet who was Levendale.

"Gracious me!" exclaimed Purdie, "it isn't—"

"Yes!" said Levendale, quietly. "But it is, though! All right, Purdie—come this way."

Purdie followed Levendale into a small room on the right of the hall—a room in which the remains of a cold, evidently impromptu supper lay on a table lighted by a shaded lamp. Two men had been partaking of that supper, but Levendale was alone. He gave his visitor another queer smile, and pointed, first to a chair and then to a decanter.

"Sit down take a drink," he said. "This is a queer meeting! We haven't seen each other since—"

"Good God, man!" broke in Purdie, staring at his host. "What's it all mean? Are you—disguised?"

Levendale laughed—ruefully—and glanced at the mean garments which Mrs. Goldmark had spoken of.

"Necessity!" he said. "Had to! Ah!—I've been through some queer times—and in queer places. Look here—what do you know?"

"Know!" cried Purdie. "You want me to tell you all I know—in a sentence? Man!—it would take a month! What do you know? That's more like it!"

Levendale passed a hand across his forehead—there was a weariness in his gesture which showed his visitor that he was dead beat.

"Aye, just so!" he said. "But—tell me! has John Purvis come looking for his brother?"

"He has!" answered Purdie. "He's in London just now."

"Has he told about that diamond?—told the police?" demanded Levendale.

"He has!" repeated Purdie. "That's all known. Stephen Purvis—where is he?"

"Upstairs—asleep—dead tired out," said Levendale. "We both are! Night and day—day and night—I could fall on this floor and sleep—"

"You've been after that diamond?" suggested Purdie.

"That—and something else," said Levendale.

"Something else?" asked Purdie. "What then?"

"Eighty thousand pounds," answered Levendale. "Just that!"

Purdie stood staring at him. Then he suddenly put a question.

"Do you know who murdered that old man in Praed Street?" he demanded.

"That's what I'm after."

"No!" said Levendale, promptly. "I don't even know that he was murdered!" He, too, stared at his visitor for a moment; then "But I know more than a little about his being robbed," he added significantly.

Purdie shook his head. He was puzzled and mystified beyond measure.

"This is getting too deep for me!" he said. "You're the biggest mystery of all, Levendale. Look here!" he went on. "What are you going to do? This queer disappearance of yours—this being away—coming back without your beard and dressed like that!—aren't you going to explain? The police—"

"Yes!" said Levendale. "Ten o'clock this morning—the police-station. Be there—all of you—anybody—anybody who likes—I'm going to tell the police all I know. Purvis and I, we can't do any more—baffled, you understand! But now—go away, Purdie, and let me sleep—I'm dead done for!"

Within ten minutes of leaving them, Purdie was back with Lauriston and Melky Rubinstein, and motioning them away from Sussex Square.

"That's more extraordinary than the rest!" he said, as they all moved off. "Levendale's there, in his own house, right enough! And he's shaved off his beard and mustache, and he's wearing tramp's clothes and he and Stephen Purvis have been looking night and day, for that confounded diamond, and for eighty thousand pounds! And—what's more, Levendale does not know who killed Daniel Multenius or that he was murdered! But, by George, sirs!" he added, as high above their heads the clock of St. James's Church struck one, "he knows something big!—and we've got to wait nine hours to hear it!"

## CHAPTER THIRTY-THREE
## SECRET WORK

The inner room of the police-station, at ten o'clock that morning, was full of men. Purdie, coming there with Lauriston at five minutes before the hour, found Melky Rubinstein hanging about the outer door, and had only just time to warn his companion to keep silence as to their midnight discovery before Guyler and John Purvis drove up in one cab and Mr. Killick in another. Inside, Ayscough, refreshed by his breakfast and an hour's rest, was talking to the inspector and the man from New Scotland Yard—all these looked enquiringly at the group which presently crowded in on them.

"Any of you gentlemen got any fresh news?" demanded the inspector, as he ran his eye over the expectant faces "No?—well, I suppose you're all wanting to know if we have?" He glanced at Ayscough, who was pointing out certain paragraphs in one of the morning newspapers to the Scotland Yard man. "The fact is," he continued, "there have been queer developments since last night—and I don't exactly know where we are! My own opinion is that we'd better wait a few hours before saying anything more definite—to my mind, these newspapers are getting hold of too much news—giving information to the enemy, as it were. I think you'd all better leave things to us, gentlemen—for a while." There was rather more than a polite intimation in this that the presence of so many visitors was not wanted—but John Purvis at once assumed a determined attitude.

"I want to know exactly what's being done, and what's going to be done, about my brother!" he said. "I'm entitled to that! That's the job I came about—myself—as for the rest—"

"Your brother's here!" said Purdie, who was standing by the window and keeping an eye on the street outside. "And Mr. Levendale with him—hadn't you better have them straight in?" he went on, turning to the inspector. "They both look as if they'd things to tell."

But Ayscough had already made for the door and within a moment was ushering in the new arrivals. And Purdie was quick to note that the Levendale who entered, a sheaf of morning papers in his hand, was a vastly different Levendale to the man he had seen nine hours before, dirty, unkempt, and worn out with weariness. The trim beard and mustache were hopelessly lost, and there were lines on Levendale's face which they concealed, but Levendale himself was now smartly groomed and carefully dressed, and business-like, and it was with the air of a man who means business that he strode into the room and threw a calm nod to the officials.

"Now, Inspector," he said, going straight to the desk, while Stephen Purvis turned to his brother. "I see from the papers that you've all been much exercised about Mr. Purvis and myself—it just shows how a couple of men can disappear and give some trouble before they're found. But here we are!—and why we're here is because we're beaten—we took our own course in trying to find our own property—and we're done! We can do no more—and so we come to you."

"You should have come here at first, Mr. Levendale," said the Inspector, a little sourly. "You'd have saved a lot of trouble—to yourselves as well as to us. But that's neither here nor there—I suppose you've something to tell us, sir?"

"Before I tell you anything," replied Levendale, "I want to know something." He pointed to the morning papers which he had brought in. "These people," he said, "seem to have got hold of a lot of information—all got from you, of course. Now, we know what we're after—let's put it in a nutshell. A diamond—an orange-yellow diamond—worth eighty thousand pounds, the property of Mr. Stephen Purvis there. That's item one! But there's another. Eighty thousand pounds in bank-notes!—my property. Now—have any of you the least idea who's got the diamond and my money? Come!"

There was a moment's silence. Then Ayscough spoke.

"Not a definite idea, Mr. Levendale—as yet."

"Then I'll tell you," said Levendale. "A Chinese fellow—one Chang Li. He's got them—both! And Stephen Purvis and I have been after him for all the days and nights since we disappeared—and we're beaten! Now you'll have to take it up—and I'd better tell you the plain truth about what's no doubt seemed a queer business from the first. Half-an-hour's talk now will save hours of explanation later on. So listen to me, all of you—I already see two gentlemen here, Mr. Killick, and Mr. Guyler, who in a certain fashion, can corroborate some particulars that I shall give you. Keep us free from interruption, if you please, while I tell you my story."

Ayscough answered this request by going to the door and leaning against it, and Levendale took a chair by the side of the desk and looked round at an expectant audience.

"It's a queer and, in some respects, an involved story," he said, "but I shall contrive to make matters plain to you before I've finished. I shall have to go back a good many years—to a time when, as Mr. Killick there knows, I was a partner with Daniel Molteno in a jewellery business in the City. I left him, and went out to South Africa, where I engaged in diamond trading. I did unusually well in my various enterprises, and some years later I came back to London a very well-to-do man. Not long after my return, I met my former partner again. He had changed his name to Multenius, and was trading in Praed Street as a jeweller and pawnbroker. Now, I had no objection to carrying on a trade with certain business connections of mine at the Cape—and after some conversation with Multenius he and I arranged to buy and sell diamonds together here in London, and I at once paid over a sum of money to him as working capital. The transactions were carried out in his name. It was he, chiefly, who conducted them—he was as good and keen a judge of diamonds as any man I ever knew—and no one here was aware that I was concerned in them. I never went to his shop in Praed Street but twice—if it was absolutely necessary for him to see me, we met in the City, at a private office which I have there. Now you understand the exact relations between Daniel Multenius and myself. We were partners—in secret.

"We come, then, to recent events. Early in this present autumn, we heard from Mr. Stephen Purvis, with whom I had had some transactions in South Africa, that he had become possessed of a rare and fine orange-yellow diamond and that he was sending it to us. It arrived at Multenius's—Multenius brought it to me at my city office and we examined it, after which Multenius deposited it in his bank. We decided to buy it ourselves—I finding the money. We knew, from our messages from Stephen Purvis, that he would be in town on the 18th November, and we arranged everything for that date. That date, then, becomes of special importance—what happened at Multenius's shop in Praed Street on the afternoon of November 18th, between half-past four and half-past five is, of course, the thing that really is of importance. Now, what did happen? I can tell you—save as regards one detail which is, perhaps, of more importance than the other details. Of that detail I can't tell anything—but I can offer a good suggestion about it.

"Stephen Purvis was to call at Daniel Multenius's shop in Praed Street between five o'clock and half-past on the afternoon of November 18th—to complete the sale of his diamond. About noon on that day, Daniel Multenius went to the City. He went to his bank and took the diamond away. He then proceeded to my office, where I handed him eighty thousand pounds in bank notes—notes of large amounts. With the diamond and these notes in his possession, Daniel Multenius went back to Praed Street. I was to join him there shortly after five o'clock.

"Now we come to my movements. I lunched in the City, and afterwards went to a certain well-known book-seller's in Holborn, who had written to tell me that he had for sale a valuable book which he knew I wanted. I have been a collector of rare books ever since I came back to England. I spent an hour or so at the book-seller's shop. I bought the book which I had gone to see—paying a very heavy price for it. I carried it away in my hand, not wrapped up, and got into an omnibus which was going my way, and rode in it as far as the end of Praed Street. There I got out. And—in spite of what I said in my advertisement in the newspapers of the following morning,—I had the book in my hand when I left the omnibus. Why I pretended to have lost it, why I inserted that advertisement in the papers, I shall tell you presently—that was all part of a game which was forced upon me.

"It was, as near as I can remember, past five o'clock when I turned along Praed Street. The darkness was coming on, and there was a slight rain falling, and a tendency to fog. However, I noticed something—I am naturally very quick of observation. As I passed the end of the street which goes round the back of the Grand Junction Canal basin, the street called Iron Gate Wharf, I saw turn into it, walking very quickly, a Chinaman whom I knew to be one of the two Chinese medical students to whom Daniel Multenius had let a furnished house in Maida Vale. He had his back to me—I did not know which of the two he was. I thought nothing of the matter, and went on. In another minute I was at the pawn-shop. I opened the door, walked in, and went straight to the little parlour—I had been there just twice before when Daniel Multenius was alone, and so I knew my way. I went, I say, straight through—and in the parlour doorway ran into Stephen Purvis.

"Purvis was excited—trembling, big fellow though he is, do you see? He will bear me out as to what was said—and done. Without a word, he turned and pointed to where Daniel Multenius was lying across the floor—dead. 'I haven't been here a minute!' said Purvis. 'I came in—found him, like that! There's nobody here. For God's sake, where's my diamond?'

"Now, I was quick to think. I formed an impression within five seconds. That Chinaman had called—found the old man lying in a fit, or possibly dead—had seen, as was likely, the diamond on the table in the parlour, the wad of bank-notes lying near, had grabbed the lot—and gone away. It was a theory—and I am confident yet that it was the correct one. And I tell you plainly that my concern from that instant was not with Daniel Multenius, but with the Chinaman! I thought and acted like lightning. First, I hastily examined Multenius, felt in his pockets, found that there was nothing there that I wanted and that he was dead. Then I remembered that on a previous visit of mine he had let me out of his house by a door at the rear which communicated with a narrow passage running into Market Street, and without a second's delay, I seized Purvis by the arm and hurried him out. It was dark enough in that passage—there was not a soul about—we crossed Market Street, turned to the right, and were in Oxford and Cambridge Terrace before we paused. My instinct told me that the right thing to do was to get away from that parlour. And it was not until we were quite away from it that I realized that I had left my book behind me!"

## CHAPTER THIRTY-FOUR
## BAFFLED

Levendale paused at this point of his story, and looked round the circle of attentive faces. He was quick to notice that two men were watching him with particularly close attention—one was Ayscough, the other, the old solicitor. And as he resumed his account he glanced meaningly at Mr. Killick.

"I daresay some of you would like to question me—and Stephen Purvis, too—on what I've already told you?" he said. "You're welcome to ask any questions you like—any of you—when I've done. But—let me finish—for then perhaps you'll fully understand what we were at.

"Purvis and I walked up and down in Oxford and Cambridge Terrace for some time—discussing the situation. The more I considered the matter, the more I was certain that my first theory was right—the Chinaman had got the diamond and the bank-notes. I was aware of these two Chinamen as tenants of Multenius's furnished house—as a matter of fact, I had been present, at the shop in Praed Street, on one of my two visits there when they concluded their arrangements with him. What I now thought was this—one of them had called on the old man to do some business, or to pay the rent, and had found him in a fit, or dead, as the result of one, had seen the diamond and the money on the table, placed there in readiness for Purvis's coming, and had possessed himself of both and made off.

Purvis agreed with me. And—both Purvis and myself are well acquainted with the characteristic peculiarities, and idiosyncrasies of Chinamen!—we knew with what we had to deal. Therefore we knew what we had to do. We wanted the diamond and my money. And since we were uncomfortably aware of the craft and subtlety of the thief who'd got both we knew we should have to use craft ourselves—and of no common sort. Therefore we decided that the very last thing we should think of would be an immediate appeal to the police.

"Now, you police officials may, nay, will!—say that we ought to have gone straight to you, especially as this was a case of murder. But we knew nothing about it being a case of murder. We had seen no signs of violence on the old man—I knew him to be very feeble, and I believed he had been suddenly struck over by paralysis, or something of that sort. I reckoned matters up, carefully. It was plain that Daniel Multenius had been left alone in house and shop—that his granddaughter was out on some errand or other. Therefore, no one knew of the diamond and the money. We did not want any one to know. If we had gone to the police and told our tale, the news would have spread, and would certainly have reached the Chinaman's ears. We knew well enough that if we were to get our property back the thief must not be alarmed—there must be nothing in the newspapers next morning. The Chinaman must not know that the real owners of the diamond and the bank-notes suspected him—he must not know that information about his booty was likely to be given to the police. He must be left to believe—for some hours at any rate—that what he had possessed himself of was the property of a dead man who could not tell anything. But there was my book in that dead man's parlour! It was impossible to go back and fetch it. It was equally impossible that it should not attract attention. Daniel Multenius's granddaughter, whom I believed to be a very sharp young woman, would notice it, and would know that it had come into the place during her absence. I thought hard over that problem—and finally I drafted an advertisement and sent it off to an agency with instructions to insert it in every morning newspaper in London next day. Why? Because I wanted to draw a red herring across the trail!—I wanted, for the time being, to set up a theory that some man or other had found that book in the omnibus, had called in at Multenius's to sell or pawn it, had found the old man alone, and had assaulted and robbed him. All this was with a view to hoodwinking the Chinaman. Anything must be done, anything!—to keep him ignorant that Purvis and I knew the real truth.

"But—what did we intend to do? I tell you, not being aware that old Daniel Multenius had met his death by violence, we did not give one second's thought to that aspect and side of the affair—we concentrated on the recovery of our property. I knew the house in which these Chinese lived. That evening, Purvis and I went there. We have both been accustomed, in our time, to various secret dealings and manoeuvres, and we entered the grounds of that house without any one being the wiser. It did not take long to convince us that the house was empty. It remained empty that night—Purvis kept guard over it, in an outhouse in the garden. No one either entered or left it between our going to it and Purvis coming away from it next morning—he stayed there, watching until it was time to keep an appointment with me in Hyde Park. Before I met him, I had been called upon by Detective Ayscough, Mr. Rubinstein, and Mr. Lauriston—they know what I said to them. I could not at that time say anything else—I had my own concerns to think of.

"When Purvis and I met we had another consultation, and we determined, in view of all the revelations which had come out and had been published in the papers, that the suspicion cast on young Mr. Lauriston was the very best thing that could happen for us; it would reassure our Chinaman. And we made up our minds that the house in Maida Vale would not be found untenanted that night, and we arranged to meet there at eleven o'clock. We felt so sure that our man would have read all the news in the papers, and would feel safe, and that we should find him. But, mark you, we had no idea as to which of the two Chinamen it was that we wanted. Of one fact, however, we were certain—whichever it was that I had seen slip round the corner of Iron Gate Wharf the previous day, whether it was Chang Li or Chen Li, he would have kept his secret to himself! The thing was—to get into that house; to get into conversation with both; to decide which was the guilty man, and then—to take our own course. We knew what to do—and we went fully prepared.

"Now we come to this—our second visit to the house in Maida Vale. To be exact, it was between eleven and twelve on the second night after the disappearance of the diamond. As on the previous night, we gained access to the garden by the door at the back—that, on each occasion, was unfastened, while the gate giving access to the road in Maida Vale was securely locked. And, as on the previous night, we quickly found that up to then at any rate, the house was empty. But not so the garden! While I was looking round the further side of the house, Purvis took a careful look round the garden. And presently he came to me and drew away to the asphalted path which runs from the front gate to the front door. The moon had risen above the houses and trees—and in its light he pointed to bloodstains. It did not take a second look, gentlemen, to see that they were recent—in fact, fresh. Somebody had been murdered in that garden not many minutes—literally, minutes!—before our arrival. And within two minutes more we found the murdered man lying behind some shrubbery on the left of the path. I knew him for the younger of the two Chinese—the man called Chen Li.

"This discovery, of course, made us aware that we were now face to face with a new development. We were not long in arriving at a conclusion about that. Chang Li had found out that his friend had become possessed of these valuable—he might have discovered the matter of the diamond, or of the bank-notes or both—how was immaterial. But we were convinced, putting everything together, that he had made this discovery, had probably laid in wait for Chen Li as he returned home that night, had run a knife into him as he went up the garden, had dragged the body into the shrubbery, possessed himself of the loot, and made off. And now we were face to face with what was going, as we knew, to be the stiffest part of our work—the finding of Chang Li. We set to work on that without a moment's delay.

"I have told you that Purvis and I have a pretty accurate knowledge of Chinamen; we have both had deep and intimate experience of them and their ways. I, personally, know a good deal of the Chinese Colony in London: I have done business with Chinamen, both in London and South Africa, for years. I had a good idea of what Chang Li's procedure would be. He would hide—if need be, for months, until the first heat of the hue and cry which he knew would be sure to be raised, would have cooled down. There are several underground warrens—so to speak—in the East End, in which he could go to earth, comfortably and safely, until there was a chance of slipping out of the country unobserved. I know already of some of them. I would get to know of others.

"Purvis and I got on that track—such as it was, at once. We went along to the East End there and then—before morning I had shaved off my beard and mustache, disguised myself in old clothes, and was beginning my work. First thing next morning I did two things—one was to cause a telegram to be sent from Spring Street to my butler explaining my probable absence; the other to secretly warn the Bank of England about the bank-notes. But I had no expectation that Chang Li would try to negotiate those—all his energies, I knew, would be concentrated on the diamond. Nevertheless, he might try—and would, if he tried—succeed—in changing one note, and it was as well to take that precaution.

"Now then, next day, Purvis and I being, in our different ways, at work in the East End, we heard the news about the Praed Street tradesman, Parslett. That seemed to me remarkable proof of my theory. As the successive editions of the newspapers came out during that day, and next day, we learnt all about the Parslett affair. I saw through it at once. Parslett, being next-door neighbour to Daniel Multenius, had probably seen Chen Li—whom we now believed to have been the actual thief—slip away from Multenius's door, and, when the news of Daniel's death came out, had put two and two together, and, knowing where the Chinamen lived, had gone to the house in Maida Vale to blackmail them. I guessed what had happened then—Parslett, to quieten him for the moment, had been put off with fifty pounds in gold, and promised more—and he had also been skilfully poisoned in such a fashion that he would get safely away from the premises but die before he got home. And when he was safe away, Chang Li had murdered Chen Li, and made off. So—as I still think—all our theories were correct, and the only thing to do was to find Chang."

But here Levendale paused, glanced at Stephen Purvis, and spread out his hands with a gesture which indicated failure and disappointment. His glance moved from Stephen Purvis to the police officials.

"All no good!" he exclaimed. "It's useless to deny it. I have been in every Chinese den and haunt in East London—I'm certain that Chang Li is nowhere down there. I have spent money like water—employed Chinese and Easterns on whom I could depend—there isn't a trace of him! And so—we gave up last night. Purvis and I—baffled. We've come to you police people—"

"You should have done that before, Mr. Levendale," said the Inspector severely. "You haven't given us much credit, I think, and if you'd told all this at first—"

Before the Inspector could say more, a constable tapped at the door and put his head into the room. His eyes sought Ayscough.

"There's a young gentleman—foreigner—asking for you, Mr. Ayscough," he said. "Wants to see you at once—name of Mr. Yada."

## CHAPTER THIRTY-FIVE
## YADA TAKES CHARGE

Ayscough had only time to give a warning look and a word to the others before Mr. Mori Yada was ushered in. Every eye was turned on him as he entered—some of the men present looking at him with wonder, some with curiosity, two, at any rate—Levendale and Stephen Purvis—with doubt. But Yada himself was to all outward appearance utterly indifferent to the glances thrown in his direction: it seemed to John Purdie, who was remembering all he had heard the night before, that the young Japanese medical student was a singularly cool and self-possessed hand. Yada, indeed, might have been walking in on an assemblage of personal friends, specially gathered together in his honour. Melky Rubinstein, who was also watching him closely, noticed at once that he had evidently made a very careful toilet that morning. Yada's dark overcoat, thrown negligently open, revealed a smart grey lounge suit; in one gloved hand he carried a new bowler hat, in the other a carefully rolled umbrella. He looked as prosperous and as severely in mode as if no mysteries and underground affairs had power to touch him, and the ready smile with which he greeted Ayscough was ingenuous and candid enough to disarm the most suspicious.

"Good morning, Mr. Detective," he began, as he crossed the threshold and looked first at Ayscough and then at the ring of attentive faces. "I want to speak to you on that little affair of last night, you know. I suppose you are discussing it with these gentlemen? Well, perhaps I can now give you some information that will be useful."

"Glad to hear anything, Mr. Yada," said Ayscough, who was striving hard to conceal his surprise. "Anything that you can tell us. You've heard something during the night, then?"

Yada laughed pleasantly, showing his white teeth. He dropped into the chair which Ayscough pushed forward, and slowly drew off his gloves.

"I assured myself of something last night—after you left me," he said, with a knowing look. "I used your card to advantage, Mr. Detective. I went to the mortuary."

Ayscough contrived to signal to the Inspector to leave the talking to him. He put his thumbs in the armholes of his waistcoat, assumed an easy attitude as he leaned against the door, and looked speculatively at the new comer.

"Aye?—and what made you do that now, Mr. Yada?" he asked, half-carelessly. "A bit of curiosity, eh?"

"Not idle curiosity, Mr. Detective," replied Yada. "I wanted to know, to make certain, which of the two Chinamen it really was who was there—dead. I saw him. Now I know. Chen Li!"

"Well?" said Ayscough.

Yada suddenly twisted round in his chair, and slowly glanced at the listening men on either side of the desk. They were cool, bold, half-insolent eyes which received face after face, showing no recognition of any until they encountered Melky Rubinstein's watchful countenance. And to Melky, Yada accorded a slight nod—and turned to Ayscough again.

"Which," he asked calmly, "which of these gentlemen is the owner of the diamond? Which is the one who has lost eighty thousand pounds in bank-notes? That is what I want to know before I say more."

In the silence which followed upon Ayscough's obvious doubt about answering this direct question, Levendale let out a sharp, half-irritable exclamation:

"In God's name!" he said, "who is this young man? What does he know about the diamond and the money?"

Yada turned and faced his questioner—and suddenly smiling, thrust his hand in his breast pocket and drew out a card-case. With a polite bow he handed a card in Levendale's direction.

"Permit me, sir," he said suavely. "My card. As for the rest, perhaps Mr. Detective here will tell you."

"It's this way, you see, Mr. Levendale," remarked Ayscough. "Acting on information received from Dr. Pittery, one of the junior house-surgeons at University College Hospital, who told me that Mr. Yada was a fellow-student of those two Chinese, and a bit of a friend of theirs, I called on Mr. Yada last night to make enquiries. And of course I had to tell him about the missing property—though to be sure, that's news that's common to everybody now—through the papers. And—what else have you to tell, Mr. Yada?"

But Yada was watching Levendale—who, on his part, was just as narrowly watching Yada. The other men in the room watched these two—recognizing, as if by instinct, that from that moment matters lay between Levendale and Yada, and not between Yada and Ayscough. They were mutually inspecting and appraising each other, and in spite of their impassive faces, it was plain that each was wondering about his next move.

It was Levendale who spoke first—spoke as if he and the young Japanese were the only people in the room, as if nothing else mattered. He bent forward to Yada.

"How much do you know?" he demanded.

Yada showed his white teeth again.

"A plain—and a wide question, Mr. Levendale!" he answered, with a laugh. "I see that you are anxious to enlist my services. Evidently, you believe that I do know something. But—you are not the owner of the diamond! Which of these gentlemen is?"

Levendale made a half impatient gesture towards Stephen Purvis, who nodded at Yada but remained silent.

"He is!" said Levendale, testily. "But you—can do your talking to me. Again—how much do you know in this matter?"

"Enough to make it worth your while to negotiate with me," answered Yada. "Is that as plain as your question?"

"It's what I expected," said Levendale. "You want to sell your knowledge."

"Well?" assented Yada, "I am very sure you are willing to purchase."

Once more that duel of the eyes—and to John Purdie, who prided himself on being a judge of expressions, it was evident that the younger man was more than the equal of the older. It was Levendale who gave way—and when he took his eyes off Yada, it was to turn to Stephen Purvis.

Stephen Purvis nodded his head once more—and growled a little.

"Make terms with him!" he muttered. "Case of have to, I reckon!"

Levendale turned once more to the Japanese, who smiled on him.

"Look you here, Mr. Yada," said Levendale, "I don't know who you are beyond what I'm told—your card tells me nothing except that you live—lodge, I suppose—in Gower Street. You've got mixed up in this, somehow, and you've got knowledge to dispose of. Now, I don't buy unless I know first what it is I'm buying. So—let's know what you've got to sell?"

Yada swept the room with a glance.

"Before these gentlemen?" he asked. "In open market, eh?"

"They're all either police, or detectives, or concerned," retorted Levendale. "There's no secret. I repeat—what have you got to sell? Specify it!"

Yada lifted his hands and began to check off points on the tips of his fingers.

"Three items, then, Mr. Levendale," he replied cheerfully. "First—the knowledge of who has got the diamond and the money. Second—the knowledge of where he is at this moment, and will be for some hours. Third—the knowledge of how you can successfully take him and recover your property. Three good, saleable items, I think—yes?"

Purdie watched carefully for some sign of greed or avarice in the informer's wily countenance. To his surprise, he saw none. Instead, Yada assumed an almost sanctimonious air. He seemed to consider matters—though his answer was speedy.

"I don't want to profit—unduly—by this affair," he said. "At the same time, from all I've heard, I'm rendering you and your friend a very important service, and I think it only fair that I should be remunerated. Give me something towards the expenses of my medical education, Mr. Levendale: give me five hundred pounds."

With the briefest exchange of glances with Stephen Purvis, Levendale pulled out a cheque-book, dashed off a cash cheque, and handed it over to the Japanese, who slipped it into his waistcoat pocket.

"Now—your information!" said Levendale.

"To be sure," replied Yada. "Very well. Chang Li has the diamond and the money. And he is at this moment where he has been for some days, in hiding. He is in a secret room at a place called Pilmansey's Tea Rooms, in Tottenham Court Road—a place much frequented by medical students from our college. The fact of the case is, Mr. Policeman, and the rest of you generally, there is a secret opium den at Pilmansey's, though nobody knows of it but a few frequenters. And there!—there you will find Chang Li."

"You've seen him there?" demanded Levendale.

"I saw him there during last night—I know him to be there—he will be there, either until you take him, or until his arrangements are made for getting out of this country," answered Yada.

Levendale jumped up, as if for instant action. But the Inspector quietly tapped him on the elbow.

"He promised to tell you how to take him, Mr. Levendale," he said. "Let's know all we can—we shall have to be in with you on this, you know."

"Mr. Police-Inspector is right," said Yada. "You will have to conduct what you call a raid. Now, do precisely what I tell you to do. Pilmansey's is an old-fashioned place, a very old house as regards its architecture, on the right-hand side of Tottenham Court Road. Go there today—this midday—a little before one—when there are always plenty of customers. Go with plenty of your plain-clothes men, like Mr. Ayscough there. Drop in, don't you see, as if you were customers—let there be plenty of you, I repeat. There are two Pilmanseys—men—middle-aged, sly, smooth, crafty men. When you are all there, take your own lines—close the place, the doors, if you like—but get hold of the Pilmansey men, tell them you are police, insist on being taken to the top floor and shown their opium den. They will object, they will lie, they will resist—you will use your own methods. But—in that opium den you will find Chang Li—and your property!"

He had been drawing on his gloves as he spoke, and now, picking up his hat and umbrella, Yada bowed politely to the circle and moved to the door.

"You will excuse me, now?" he said. "I have an important lecture at the medical school which I must not miss. I shall be at Pilmansey's, myself, a little before one—please oblige me by not taking any notice of me. I do not want to figure—actively—in your business."

Then he was gone—and the rest of them were so deeply taken with the news which he had communicated that no one noticed that just before Yada fastened his last glove-button, Melky Rubinstein slipped from his corner and glided quietly out of the room.

## CHAPTER THIRTY-SIX
## PILMANSEY'S TEA ROOMS

Two hours later, it being then a quarter-to-one o'clock, Purdie and Lauriston got out of a taxi-cab at the north-end of Tottenham Court Road and walked down the right-hand side of that busy thoroughfare, keeping apparently careless but really vigilant eyes open for a first glimpse of the appointed rendezvous. But Pilmansey's Tea Rooms required little searching out. In the midst of the big modern warehouses, chiefly given up to furniture and upholstery, there stood at that time a block of old property which was ancient even for London. The buildings were plainly early eighteenth century: old redbrick erections with narrow windows in the fronts and dormer windows in the high, sloping roofs. Some of them were already doomed to immediate dismantlement; the tenants had cleared out, there were hoardings raised to protect passers-by from falling masonry, and bills and posters on the threatened walls announced that during the rebuilding, business would be carried on as usual at some other specified address. But Pilmansey's, so far, remained untouched, and the two searchers saw that customers were going in and out, all unaware that before evening their favourite resort for a light mid-day meal would attain a fame and notoriety not at all promised by its very ordinary and commonplace exterior.

"An excellent example of the truth of the old saying that you should never judge by appearances, Andie, my man!" remarked Purdie, as they took a quick view of the place. "Who'd imagine that crime, dark secrets, and all the rest of it lies concealed behind this?—behind the promise of tea and muffins, milk and buns! It's a queer world, this London!—you never know what lies behind any single bit of the whole microcosm. But let's see what's to be seen inside."

The first thing to be seen inside the ground floor room into which they stepped was the man from New Scotland Yard, who, in company with another very ordinary-looking individual was seated at a little table just inside the entrance, leisurely consuming coffee and beef sandwiches. He glanced at the two men as if he had never seen them in his life, and they, preserving equally stolid expressions with credit if not with the detective's ready and trained ability, passed further on—only to recognize Levendale and Stephen Purvis, who had found accommodation in a quiet corner half-way down the room. They, too, showed no signs of recognition, and Purdie, passing by them, steered his companion to an unoccupied table and bade him be seated.

"Let's get our bearings," he whispered as they dropped into their seats. "Looks as innocent and commonplace within as it appeared without, Andie. But use your eyes—it ought to make good copy for you, this."

Lauriston glanced about him. The room in which they sat was a long, low-ceiling apartment, extending from the street door to a sort of bar-counter at the rear, beyond which was a smaller room that was evidently given up to store and serving purposes. On the counter were set out provisions—rounds of beef, hams, tongues, bread, cakes, confectionery; behind it stood two men whom the watchers at once set down as the proprietors. Young women, neatly gowned in black and wearing white caps and aprons, flitted to and fro between the counter and the customers. As for the customers they were of both sexes, and the larger proportion of them young. There was apparently no objection to smoking at Pilmansey's—a huge cloud of blue smoke ascended from many cigarettes, and the scent of Turkish tobacco mingled with the fragrance of freshly-ground coffee. It was plain that Pilmansey's was the sort of place wherein you could get a good sandwich, good tea or coffee, smoke a cigarette or two, and idle away an hour in light chatter with your friends between your morning and afternoon labours.

But Lauriston's attention was mainly directed to the two men who stood behind the bar-counter, superintending and directing their neat assistants. Sly, smooth, crafty men—so they had been described by Mr. Mori Yada: Lauriston's opinion coincided with that of the Japanese, on first, outer evidence and impression. They were middle-aged, plump men who might be, and probably were, twins, favouring mutton chop whiskers, and good linen and black neckcloths—they might have been strong, highly-respectable butlers. Each had his coat off; each wore a spotless linen apron; each wielded carving knives and forks; each was busy in carving plates of ham or tongue or beef; each contrived, while thus engaged, to keep his sharp, beady eyes on the doings in the room in front of the counter. Evidently a well-to-do, old-established business, this, and highly prosperous men who owned it: Lauriston wondered that they should run any risks by hiding away a secret opium den somewhere on their ancient premises.

In the midst of their reflections one of the waitresses came to the table at which the two friends sat: Lauriston quicker of wit than Purdie in such matters immediately ordered coffee and sandwiches and until they came, lighted a cigarette and pretended to be at ease, though he was inwardly highly excited.

"It's as if one were waiting for an explosion to take place!" he muttered to Purdie. "Even now I don't know what's going to happen."

"Here's Ayscough, anyway," said Purdie. "He looks as if nothing was about to happen."

Ayscough, another man with him, was making his way unconcernedly down the shop. He passed the man from New Scotland Yard without so much as a wink: he ignored Levendale and Stephen Purvis; he stared blankly at Purdie and Lauriston, and led his companion to two vacant seats near the counter. And they had only just dropped into them when in came Mr. Killick, with John Purvis and Guyler and slipped quietly into seats in the middle of the room. Here then, said Lauriston to himself, were eleven men, all in a secret—and there were doubtless others amongst the company whom he did not know.

"But where's Melky Rubinstein?" he whispered suddenly. "I should have thought he'd have turned up—he's been so keen on finding things out."

"There's time enough yet," answered Purdie. "It's not one. I don't see the Jap, either. But—here's the Inspector—done up in plain clothes."

The Inspector came in with a man whom neither Purdie nor Lauriston had ever seen before—a quietly but well-dressed man about whom there was a distinct air of authority. They walked down the room to a table near the counter, ordered coffee and lighted cigarettes—and the two young Scotsmen, watching them closely, saw that they took a careful look round as if to ascertain the strength of their forces. And suddenly, as Lauriston was eating his second sandwich, the Inspector rose, quietly walked to the counter and bending over it, spoke to one of the white-aproned men behind.

"The game's begun!" whispered Lauriston. "Look!"

But Purdie's eyes were already fixed on the Pilmanseys, whom he recognized as important actors in the drama about to be played. One of them slightly taller, slightly greyer than the other, was leaning forward to the Inspector, and was evidently amazed at what was being said to him, for he started, glanced questioningly at his visitor, exchanged a hurried word or two with him and then turned to his brother. A second later, both men laid down their great knives and forks, left their counter, and beckoned the Inspector to follow them into a room at the rear of the shop. And the Inspector in his turn, beckoned Ayscough with a mere glance, and Ayscough in his, made an inviting movement to the rest of the party.

"Come on!" said Purdie. "Let's hear what's happening."

The proprietors of the tea-rooms had led the Inspector and the man who was with him into what was evidently a private room—and when Lauriston and Purdie reached the door they were standing on the hearth rug, side by side, each in a very evident state of amazement, staring at a document which the Inspector was displaying to them. They looked up from it to glance with annoyance, at the other men who came quietly and expectantly crowding into the room.

"More of your people?" asked the elder man, querulously. "Look here, you know!—we don't see the need for all this fuss, not for your interrupting our business in this way! One or two of you, surely, would have been enough without bringing a troop of people on to our premises—all this is unnecessary!"
"You'll allow us to be the best judge of what's necessary and what isn't, Mr. Pilmansey," retorted the Inspector. "There'll be no fuss, no bother—needn't be, anyway, if you tell us what we want to know, and don't oppose us in what we've got power to do. Here's a warrant—granted on certain information—to search your premises. If you'll let us do that quietly."
"But for what reason?" demanded the younger man. "Our premises, indeed! Been established here a good hundred years, and never a word against us. What do you want to search for?"
"I'll tell you that at once," answered the Inspector. "We want a young Chinaman, one Chang Li, who, we are informed, is concealed here, and has valuable stolen property on him. Now, then, do you know anything about him? Is he here?"
The two men exchanged glances. For a moment they remained silent—then the elder man spoke, running his eye over the expectant faces watching him.
"Before I say any more," he answered, "I should just like to know where you got your information from?"
"No!" replied the Inspector, firmly. "I shan't tell you. But I'll tell you this much—this Chang Li is wanted on a very serious charge as it is, and we may charge him with something much more serious. We've positive information that he's here—and I'm only giving you sound advice when I say that if he is here, you'll do well to show us where he is. Now, come, Mr. Pilmansey, is he here?"
The elder Pilmansey shook his head—but the shake was more one of doubt than of denial.
"I can't say," he answered. "He might be."
"What's that mean?" demanded the Inspector. "Might be? Surely you know who's in your own house!"
"No!" said the elder man, "I can't say. It's this way—we've a certain number of foreigners come here. There are few—just a few—Chinese and Japanese—medical students, you know. Now, some time ago—a couple of years ago—some of them asked us if we couldn't let them have three or four rooms at the top of the house in which to start a sort of little club of their own, so that they could have a place for their meetings, you

understand. They were all quiet, very respectable young fellows—so we did. They have the top floor of this house. They furnished and fitted it up themselves. There's a separate entrance—at the side of the shop. Each of them has a latch-key of his own. So they can go in and out as they like—they never bother us. But, as a matter of fact, there are only four or five of them who are members now—the others have all left. That's the real truth—and I tell you I don't know if Mr. Chang Li might be up there or not. We know nothing about what they do in their rooms—they're only our tenants."

"Let me ask you one question," said the Inspector, "Have either of you ever been in those rooms since you let them to these people!"

"No!" answered the elder man. "Neither of us—at anytime!"

"Then," commanded the Inspector, "I'll thank you to come up with us to them—now!"

## CHAPTER THIRTY-SEVEN
## CHANG LI

Not without some grumbling as to waste of time and interference with business, the Pilmansey brothers led the way to a side door which opened into a passage that ran along the side of the shop and from whence a staircase rose to the upper regions of the house. The elder pointed, significantly, to the street door at the end.

"You'll take notice that these young fellows I told you of get to the rooms we let them through that?" he observed. "That door's always locked—they all have latch-keys to it. They never come through the shop—we've nothing to do with them, and we don't know anything about whatever they may do in their rooms—all we're concerned with is that they pay their rent and behave themselves. And quiet enough they've always been—we've had no reason to complain."

"And, as they all have latch-keys, I suppose they can get into the place at any hour of the day—or night?" suggested the Inspector. "There's no bar against them coming here at night?"

"They can come in—and go out—whenever they please," answered the elder man. "I tell you we've nothing to do with them—except as their landlords."

"Where do you live—yourselves?" asked the Inspector. "On these premises?"

"No, we don't," replied the younger brother, who, of the two, had showed the keenest, if most silent, resentment at the police proceedings. "We live—elsewhere. This establishment is opened at eight in the morning, and closed at seven in the evening. We're never here after seven—either of us."

"So that you never see anything of these foreigners at night-time?" asked the Inspector. "Don't know what they do, I suppose?"

"We never see anything of 'em at any time," said the elder brother. "As you see, this passage and staircase is outside the shop. We know nothing whatever about them beyond what I've told you."

"Well—take us up, and we'll see what we can find out," commanded the Inspector. "We're going to examine those rooms, Mr. Pilmansey, so we'll get it done at once."

The intervening rooms between the lower and the top floors of the old house appeared to be given up to stores—the open doors revealed casks, cases, barrels, piles of biscuit and confectionery boxes—nothing to conceal there, decided the lynx-eyed men who trooped up the dingy stairs after the grumbling proprietors. But the door on the top floor was closed—and when Ayscough turned its handle he found it to be locked from within.

"They've keys of their own for that, too," remarked the younger Pilmansey. "I don't see how you're going to get in, if there's nobody inside."

"We're going in there whether there's anybody or not," said the Inspector. "Knock, Ayscough!—knock loudly!"

The group of men gathered behind the leaders, and filling the whole of the lobby outside the closed door, waited, expectant and excited, in the silence which followed on Ayscough's loud beating on the upper panel. A couple of minutes went by: the detective knocked again, more insistently. And suddenly, and silently, the door was opened—first, an inch or two, then a little wider, and as Ayscough slipped a stoutly booted foot inside the crack a yellow face, lighted by a pair of narrow-slitted dark eyes, looked out—and immediately vanished.

"In with you!" said the Inspector. "Careful, now!"

Ayscough pushed the door open and walked in, the rest crowding on his heels. And Purdie, who was one of the foremost to enter, was immediately cognizant of two distinct odours—one, the scent of fragrant tea, the other of a certain heavy, narcotic something which presently overpowered the fragrance of the tea and left an acid and bitter taste.

"Opium," he whispered to Lauriston, who was close at his elbow. "Opium!

Smell it?"

But Lauriston was more eyes than nose just then. He, like the rest of his companions, was staring at the scene on which they had entered. The room was of a good size—evidently, from its sloping ceilings, part of the attic story of the old house. The walls were hung with soft, clinging, Oriental draperies and curtains; a few easy chairs of wickerwork, a few small tables of like make, were disposed here and there: there was an abundance of rugs and cushions: in one corner a gas-stove was alight, and on it stood a kettle, singing merrily.

The young man who had opened the door had retreated towards this stove; Purdie noticed that in one hand he held a small tea-pot. And in the left-hand corner, bent over a little table, and absorbed in their game, sat two other young men, correctly attired in English clothes, but obviously Chinese from their eyebrows to their toes, playing chess.

The holder of the tea-pot cast a quick glance at the disturbance of this peaceful scene, and set down his tea-pot; the chess-players looked up for one second, showed not the faintest sign of perturbation—and looked down again. Then the man of the tea-pot spoke—one word.

"Yes?" he said.

"The fact is, Mister," said the elder Pilmansey, "these are police-officers. They want one of your friends—Mr. Chang Li."

The three occupants of the room appeared to pay no attention. The chess-players went on playing; the other man reached for a canister, and mechanically emptied tea out of it into his pot.

"Shut and lock that door, Ayscough," said the Inspector. "Let somebody stand by it. Now," he continued, turning to the three Chinese, "is one of you gentlemen Mr. Chang Li?"

"No!" replied one of the chess-players. "Not one of us!"

"Is he here?" demanded the Inspector. Then seeing that he was to be met by Oriental impassivity, he turned to the Pilmanseys. "What other rooms are there here?" he asked.

"Two," answered the elder brother, pointing to the curtains at the rear of the room. "One there—the other there. Behind those hangings—two smaller rooms."

The Inspector strode forward and tore the curtains aside. He flung open the first of the doors—and started back, catching his breath.

"Phew!" he said.

The heavy, narcotic odour which Purdie had noticed at once on entering the rooms came afresh, out of the newly-opened door, in a thick wave. And as the rest of them crowded after the Inspector, they saw why. This was a small room, hung like the first one with curiously-figured curtains, and lighted only by a sky-light, over which a square of blue stuff had been draped. In the subdued life they saw that there was nothing in that room but a lounge well fitted with soft cushions and pillows—and on it, his spare figure wrapped in a loose gown, lay a young Chinaman, who, as the foremost advanced upon him, blinked in their wondering faces out of eyes the pupils of which were still contracted. Near him lay an opium pipe—close by, on a tiny stand, the materials for more consumption of the drug.

The man who had accompanied the Inspector in his entrance to the tea-shop strode forward and seized the recumbent figure by the shoulder, shaking him gently.

"Now then!" he said, sharply, "wake up, my man! Are you Chang Li?"

The glazed eyes lifted themselves a little wonderingly; the dry lips moved.

"Yes," he muttered. "Chang Li—yes. You want me?"

"How long have you been here?" demanded the questioner.

"How long—yes? Oh—I don't know. What do you want?" asked Chang Li. "I don't know you."

The tea-maker thrust his head inside the room.

"He can't tell you anything," he said, with a grin. "He has been—what you call on the break-out—with opium—ever so many days. He has—attacks that way. Takes a fit of it—just as some of your people take to the drink. He's coming out of it, now—and he'll be very, very unhappy tomorrow."

The Inspector twisted round on the informant.

"Look here!" he said. "Do you know how long he's been here—stupifying himself? Is it a day—or days?"

One of the chess-players lifted a stolid face.

"He has been here—like that—several days," he said. "It's useless trying to do anything with him when he takes the fit—the craving, you understand?—into his head. If you want any information out of him, you'd better call again in a few hours."

"Do you mean to tell me he's been here—like that—several days?" demanded the Inspector.

The young man with the tea-pot grinned again.

"He's never been at a class at the medical school since the 17th," he announced. "I know that—he's in some classes with me. He's been here—all the time since then."

The Inspector turned sharply on Ayscough.

"The 17th!" he exclaimed. "And that affair was on the 18th! Then—"

Chang Li was fumbling in a pocket of his gown. He found something there, raised a hand to his lips, swallowed something. And in a few seconds, as his eyes grew brighter, he turned a suspicious and sullen glance on the group which stood watching him.

"What do you want?" he growled. "Who are you?"

"We want some information from you," said the Inspector. "When did you last see your brother, or friend, or whatever he is—Chen Li?"

Chang Li shook his head—it was obvious that he had no clear recollection.

"Don't know," he answered. "Perhaps just now—perhaps tomorrow—perhaps not for a long time."

"When were you last at home—in Maida Vale?" asked the Inspector.

But Chang Li gave no answer to that beyond a frown, and it was evident that as his wits cleared his temper was becoming ugly. He began to look round with more intelligence, scanning one face after another with growing dislike, and presently he muttered certain observations to himself which, though not in English, sounded anything but complimentary to those who watched him. And Ayscough suddenly turned to the superior officials.

"If this man's been here ever since the 17th," he said, "he can't have had anything to do with the affairs in Praed Street and Maida Vale! Supposing, now—I'm only supposing—that young Jap's been lying all the time?" He turned again—this time on the two chess-players, who had now interrupted their game and were leaning back in their chairs, evidently amused at the baffled faces of the searchers. "Here!" he said, "do you know one Yada—Mori Yada—a Japanese? Is he one of you?"

"Oh, yes!" answered one of the chess-players. "Yada,—yes! We know him—a very smart fellow, Yada. You know him—too?"

But before Ayscough could reply to this somewhat vexatious question, a man who had been left in the tearooms came hurrying up the staircase and burst in upon them. He made straight for the Inspector.

"Man from the office, sir, outside in a taxi!" he exclaimed breathlessly. "You're on the wrong track—you're to get to Multenius's shop in Praed Street at once. The real man's there!"

## CHAPTER THIRTY-EIGHT
## THE JEW AND THE JAP

When Melky Rubinstein slipped quietly out of the police-station, he crossed the street, and taking up a position just within a narrow alley on the other side, set himself to watch the door which he had just quitted. There was a deep design in his mind, and he meant to carry it out—alone. Mr. Mori Yada, apparently as cool and unconcerned as ever, presently tripped down the steps of the police-station and went leisurely off, swinging his neatly rolled umbrella. As long as he was within sight of the police-station windows he kept up the same gentle pace—but as soon as he had turned the first corner his steps were quickened, and he made for a spot to which Melky had expected him to make—a cab-rank, on which two or three taxi-cabs were drawn up. He had reached the first, and was addressing the driver, when Melky, who had kept a few yards in the rear, stole gently up to his side and tapped him on the shoulder.

"Mister!" said Melky. "A word—in private!"

Yada turned on his interrupter with the swiftness of a snake, and for a second his white teeth showed themselves in an unmistakable snarl, and a savage gleam came into his dark eyes. Both snarl and gleam passed as quickly as they had come, and the next instant he was smiling—as blandly as ever.

"Oh, yes!" he said. "It is you—how do you do? Perhaps you are going my way—I can give you a lift—Yes?"

Melky drew his man away a yard or two, and lowered his voice to a whisper.

"Mister!" he said, with a note of deep confidence which made Yada look at him with a sudden sense of fear. "Mister!—I wouldn't go no way at all if I was you—just now. You're in danger, mister—you shoved your head into the lions' den when you walked in where I've just seen you! Deep, deep is them fellows, mister!—they're having you on toast. I know where you're thinking of going, mister, in that cab. Don't go—take my tip!"

"How do you know where I'm going?" demanded Yada.

"I was looking over Levendale's shoulder when he wrote that bit of a cheque, mister," answered Melky, in his quietest accents. "You're off to his bank to turn it into cash. And—if you walk into that bank—well, you'll never walk out again, alone! Mister!—they're going to collar you there—there's a trap laid for you!"

Melky was watching Yada's face out of his own eye-corners, and he saw the olive-tinted skin pale a little, and the crafty eyes contract. And on the instant he pursued his tactics and his advantage. He had purposely steered the Japanese into a more crowded part of the street, and now he edged him into a bye-alley which led to a rookery of narrow bye-streets beyond. He felt that Yada was yielding—oppressed by a fear of the unknown. But suddenly Yada paused—drawing back from the hand which Melky had kept on his arm.

"What are you after?" he demanded. "What is your game, eh? You think to alarm me!—what do you want?"

"Nothing unreasonable, mister," answered Melky. "You'll easily satisfy me. Game? Come, now, mister—I know your game! Bank first—to get some ready—then somewhere to pick up a bit of luggage—then, a railway station. That's it, ain't it, now? No blooming good, mister—

they're ready for you the minute you walk into that bank! If they don't take you then, they'll only wait to follow you to the station. Mister!—you ain't a cat's chance!—you're done—if you don't make it worth my while to help you! See?"

Yada looked round, doubtfully. They had turned two or three corners by that time, and were in a main street, which lay at the back of Praed Street. He glanced at Melky's face—which suggested just then nothing but cunning and stratagem.

"What can you do for me?" he asked. "How much do you want? You want money, eh?"

"Make it a hundred quid, mister," said Melky. "Just a hundred of the best, and I'll put you where all the police in London won't find you for the rest of today, and get you out of it at night in such a fashion that you'll be as safe as if you was at home. You won't never see your home in Japan, again, mister, if you don't depend on yours truly! And a hundred ain't nothing—considering what you've got at stake."

"I haven't a hundred pounds to give you," answered Yada. "I have scarcely any money but this cheque."

"In course you ain't, mister!" agreed Melky. "I twigged your game straight off—you only came there to the police-station to put yourself in funds for your journey! But that's all right!—you come along of me, and let me put you in safety—then you give me that cheque—I'll get it cashed in ten minutes without going to any banks—see? Friend o' mine hereabouts—he'll cash it at his bank close by—anybody'll cash a cheque o' Levendale's. Come on, now, mister. We're close to that little port o' refuge I'm telling you about."

The bluff was going down—Melky felt, as much as saw, that Yada was swallowing it in buckets. And he slipped his hand within his companion's arm, piloted him along the street, across Praed Street, round the back of the houses into the narrow passage which communicated with the rear of the late Daniel Multenius's premises, and in at the little door which opened on the parlour wherein so many events had recently taken place.

"Where are you taking me?" asked Yada, suspiciously, as they crossed the threshold.

"All serene, mister!" answered Melky, reassuringly. "Friend o' mine here—my cousin. All right—and all secure. You're as safe here as you will be in your grave, mister—s'elp me, you are! Zillah!"

Zillah walked into the parlour and justified Melky's supreme confidence in her by showing no surprise or embarrassment. She gave Yada the merest glance, and turned to Melky.

"Bit o' business with this young gentleman, Zillah," said Melky. "That little room, upstairs, now—what?" "Oh, all right!" said Zillah, indifferently. "You know your way—you'll be quiet enough there."

Melky signed to Yada to follow him, and led the way up the stairs to the very top of the house. He conducted the Japanese into the small room in which were some ancient moth-and-worm-eaten bits of furniture, an old chest or two, and a plenitude of dust—and carefully closed the door when he and his captive had got inside.

"Now, mister!" he said, "you're as safe here as you could be in any spot in the wide world. Let's get to business—and let's understand each other. You want that cheque turned into cash—you want to get out of London tonight? All right—then hand over your cheque and keep quiet till I come back. Is there anything else now—any bit of luggage you want?"

"You do all this if I pay you one hundred pounds?" asked Yada.

"That'll do me, mister," answered Melky. "I'm a poor fellow, d'ye see?—I don't pick up a hundred quid every day, I assure you! So if there is anything—"

"A suit-case—at the luggage office at Oxford Circus Tube," said Yada. "I must have it—papers, you understand. If you will get me that—"

"Give me the ticket—and that cheque," said Melky. He slipped the two bits of paper into his pocket, and made for the door. "I'll turn the key outside," he said. "You'll be safer. Make yourself comfortable, mister—I'll be back in an hour with the money and the goods."

Two minutes later Melky confronted Zillah in the parlour and grinned at her. Zillah regarded him suspiciously.

"What's this, Melky?" she demanded. "What're you up to?"

"Zillah!" said Melky, "you'll be proud of your cousin, Melky Rubinstein, before ever it's dinner-time—you will do, Zillah! And in the meantime, keep your counsel, Zillah, while he fetches a nice large policeman."

"Is that Japanese locked in that little room?" asked Zillah.

Melky tapped the side of his nose, and without a word looked out into the street. A policeman, large enough for all practical purposes, was lounging along the side-walk; another, equally bulky, was looking into a shop-window twenty yards away across the street. Within a couple of minutes Melky had both in the back-parlour and was giving them and Zillah a swift but particular account of his schemes.

"You're sure you're right, Melky?" asked Zillah. "You're not making any mistake?"

"Mistake!" exclaimed Melky, satirically. "You'll see about that in a minute! Now," he added, turning to the policemen, "you come quietly up—and do exactly what I've told you. We'll soon know about mistakes, Zillah!"

Yada, left to himself, had spent his time in gazing out of the dirty window of his prison. There was not much of a prospect. The window commanded the various backyards of that quarter. As if to consider any possible chance of escape, he looked out. There was a projection beneath him, a convenient water-pipe—he might make a perilous descent, if need arose. But, somehow, he believed in that little Jew: he believed, much more, in the little Jew's greed for a hundred pounds of ready money. The little Jew with the cunning smile had seen his chance of making a quiet penny, and had taken it—it was all right, said Yada, all right. And yet, there was one horrible thought—supposing, now that Melky had got the cheque, that he cashed it and made off with all the money, never to return?

On top of that thought, Melky did return—much sooner than Yada had expected. He opened the door and beckoned the prisoner out into the dark lobby at the top of the stairs.

"Come here a minute, mister," said Melky, invitingly. "Just a word!"

Yada, all unsuspecting, stepped out—and found his arms firmly gripped by two bulky policemen. The policemen were very quiet—but Melky laughed gleefully while Yada screamed and cursed him. And while he laughed Melky went through his prisoner's pockets in a knowing and skilful fashion, and when he had found what he expected to find, he made his helpers lock Yada up again, and taking them downstairs to the parlour laid his discoveries on the table before them and Zillah. There was a great orange-yellow diamond in various folds of tissue-paper, and a thick wad of bank-notes, with an indiarubber band round them.

These valuables lay, carelessly displayed, on the table when the party from Pilmansey's Tea Rooms came tumbling into the shop and the parlour, an hour later. Melky was calmly smoking a cigar—and he went on smoking it as he led the Inspector and his men upstairs to the prisoner. He could not deprive himself of the pleasure of a dig at Ayscough.

"Went one better than you again, Mr. Ayscough," he said, as he laid his hand on the key of the locked room. "Now if I hadn't seen through my young gentleman—"

But there, as Melky threw open the door, his words of assurance came to an end. His face dropped as he stared into an empty room. Yada had risked his neck, and gone down the water-pipe.

## CHAPTER THIRTY-NINE
## THE DIAMOND NECKLACE

For the better part of a fortnight the sleuth-hounds of New Scotland Yard hunted for Mr. Mori Yada in all the likely and unlikely places in London and sent out their enquiries much further afield. They failed to find him. One small clue they got, with little difficulty. After the hue-and-cry was fairly out, an Edgware Road pawnbroker came forward and informed the police that at two o'clock, or thereabouts, on the afternoon of the day on which Yada had made his escape from the window, a young Japanese gentleman who gave his name as Mr. Motono and his address at a small hotel close by and who volunteered the explanation that he was temporarily short of cash until a remittance arrived, had borrowed five pounds from him on a pearl tie-pin which he had drawn from his cravat. That was Yada, without a doubt—but from that point Yada vanished.

But hunger is the cleverest detective, and at the end of the fortnight, certain officials of the Japanese embassy in London found themselves listening to a strange tale from the fugitive, who had come to the end of his loan, had nowhere to turn and no one but the representatives of his nation to whom he could appeal. Yada told a strange tale—and all the stranger because, as the police officials who were called in to hear it anew recognized that there was probably some truth in it. It amounted, when all was heard, to this—Yada was willing to confess that for a few days he had been a successful thief, but he stoutly denied that he was a murderer.

This was his story:—On the 18th November, in the evening, he was at the club which housed itself in Pilmansey's attic. There he saw Chang Li, who, according to the other members who were there, was beginning one of his periodic fits of opium smoking, and had been in the inner room, stupifying himself, since the previous day. Yada knew that it was highly necessary that Chang Li should be in attendance at certain classes at the medical school during the next few days, and tried to rouse him out of his debauch, with no result. Next day, the 19th, he went to Pilmansey's again—Chang Li was still in the realms of bliss and likely to stop there until he had had enough of them. For two days nobody at the club nor at the school had seen Chen Li—and Chen Li was the only person who could do anything with Chang. So, late that night of the 19th November, Yada went up to Maida Vale, taking Chang Li's keys with him. He admitted himself to garden and house and found the house empty. But just as he was entering the front door he heard the voice of Chen Li at the garden gate; he also heard the voice of an Englishman. Also he caught something of what that Englishman said. He was telling Chen Li that he'd better take him, the Englishman, inside, and settle with him—or things would be all the worse. And at that, he, Yada, had slipped into the house, quietly closed the front door behind him, gone into the front room, hidden himself behind a curtain and waited.

Into that front room, Chen Li had presently conducted a man. He was, said Yada, a low-class Englishman—what is called a Cockney. He had begun to threaten Chen Li at once. He told his tale. He was, said this fellow, next door neighbour to Mr. Daniel Multenius, in Praed Street, Chen Li's landlord: his name, if Chen Li wanted to know it, was Parslett, fruitier and green-grocer, and it was there, bold as brass, over his shop-door, for him or anybody to look at. He had a side-door to his house: that side-door was exactly opposite a side-door in Mr. Multenius's house, opening into his back-parlour. Now, the previous afternoon, he, Parslett, had had a consignment of very fine mushrooms sent in—rare things at that time of year—and knowing that the old man had a great taste for them and didn't mind what price he paid, he stepped across with a dish of them to tempt him. He found Mr. Multenius in his parlour—he was counting a lot of bank-notes—they must, said Parslett, have represented a large sum. The old man bade him leave the mushrooms, said he'd send him the money across presently, and motioned him out. Parslett put the dish of mushrooms aside on a chiffonier and went away. Somewhat later, chancing to be at his front door and looking out into the street, he saw Chen Li open the door of Multenius's shop and go swiftly away. Half-an-hour after that he heard that something had happened at Multenius's—later in the evening he heard definitely that the old man had been assaulted under circumstances which pointed to murder for the sake of robbery. And then he, Parslett, now put two and two together—and had fixed on Chen Li as the culprit. And now—how much was Chen Li going to pay for silence?

According to Yada, Chen Li had had little to say—his chief anxiety, indeed, had been to find out what the man wanted. Parslett was definite enough about that. He wanted a thousand pounds—and he wanted it in gold, and as much of it as Chen Li could hand out there and then. He refused to believe that Chen Li hadn't gold in considerable quantity somewhere about—he must, said Parslett, have changed some of those notes since he had stolen them the previous day. Chen Li protested that he had but some fifty or sixty pounds in gold available—but he promised to have the rest of the thousand ready on the following evening. Finally, he handed Parslett fifty pounds, arranged that he should call the next night—and then invited him to take a drink. Parslett pocketed the money and accepted the invitation—and Yada, from his hiding-place, saw Chen Li go to the sideboard, mix whisky and soda and pour into the mixture a few drops from a phial which he took from his waistcoat pocket. Parslett drank off the contents of the glass—and Chen Li went down to the gate with him.

Yada followed to the front door and, through a slight opening, watched. The garden was fairly well lighted by the moon, which had recently risen. He saw Chen Li let the man out. He saw him turn from the gate and slowly come back towards the house. And then he saw something else—the sudden spring, from behind a big laurel bush, of a man—a short-statured, slight-figured man, who leapt on Chen Li with the agility of a panther. He saw the flash of a knife in the moonlight—he heard a muffled cry, and startled groan—and saw Chen Li pitch forward and lie evidently lifeless, where he fell. He saw the assailant stoop, seize his victim by the shoulders and drag him behind the shrubbery. Then, without further delay, the murderer hurried to the gate. Evidently assured himself that there was no one about, let himself out, and was gone.

By all the solemn oaths that he could think of, Yada swore that this was true. Of another thing he was certain—the murderer was a Chinese.

Now began his own career of crime. He was just then very hard up. He had spent much more than his allowance—he was in debt at his lodgings and elsewhere. Somewhere, he felt sure, there was, in that house, the money which Chen Li had evidently stolen from old Multenius. He immediately set to work to find it. But he had no difficulty—the bank-notes were in the drawer from which he had seen Chen Li take the gold which he had given to the blackmailer, Parslett. He hurriedly transferred them to his own pocket, and got away from the house by the door at the back of the garden—and it was not until late that night, in the privacy of his own rooms, that he found he had nearly eighty thousand pounds in his possession.

For some days, said Yada, he was at a loss what to do with his booty. He was afraid of attempting to change five hundred pound notes. He made cautious enquiries as to how that could be done—and he began to think that the notes were so much waste paper to him. And then Ayscough called on him—and for the first time, he heard the story of the orange-yellow diamond.

That gave him an idea. He had a very accurate knowledge of Chinese habits and characteristics, and he felt sure that Chen Li would have hidden that diamond in his pig-tail. So he took advantage of his possession of the detective's card to go to the mortuary, to get a minute or two alone with the body, and to slip his hand underneath the dead man's silk cap. There he found the diamond—and he knew that whether the bank-notes were to be of any value to him or not, the diamond would be if he could only escape to the Continent.

But—he wanted funds; wanted them badly. He thereupon conceived the bold idea of getting a reward for his knowledge. He went to the police-station with a merely modest motive in his mind—fifty pounds would carry him to Vienna, where he knew how to dispose of the diamond at once, with no questions asked. But when he found the owners of the diamond and the bank-notes present he decided to play for higher stakes. He got what he asked for—and, if it had not been for that little Jew, he said malevolently, he would have got out of England that eventful afternoon. But—it was not so written—and the game was up. Only—what he had said was true. Now let them do what they could for him—but let them search for Chen Li's murderer.

\* \* \* \* \*

The folk who had been chiefly concerned about the orange-yellow diamond and the eighty thousand pounds' worth of Bank of England notes were not so much troubled about proving the truth of Yada's strange story as Yada himself was—the main point to them was that they had recovered their property. Naturally they felt remarkably grateful to Melky Rubinstein for his astuteness in circumventing Yada at what might have been the last moment. And one day, at that portion of it when business was slack and everybody was feeling comfortable after dinner, Melky called on Mrs. Goldmark and became confidentially closeted with her in a little parlour behind her establishment which she kept sacred to herself. Mrs. Goldmark, who had quick eyes, noticed that Melky was wearing his best clothes, and a new silk hat, and new gloves, and had put his feet into patent-leather boots which she secretly and sympathizingly—felt to be at least a size too small for him. He sighed as he sat near her on the sofa—and Mrs. Goldmark looked at him with concern.

"Such a time you have lately, Mr. Rubinstein, don't you?" she said feelingly. "Such worries—such troubles! And the risk you ran taking that wicked young man all by yourself—so brave of you! You'd ought to have one of these medals what they give to folks, so!"

"You think that?" responded Melky, brightening suspiciously. "Oh, Mrs. Goldmark, your words is like wine—all my life I been wishing some beautiful woman would say them things to me! Now I feel like I was two foot taller, Mrs. Goldmark! But I don't want no medals—not me. Mr. Levendale and Mr. Purvis, they came to me and say they must give me a reward—handsome reward, you understand, for getting back their goods. So I say no—I won't have nothing for myself—nothing. But, I say, just so—there is one that should be rewarded. Mrs. Goldmark!—do you know what? I think of you when I say that!"

Mrs. Goldmark uttered a feeble scream, clasped her hands, and stared at Melky out of her melting eyes.

"Me?" she exclaimed. "Why—I ain't done nothing, Mr. Rubinstein!"

"Listen to me," persisted Melky. "What I says to Mr. Levendale is this here—if Mrs. Goldmark hadn't had her eating establishment, and if Mr. Purvis hadn't gone into it to eat a chop and to drop his platinum solitaire on the table, and if Mrs. Goldmark hadn't taken care of that platinum solitaire, and if things hadn't sprung from it—eh, what then, I should like to know? So Mrs. Goldmark is entitled to whatever little present there is!—that's how I put it, Mrs. Goldmark. And Mr. Levendale and Mr. Purvis, they agreed with me—and oh, Mrs. Goldmark, ain't you going to be nice and let me put this round your beautiful neck?"

Mrs. Goldmark screamed again as Melky produced a diamond necklace, lying in a blue velvet bed in a fine morocco case. The glitter of the diamonds turned both beholders hoarse with emotion.

"Do you know what, Mrs. Goldmark!" whispered Melky. "It cost a thousand guineas—and no error! Now you bend your lovely head, and I puts it on you—oh, ain't you more beautiful than the Queen of Sheba! And ain't you Melky's queen, Mrs. Goldmark—say you was!"

"Lor', Mr. Rubinstein!" said Mrs. Goldmark, coyly. "It's as if you was proposing to me!"

"Why, ain't I?" exclaimed Melky, gathering courage. "Don't you see I'm in all my best clothes? Ain't it nothing but weddings, just now? There's Mr. Lauriston a-going to marry Zillah, and Mr. Purdie's a-fixing it up with Levendale's governess, and—oh, Mrs. Goldmark, ain't I worshipped you every time I come to eat my dinner in your eating house? Ain't you the loveliest woman in all Paddington. Say the word, Mrs. Goldmark—don't you see I'm like as if I was that hungry I could eat you?"

Then Mrs. Goldmark said the word—and presently escaped from Melky's embrace to look at herself and her necklace in the mirror.

**THE END**

# Freeriver Community

Freeriver is a community project working to create a place for people to visit and potentially live, long-term, in peace, free from the normal stresses of modern life.

We aim to provide a place where people can spend time discovering themselves and discovering nature. We aim to focus on creativity, health and wellbeing. We plan to provide events and classes for people in the local area and enhance the community.

Please visit our website for more details

www.freerivercommunity.com
freerivercommunity@hotmail.com

www.freerivercommunity.com

This book is in the public domain as the author died over 70 years ago and also the original was first published before 1923. No persons, organisation or establishment accept any ownership, liability or responsibility for the content of this book as it is in the public domain. Every attempt has been made to present you with an accurate version of the text, however there may be very subtle differences in text type, punctuation etc due to the editing process.

**J.S. Fletcher died 1935**

Any profits generated from the sale of this book will go towards the Freeriver Community project, a project designed to promote harmonious community living and well-being in the world. To learn more about the Freeriver project please visit the website - www.freerivercommunity.com

Printed in Great Britain
by Amazon